THE DRAGON COLLECTIVE

Lochguard Highland Dragons #8

JESSIE DONOVAN

Mythical Lake Press, LLC

Books in this series:

The Dragon Collective Synopsis

Over the last ten years Lachlan MacKintosh has kept his sobriety through hard work, focus, and strict routines. Then he meets one dragonwoman a year prior, a woman with easy smiles and humor, and he starts to wonder if his routines are enough. When he's assigned a major project on Lochguard, one to bring together human and dragon artists, he's forced to live with the dragon-shifters and work with the woman who caught his eye all those months ago. He tries to resist her, knowing temptation could be his downfall. But instead he falls more under her charm with each passing day, making him wonder if he's strong enough to overcome his demons so he can have her.

Despite Cat MacAllister's never-ending schedule of helping her family, art is her true passion and so when she's asked to help with a major human-dragon art collective, she jumps at the chance. The only downside is the human male in charge—he's the one she met the year before and has been constantly sketching ever since. She attempts to keep their relationship professional, but soon she asks him to kiss her and it changes her life forever.

As the pair try to figure out if they fit together, they not only have to face Lachlan's past but a new threat emerges before the start of the art project. Will they find a way to stay together, or will Lachlan have to give up everything to protect those he cares about?

The Stonefire and Lochguard series intertwine with one another. (As well as with one Tahoe Dragon Mates book.) Since so many readers ask for the overall reading order, I've included it with this book. (This list is as of May 2021 and you can view the most up-to-date version here on my website.)

Winning Skyhunter (Stonefire Dragons Universe #1)
The Dragon's Discovery (Lochguard Highland Dragons #6)
Transforming Snowridge (Stonefire Dragons Universe #2)
The Dragon's Pursuit (Lochguard Highland Dragons #7)
Persuading the Dragon (Stonefire Dragons #12)
Treasured by the Dragon (Stonefire Dragons #13)
The Dragon Collective (Lochguard Highland Dragons #8)
The Dragon's Bidder (Tahoe Dragon Mates #3)
The Dragon's Chance (Lochguard Highland Dragons #9, September 16, 2021)
Trusting the Dragon (Stonefire Dragons #14, Jan 20, 2022)

Short stories that lead up to *Persuading the Dragon* / *Treasured by the Dragon*:

Meeting the Humans (Stonefire Dragons Shorts #1)
The Dragon Camp (Stonefire Dragons Shorts #2)
The Dragon Play (Stonefire Dragons Shorts #3)

Semi-related dragon stories set in the USA, beginning sometime around *The Dragon's Discovery* / *Transforming Snowridge*:

The Dragon's Choice (Tahoe Dragon Mates #1)

Chapter One

Catherine "Cat" MacAllister sat at the large table in one of the rooms of the newly rebuilt great hall on Lochguard and tried to sketch out her latest painting idea while simultaneously keeping an eye on the female opposite her.

One of her many jobs inside the clan was to help the poor lass named Aimee King, one who'd suffered abuse by a former dragon leader down south in England on Clan Skyhunter. She'd been sent to Lochguard to heal, and art therapy had been working well over the past few months, helping to calm her down for longer and longer periods of time.

True, the female wasn't any sort of brilliant artist, but she relaxed as she filled in the paint-by-numbers project Cat had created. So much so that it was hard to remember the lass had suffered so much while still so young, not to mention the fact she had a silent dragon.

Which, to a dragon-shifter, was akin to missing half of one's soul.

Cat could feel her own inner beast stirring inside her mind as if to reassure Cat she was still there, but her dragon knew better than to talk. When her inner beast spoke, Cat's pupils changed to slits temporarily. And flashing dragon eyes sometimes still scared Aimee—related to something that had happened to her while Aimee had been imprisoned, although the female didn't talk about it—and not even Cat's rather chatty dragon would risk spooking the poor female.

Especially since Cat would soon become even busier and didn't want someone to have to start from ground zero when it came to building trust with Aimee.

Besides helping at her mother's restaurant, Cat's own art projects, art lessons with the children, and her sessions with Aimee, she would soon be working with a human male named Lachlan MacKintosh.

Aye, she looked forward to the month-long joint art project between humans and dragon-shifters. But she was a wee bit worried about saying something she shouldn't to the male in charge.

Or, at least, she'd always had a problem with that during their past meetings.

Her dragon moved again, and for once, Cat

The Dragon Collective   11

wished she could speak to her inner beast beyond murmuring, *Soon*, inside her mind.

She watched Aimee dip her paintbrush into a dark blue just as the door banged open and her younger brother Connor barged in. "Cat—"

Cat barely noticed her brother and instead focused on Aimee.

The lass had trouble around males.

But instead of running to the far side of the room, Aimee stared at Connor. Her brother stared back.

Knowing how Connor wouldn't stay quiet for long—no one in her family could—she stood and shooed him out the door. She grabbed the doorknob and looked at Aimee. "I'll be right back, aye?"

Once the other female nodded, Cat shut the door and said in a scolding whisper, "What the bloody hell were you doing? You know not to barge in when I'm with her."

Connor crossed his arms over his chest. "It's Tuesday, not Thursday, so how the hell was I to know she'd be in there with you?"

She frowned. "Since when do you know my schedule?"

He raised his brows. "Since when don't you know mine?"

She grumbled, "That's different. If I don't keep track of you lot, then trouble is bound to happen."

He growled, "I'm not fifteen anymore, Cat. Stop treating me like a lad green behind the ears."

Her inner dragon spoke up. *He has a point.*

Now you decide to start talking?

Her beast sniffed. *Aimee's not here, so why not?*

Ignoring her dragon, she took a deep breath and murmured, "Sorry. Old habits die hard, and all that."

He grinned, and Cat nearly groaned. There was no way her brother wouldn't tease her about her apology at some point. Or, more likely, use it as proof that he was indeed the male of the house, being the eldest male of the siblings.

In other words, Connor would become even more insufferable than normal.

Needing to change the topic, she asked, "So why did you barge in like that? I hope there's a good reason, or I may have to take my apology back."

Uncrossing his arms, he rocked back on his heels, his grin growing wider. "As if I'd let that happen."

She growled, "Connor."

He shrugged. "Fine. The human male arrived, that DDA bloke, and he's waiting for you at Finn's house. You're supposed to go meet him about something or other, as soon as possible. They didn't tell me the details."

Finn was Lochguard's clan leader, which meant she couldn't say no or delay going until Aimee's session was finished. "Just let me get Aimee packed up and I'll go."

The lass had often been staying with Finn and his mate, Arabella. So her clan leader couldn't get mad at her for taking a few minutes to get Aimee sorted and home safely.

Connor cleared his throat. "I can stay until she's finished. I'll even try to stay quiet."

She looked at him askance. "I doubt that's possible. Besides, she doesn't do well with males." He opened his mouth, but she beat him to it. "Not right now, Connor. The longer you argue with me, the tardier I'll be. And do you really want to explain to Finn why that is?"

He rolled his eyes. "Just trying to be helpful, but whatever. I'll let them know you're coming."

As her brother walked away, she wondered a second about his sudden interest in Aimee.

But then she remembered she needed to hurry—Lachlan would no doubt already give her a superior look for taking so long—and she focused on getting the room cleaned up and guiding Aimee toward Finn's house.

Lachlan MacKintosh sat in a chair opposite Lochguard's blond clan leader, Finn Stewart, and did his best not to tap his fingers against his thigh.

All he wanted to do was get started. There were a million things he needed to research on the Scottish dragons' land before he could start setting up the accommodations and workspaces for the artists due to come in the fall.

Two months. That was all he had to learn everything he could about this clan and find a way to make it work for his pet project.

If Lachlan's plan to invite human and dragon artists to this place failed, he could lose his job. He'd bet everything on this event, which meant it needed to go smoothly.

And Lachlan refused to fail.

His job was his life, his purpose, and kept him from returning to his former way of life—that of an angry, irresponsible drunk who hurt everyone close to him.

No. He wouldn't go back there. He couldn't.

So as Finn stared at him silently—going against everything Lachlan had heard about the Scottish dragonman's chattiness—he stared back. He'd worked with dragon-shifters long enough not to be intimidated by them very often.

But as even more minutes ticked by, Lachlan finally cleared his throat and said, "She's late. I'm more than happy to talk with someone else, someone less busy."

Finn raised his dark blond brows. "Are you telling me that you never had something unexpected come up? It's only five minutes, MacKintosh. The world won't end."

True, it wouldn't. But Lachlan needed structure. Ten minutes late one day, then an hour another, making excuses for the little things until he eventually ended up pissed in a pub somewhere, losing track of not only time but also himself.

Maybe someone would say it was hyperbole, given how he'd been sober for ten years. But Lachlan knew himself, and he also refused to tempt himself again. Because next time, he might not ask for help or have the strength to fight his self-imposed hell.

And the next time, he could end up like his father.

Not wanting to go down that road—he needed to keep his wits around the dragons—he replied, "I'm sure you don't need me to repeat how important this is and how we both need to get it right. If this is my first impression of working with Ms. MacAllister on this project, I may need another contact."

Finn leaned back in his chair. "Cat has more on her plate than almost anyone else not in a leadership position, and yet she somehow still finds a way to balance it all." An almost warning threaded through Finn's voice as he said, "Don't dare question her work ethic."

Lachlan knew firsthand from the previous exhibition event she'd participated in that Cat did what needed to be done, even if she did it in a laissez-faire way he didn't quite understand.

But there was another reason he was harsh

concerning her tardiness, something he'd never tell
the dragon leader, not even if he threatened to cut
off his bollocks.

He'd spent a full month after his last encounter
with Cat dreaming of her smile, her laughter, and
how she teased him.

Dreams resulting in him doing much more than
kissing her, leaving him hard and frustrated with only
his hand for comfort.

She was everything he should avoid, and yet his
dreams didn't seem to care.

No, more accurately, his lust and desire didn't
care.

So working with her for months on end would
most definitely test his resolve. And he needed to
resist her. Not only because he wasn't sure how to
deal with a relationship since it meant revealing his
sordid past, but she was also a dragon-shifter. Merely
kissing her could result in him losing his job. A few—
very few—kept their positions in the Department of
Dragon Affairs, or DDA, after getting involved with a
dragon-shifter.

However, Lachlan wouldn't risk it. His job was his
life. Without it, he would be lost.

Which is why you need to pull yourself together and focus.

He was about to apologize since he *was* being
unduly harsh, but a knock on the door stopped him.
Finn yelled, "Come in."

While he probably shouldn't have turned, Lachlan did. As the door opened, revealing the lovely dark-haired, pale-skinned form of Catherine MacAllister, his dream of her laughing as he kissed her neck rushed forth.

Except unlike his dream, she was so much lovelier in person.

Stop it. If he could handle facing everyone he'd hurt in his life and owning up to his mistakes, he could handle one woman and her smiles.

Cat shut the door and said, "Sorry I'm late. I was in the middle of something."

Finn nodded, clearly knowing what it was, but didn't think to share it with Lachlan. The clan leader said, "Aye, I know. Come, sit down, Cat."

Lachlan stood. "I'd rather not waste time with small talk. We can merely get started instead."

Finn raised an eyebrow, but it was Cat who spoke up. "Aye, that's fine with me. I have a half-dozen things to do today, so the sooner we finish, the better. Ready Lachlan?"

He nearly blinked at her directness. "Yes. That would be excellent, Miss MacAllister."

She sighed. "Again with being formal. You're going to be this way the whole time, aren't you?"

If not in the presence of Lochguard's clan leader, he might be tempted to throw back the words she'd said to him months and months ago, back at the art exhibition, about getting shit done. Her expression would be priceless.

But he quickly pushed the temptation away. Even if it would probably make her smile or even laugh— something he'd love to see again to compare to his memories—there was far too much to do. "Shall we go or continue talking about my word choices?"

Cat waved a hand in dismissal. "Fine, fine, speak how you like. But call me Cat because if you use Miss MacAllister, I won't answer."

Finn snorted, but Lachlan ignored him. He asked, "How about Catherine?"

She scrunched her nose. "Definitely not. It makes me think of my grandmother, whom I'm named after."

Lachlan knew a thing or two about not wanting to be associated with a family member. He doubted the dragonwoman had anything as bad as his father in her family tree, but for expediency, he gave a curt nod. "Cat it is. Now, let's go."

Cat studied him a second, her eyes full of questions, but she merely shrugged. "As you wish." She looked at Finn. "I'll stop by later, Finn."

He had no idea what for, but Lachlan didn't really care. And as Cat led him out of the room and then out of the cottage, he did his best to match her pace and stare straight ahead.

Otherwise he might notice how the sun

highlighted the red parts of her dark hair or how she walked with a confidence he didn't see very often.

No, best to focus on the job. And the sooner he saw the spaces he'd be working with, the sooner he could get to work and dismiss her from his sight.

Chapter Two

During the entire walk to the warehouse—the one that would be used for the art collective project—Cat stole glimpses of Lachlan's profile from the corner of her eye.

She only looked for artistic reasons, of course. She'd painted him quite a lot over the last however many months, but she always seemed to have trouble with his lips and the intensity of his gaze.

Maybe some could settle for "mostly okay," but not her. It had almost become her obsession, to paint him as she saw him.

But to truly capture him, she'd need for him to sit and model for her, especially since he'd cut his hair short since the last time she'd seen him. However, she couldn't ask him to do that, even if she thought he might agree to it, which he wouldn't.

And even if he did somehow surprise her and

offer to model, she wasn't entirely sure she trusted herself alone with him.

Despite the fact he was overly formal, strung tight, and close-lipped—the complete opposite of her family—something about him was magnetic.

Almost as if he were full of secrets, and she wanted nothing more than to get to the bottom of them.

Not for the first time, she asked her inner dragon, *Are you sure you can't tell if he's our true mate?*

A dragon-shifter's true mate was their best chance at happiness. Not always, but most of the time. And a kiss would set off a mate-claim frenzy until the female was pregnant.

Cat had often wondered if Lachlan was hers, strange as the pairing seemed to her.

Her beast yawned before replying, *You know as well as I do that male dragons can recognize true mates. As bloody unfair as it is, the best I can do is guess. And I have no blasted idea. Although if you want to kiss him and ride him all night long, I'm on board for it. I want more sex.*

She mentally sighed. *You know we've been busy. I simply don't have time for it.*

And yet you're asking about this human male. Maybe it's because you want him yourself.

He was attractive, sure, what with his dark hair, strong jaw, and broad shoulders that would make any female attracted to males rush to jump him. She probably wasn't the only female—or male, for that matter—on Lochguard to notice.

But Lachlan was secretive, and quiet, and reserved in a way she couldn't even begin to imagine.

Some people liked that sort of thing, wanted to prod and gently push to extract the truth.

However, Cat didn't have enough hours in the day for all her jobs as it was. She'd prefer to find a mate like Finn, or Fraser MacKenzie, or any of the charming, happy-go-lucky males on Lochguard.

Her dragon snorted. *They're all taken or not interested.*

Well, maybe not all. There are a few MacKay brothers still single.

And they all live on Seahaven. It's too bloody cold that close to the sea for me.

Seahaven was a smaller splinter clan, the members originally from Lochguard but banished decades ago for having human mates. Cat had only recently started giving art lessons to a few of the Seahaven children. *Which, in a way, works in my favor that they don't live on Lochguard. At least for now. With our regular duties, plus the joint human-dragon project, I don't have time to waste on dating regularly. But a trip once a month or every two weeks, that I could do.*

That's not enough.

It's all I can manage right now, and you know it.

Her dragon sniffed at her reply. She clearly didn't want to argue about this yet again.

She did feel a little guilty about denying her beast sex—inner dragons craved it. And it wasn't that Cat didn't want to find a male to claim as her own and start a family one day. She loved her own family dearly and wanted that for herself too.

However, now wasn't the right time for it. She was twenty-six; Cat had plenty of time left.

The small warehouse came into view, and she realized they'd walked the entire time in silence. Hoping to give a better impression of Lochguard's hospitality, she stated, "If you have any questions, you can ask me any time."

He grunted, bobbing his head but never looking at her.

And for some reason, that irritated her.

Her clan had scrambled to help out Cat's mother with running the restaurant so that Cat would have enough time to plan and set up the joint art program between humans and dragon-shifters. And he couldn't even bloody bother to look at her, let alone say a sentence or two.

But more than that, Cat wasn't used to being ignored. She rather enjoyed being liked by all, and she couldn't recall doing anything to upset Lachlan MacKintosh. She'd teased him, aye, but no more than she'd done with any of the others during that exhibition about a year ago.

Her dragon spoke up. *Why don't you tell him? Fuming isn't your way.*

I was trying to be nice.

Her beast snorted. *Aye, because that won't backfire eventually, when your temper flares in all its glory.*

Her dragon was right—Cat liked tackling things head-on. It was better to say something now than later. She didn't yell often, but it wasn't pretty when it happened.

So even though they were nearly at the warehouse, she stopped and reached out a hand to take his wrist. Lachlan could've kept walking, but he stopped. He still didn't look at her but asked, "What?"

She stood directly in front of him and demanded, "Do you have a problem with me?"

His eyes finally met hers, the blue much deeper than she'd noticed before. There were also flecks of gold around the center, almost like the embers of a fire.

And for a split second, she thought she saw heat there.

But if so, all she could see was a hard, cold look the next second. She asked, "So, do you?"

"I'm not the most loquacious of individuals. If I have a question, I'll ask."

She leaned closer, raising her head to meet his eyes better. "Can you stop with all the fancy talk? It drives me mad, and I can assure you that it'll annoy everyone here. And I'm fairly sure that's the opposite of what you're supposed to do, aye? Annoy a large clan of dragon-shifters?"

He hesitated a moment, but then determination flashed in his eyes, and he said, "What the fuck should I say instead, lass? That I'm not a talkative bastard, I don't like blabber, and that you should stop your bloody pestering?"

She blinked at the change in him. It was the first time she'd heard any emotion from Lachlan MacKintosh.

And she much preferred it.

Not one to back down—to do that in her family spelled disaster and ridicule—she moved her head even closer to his. "Aye, I'd like that better. Gets to the point and shows me and my dragon a bit of who you are."

Her dragon snorted. *Leave me out of it.*

If Lachlan noticed her flashing dragon eyes, he didn't show it. Instead, he narrowed his gaze and murmured, "Be careful, lass. Because you may not like what you see."

And she stared at him a minute, trying to figure out what the bloody hell that meant.

LACHLAN RARELY SLIPPED UP when it came to his carefully crafted demeanor, but something about

Cat's words had released the dam he'd been holding back.

The way he'd once spoke, full of fire and swear words, had rushed forth. And then the bloody woman had to go and say she liked it.

Fear, anxiety, or both should've rushed over him at the dragonwoman's words. He'd worked so damn hard to change who he'd been, to be something better.

And usually, when his carefully constructed façade cracked, he caught himself and quickly locked away that former version of himself.

Whenever he hadn't been able to do so, in the early weeks and months of his recovery, he'd panicked, constantly afraid he'd relapse and go back to hurting everyone around him.

Despite the years and years of control, Lachlan should also be panicking now at his slipup. Because controlling his behavior and resisting addiction was a lifelong endeavor.

And yet deep down he knew he could put up the mask of refinement and control back up again without much effort. As soon as he wasn't around Cat, at any rate.

It was almost as if he wanted to drive her a wee bit mad on purpose.

Which was ridiculous.

And so to try and dissuade her, he murmured,

"Be careful, lass. Because you may not like what you see."

But rather than answer, she stared at him. Not in an angry or disapproving way. No, more like she was trying to reach inside and discover what made him tick.

Aye, it could merely be her studying him the way artists did. He'd been around enough to know they stared as if to puzzle out how a face was made, often without thinking.

However, he didn't think Cat did that now.

Lachlan barely resisted shifting his feet. He was the one usually in charge, directing everything about his job and his life, only showing what he wanted to show.

Even just the whisper of "what if she discovers those secrets?" running through his mind was enough for him to hurry up and compose himself again. The less he showed her, the better.

He was about to apologize for his outburst and hopefully restore the formality from before when Cat's pupils flashed between round and slits and back again. Hoping to change the topic and steer the attention away from him, he asked, "What does your dragon have to say?"

She raised an eyebrow. "Isn't it DDA training 101 to not ask something so personal to a dragon-shifter you barely know?"

He shrugged. "If we're to work together, I suspect I should learn how to not anger your dragon."

She rolled her eyes. "Back to being formal, I see."

Good. The distance would help protect him. From what, he didn't know. However, he sensed he needed to keep formality and distance between him and this woman.

Ignoring her comment, he repeated, "Your dragon? What did she say?"

Cat's eyes flashed again, and then she smiled. "You really don't want to know."

Maybe he shouldn't react given how he wanted to be formal. However, if she was going to try unsettling him, he'd do the same. She might think twice about doing it again in the future. "Given what I've learned about dragon-shifters, I suspect it's about me, and maybe even my lack of clothes. And perhaps a bed?"

Cat's jaw dropped, and his lips curved into a small smile.

Aye, he quite liked unnerving her. He was tempted to wink just to provoke her further, but resisted.

She closed her mouth, cleared her throat, and whispered, "Wouldn't you like to know." Then she released his wrist and walked toward the warehouse.

He should be thrilled about getting back to the project. Lachlan had so much riding on it and its success.

And yet, he wished he could talk with Cat a little longer.

Which, of course, he shouldn't do.

So he swiftly packed up his emotions and desires, checking he was in control once more, before he followed her.

One conversation teasing her he could allow. Another, however, would be dangerous.

Remember the project, remember it.

Right. He soon caught up to her and walked the rest of the way to the warehouse in silence.

CAT WAS FAIRLY sure Lachlan had flirted with her, or at the very least had teased her about sex fantasies.

Lachlan, the stuffiest, most formal person she'd probably ever met.

Maybe she'd misjudged him completely.

Her dragon laughed. *If you'd merely told him how I want to show my dragon form, you could've avoided it.*

Cat didn't usually lie about what her dragon said, unless it was something like a naked fantasy that she would most definitely *never* share with her family. *I couldn't help it. He's all but begging to be teased, and it's better for it to come from me than someone else.*

And why is that?

Her dragon played coy, but Cat ignored the bait.

It's part of our job to help him acclimate. So that's what I'm doing.

Aye, I'm sure that's the reason, her dragon drawled. *And does that acclimation include helping him to relax? You know, in the naked and moaning capacity?*

An image flashed of Lachlan's intense gaze focused solely on her, conveying all the things he wanted to do with her—licking, sucking, biting—before doing them in truth.

Just the thought of all that intensity on her made Cat shiver.

She quickly pushed the image aside. *No, I'm not thinking of shagging him. Maybe I should go find one of the MacKay brothers and try to seduce him. Then you'd stop bombarding me with sexy images.*

I haven't done it today. That's all you.

Whenever she didn't want to admit her dragon was correct, Cat ignored her.

Not that she had to ignore her beast for long since in the next minute, they'd reached the warehouse. After putting in a code—Lochguard had suffered too many attacks and threats to not have heightened security—she motioned Lachlan inside.

Once the door closed, she said, "This way. I'll give you a tour of all the smaller rooms later. I want to show you the main workspace first."

He inclined his head in answer, the action so formal it was hard to believe he'd teased and cursed not five minutes ago.

Lachlan MacKintosh had turned out to be more of an enigma than she'd thought.

The project, Cat. Focus on the project. Striding ahead, she finally reached the main room. All of the doubts and surprises from during her walk with Lachlan faded, replaced with a bubbling sense of excitement.

Whenever she could share her art with someone, she always felt this way—anxious and happy with a sense of accomplishment. But today was extra special since Lachlan would be the first to see her mural on the wall.

And while Cat knew she had talent, a gift, even, for painting, her stomach churned a little. She'd never done a mural before, and she hoped Lachlan saw it the way she did.

Pushing aside the blasted doubts, Cat walked into the room and flipped on the lights.

It was one large, open space with various worktables, easels, and empty carts ready for supplies, with several sinks dotted along one edge.

However, she focused solely on the patch of wall she'd claimed as her own, on the far side of the room.

She'd painted a pair of dragons flying through the stars in the night sky, the moon glinting off their hides, and items related to Lochguard's history hidden as constellations.

An old brooch, an old-fashioned crest, and even

her imagining of their very first clan leader were all there.

It was very Lochguard-specific, but that was the point. Her aim was for every artist to paint their own mural, representing something from their hometowns or clans. Not only so they could learn from one another, but the rest of her clan and any visitors could learn a little too.

Lachlan walked closer to her mural, his hands behind his back, until he stopped near it but still far enough away he could see the whole thing.

Her first instinct was to rush over and explain everything. However, if the point was for others to look and interpret, she needed to allow time for that.

So she casually walked over to him. After a few minutes, she asked, "What do you think?"

"It's different."

She resisted biting her lip to hold her tongue and asked, "Different how?"

He gestured toward the mural. "It's a bit more fantastical than the other things I've seen of yours. Not that it's bad but just different."

"I know, but it was the only way to get so much in and not have it look forced."

He pointed toward the crest. "Like your clan's original crest."

Pleasure shot through her at him recognizing the small detail. She nodded. "Aye, there are eight things hidden in the stars. While I think it looks fantastic, it's also engaging. Something I hope the old and young can appreciate when you start giving tours."

He finally looked at her, but Cat couldn't read his expression. "You thought that far ahead?"

"Aye, of course I did. I almost always do. Well, at least since my father died and I had to help my mother raise my siblings. Trust me, any of those rascals would take any advantage they could find if I left them an opening. Which meant I always had to plan two steps ahead of them."

He continued to look at her and asked quietly, "When did your father pass away?"

She paused a beat, debating if she should answer. It'd been more than ten years, but talking about her father still made her throat tighten.

Lachlan quickly added, "You don't have to tell me."

No, she didn't. And yet, the words tumbled from her lips before she could stop herself. "I'm surprised it didn't come up in your research. A little over ten years ago, he was…" She paused, took a deep breath, and then added, "He was captured by dragon hunters and later found drained of blood."

Lachlan said softly, "I had no idea. Apologies."

She shrugged, trying her best to ignore how formal and cold the words sounded. "It's better you find out now instead of politely asking my mother."

Rather than point out how he didn't need to meet

her mother to finish his tasks for the project, he just nodded and looked back at the mural.

And since she'd shared so much already, she decided what the hell and murmured, "The blue dragon in the mural is my father. The other is his friend, who'd been missing and my father had been searching for when he was captured."

Lachlan never looked away from the two dragons. "His friend suffered the same fate."

"Aye."

They stood in silence. Not an awkward one, but just as if they were both honoring the two dragonmen for a minute, remembering them and how they should still be alive if not for greed.

And aye, it'd been greed. Dragon's blood had healing properties and sold for huge amounts on the black market.

Not that Cat ever tried to think about that, or how the hunters had seen her father and his friend as nothing more than disposable beings, unworthy of life if it meant they could get rich.

Lachlan's voice interrupted her thoughts. "I'm sorry. I can't imagine what it's like losing a father you cared for."

His words seemed an odd choice to her—not just sorry for her loss, but for someone she cared for. However, before she could even debate asking for more information, Lachlan cleared his throat and gestured toward the door. "How about you show me the rest of the place?"

Grateful for the change in topic—she would always love her father, but thinking about him still made her sadder than she would ever like to admit—she strode over toward the exit.

Once she'd shown Lachlan every room in the building and left him in his temporary office, Cat quickly exited the warehouse and soon jogged toward her small studio space.

She only had an hour before she had to help at the restaurant, but she itched to work on something, anything, to help restore her spirits.

Without realizing it, she ended up working the whole time on another sketch of Lachlan. But this time, he had fire in his eyes, making the drawing more animated somehow.

More than that, it was more *him* instead of just a two-dimensional being. Still full of mystery, but a little less icelike than all the other times she'd drawn him. Maybe once she finally painted a piece that seemed more him, she could forget about the male.

Aye, that had to be it. She was stubborn and determined when it came to getting something just right in her art. Once she did it for Lachlan, she could mostly forget about him and stop trying to figure out his secrets.

Chapter Three

Lachlan spent the rest of the day settling into both his new office and then the cottage he would call home for the next few months, keeping himself busy enough to not slip up and think of Cat.

Aye, well, at least when he was awake.

By the next morning, he pushed all those visions of him fucking her in her studio space—over a table, against a wall, sitting on a counter—and attended a meeting with some of Lochguard's security team, better known as the Protectors.

He'd worked with both the ones on Lochguard and others in the UK before, although his current experience was filled with more questions, forms, and borderline lectures than in the past. Usually, he received any sort of instructions or lectures from the sole dragonman in charge—labeled head Protector— but Lochguard had two people in charge of clan security. And while both had conducted the most recent meeting, along with a few of their colleagues in attendance, the animated one with wild, curly hair named Faye MacKenzie had done most of the talking.

All while carrying her baby in some sort of contraption on her chest.

Eventually, the group meeting finished, although Faye and her mate and co-head Protector, Grant, signaled for him to stay. Once they were alone, Faye spoke. "Whilst the main celebration will be held when all the artists arrived, Finn wants to welcome you properly to the clan with a smaller gathering tonight, to ease you into it all."

Given how big most of the families on Lochguard were, Lachlan wondered if "small" was the right word. "I can spare an hour or two, but I still have a lot of work to do before the artists arrive in two months."

Faye raised her dark brows. "One night won't kill you. Besides, not only is it rare to get people we trust to watch all the bairns for an evening, but also Sylvia MacAllister worked hard to get a huge dinner ready for the event."

At the name MacAllister, Lachlan perked up a little. He went through the names in his head and remembered that she was Cat's mother. Still, he couldn't resist pointing out, "If someone had to prepare a huge meal, then I'm not sure the gathering counts as small."

Faye glared, but Grant tried not to smile as he said, "It's small by her family's standards. But regardless, part of your assignment is to better know the clan, aye? Hiding away in your work won't accomplish that."

Lachlan was aware of that. But most of the time, getting to know someone in the UK meant going to a pub. And while he could, technically, make it through a night surrounded by a room full of people drinking alcohol and not relapse, it was a strain he didn't much care for.

And hence why he spent so much time on his work and not on socializing.

Grant motioned for Faye to leave them, and she did so without a word.

Quite the feat, that, given how the dragonwoman had been in charge most of the meeting. He'd heard about the strong bonds between dragon mates, and apparently, that had to be the case with Faye and Grant. He doubted Faye would so easily be dismissed by anyone else.

Once they were alone, Grant cleared his throat and said, "I'm not going to beat around the bush. We did a background check on you and are more than aware of your past." Lachlan had long ago learned to keep his face passive when someone casually mentioned his blackout-drunk phase, and nodded.

Grant continued, "But don't worry, we don't have a pub here and rarely have alcohol. Lochguard had an incident about twenty years ago, something that involved a few people dying, and it's been clan law since then to keep alcohol to a minimum to avoid a repeat occurrence. Sometimes we have it for big celebrations, but tonight isn't one of those."

In other words, if Lachlan attended the gathering, he wouldn't have to worry about more than handling a room full of dragon-shifters. There wouldn't be any alcohol to consciously resist.

Apart from his sister, few bothered to care about such details.

And maybe he should be embarrassed—at one time, discussing his biggest weakness would've done exactly that—but instead, all Lachlan felt was greater respect for Grant. "Thank you for telling me that."

The dragonman waved a hand in dismissal and stood. "No worries." He grinned slowly. "But now you have no excuse not to attend. And if I were you, I wouldn't even try to weasel out of it. You've worked with Faye before, but trust me, when her entire family gets together, it's madness. They'll hunt you down and drag you to the event, if need be."

He blinked. Surely he had to be joking.

Grant said, "And they will too. So be at the great hall by six, aye? And dress casually. No need for the tie."

Lachlan resisted straightening his. In a way, his suit and tie were a type of armor for him.

But since he'd have to attend many casual events in the future once the artists arrived, he needed to get used to being without it.

Standing, Lachlan nodded. "I'll be there, and I can bring some dessert."

Grant raised his eyebrows. "You can cook?"

He shrugged. When someone had as much time alone as Lachlan, a person picked up a few hobbies. Not that he was going to go into detail with a dragonman he barely knew.

Grant opened the door. "If you can make a strawberry cheesecake, you'll win over both my mate and her brothers. And trust me, they are good people to have as allies."

Lachlan didn't have a bloody clue what Grant was talking about since, apart from Faye, he wouldn't have any dealings with the MacKenzies. However, he thought nodding was the best course of action.

And as they exited the security building and Lachlan headed toward his cottage, he wondered what constituted madness for a dragon-shifter family.

Cat laid out the last of the food she, Connor, and her mother had brought to the great hall and wondered if it'd be enough.

Between her family, the MacKenzies, Finn's family, and Chase and Layla McFarland, she doubted the spread would last very long.

Her mother snorted and said, "Don't worry, Cat. I have more keeping warm in the wee kitchen in the back. But if there's one thing I learned with five children, it's that you always hold some in reserve just in case you need it."

She smiled at her mum. "Especially with Connor."

Her mother laughed. "Aye, although all of you eat your weight in food. Or, at least you did when you were younger."

Connor's voice came from behind her. "I heard that. And you're wrong—I eat the most. It's why I'm the tallest."

Cat rolled her eyes. "That's not how it works."

Her brother winked. "Says the shortest of us all, the one who sometimes forgets to eat when lost in an art project."

It was true—she lost track of time when an idea struck. That's why she had alarms everywhere. Sometimes it took two to get her head out of the clouds. "I'm the same height as Mum. It's called genetics."

Connor swiped a roll, and their mother raised her brows before saying, "Take anything else from this table before the others get here, Connor Archibald, and you'll eat last, only getting whatever wee scraps you can find." Amusement twinkled in her mum's eyes as she added, "And who knows, maybe you'll start shrinking without so much food."

As her brother tried to play the wounded son—his hand over his heart as if he'd been stabbed—Cat couldn't stop smiling. Aye, because her brother was an idiot sometimes, and she couldn't help it. But also because her mother had been feeling better the last few weeks, acting almost like her old self.

She and her siblings knew their mother had suffered an illness for over a year, but not much more than that. Her mum refused to elaborate. But she was tired a lot and was too thin, and until recent weeks, had been even quieter than normal.

And since Cat couldn't very well corner any of the doctors and demand answers because of privacy rules, her mind kept coming up with possible scenarios. Dragon-shifters didn't get cancer, but there were always other diseases that could make them quite ill and even die.

Stop. Not tonight. No, she wouldn't worry about that for once. This evening was all about a little fun.

Well, for her and the other dragon-shifters, anyway. She wasn't entirely sure Lachlan would enjoy it.

She wanted to see how he did when surrounded by the craziness of the four families. She hadn't lied when she'd told him his formality would annoy almost everyone on Lochguard. And many of those attending the gathering weren't exactly what she'd call tactful.

And she hoped their bluntness taught him to trust her word when it came to fitting in better with the Scottish dragons. After all, that was part of the reason he was here early—to learn how to better bridge between Lochguard and the human visitors who would attend the art exhibition.

However, all thoughts of the project vanished as her youngest brother, Jamie, rushed into the room and shouted, "Everyone's just about to come in! Can I start the music now?"

Her mother answered, "Aye, as long as it's not some sort of booming dance music to give us all headaches, then you can start playing it."

Jamie raced over to the little computer-slash-deejay station on the side of the room. Cat murmured to her mother, "Clever to have him occupied for the night."

Her mum laughed. "I love all my children, but Finn said this DDA lad was somewhat reserved. I thought it best to save him from Jamie, at least for tonight."

She smiled and glanced at her youngest brother. Jamie loved to talk, so much so, even their grandfather Archie would find ways to excuse himself.

And considering her granddad had once dropped a boulder on his neighbor's barn over a minor dispute, he wasn't exactly the model of decorum.

Which reminded her. "Granddad isn't bringing his, er, thruple tonight is he?"

Her mother looked at the ceiling. "No, thank goodness. He said he couldn't make it tonight."

Her grandfather was in a complicated relationship with another female and male. The three were inseparable.

And while Lochguard was used to it, she doubted Lachlan would be.

To be honest, she'd rather like to be the one to explain that situation to him. Maybe then he'd show some surprise for a change.

Or any emotion, really. His cool demeanor—or was it a façade?—only irritated her, and she had no idea why. She'd certainly met reserved people before.

Her dragon spoke up. *It's because he's keeping his true self tamped down. He showed us what he could be with that one outburst, and you want more of that side of him.*

Rather than discuss the point with her inner beast, she focused on her twin siblings, Ian and Emma, as they walked inside the room and stopped near them. Emma said, "You should see that human male. Didn't you say he was stuffy, Cat?" Her sister fanned herself. "Something must've happened because he's looking dead sexy tonight."

She blinked at her sister's words. Had Lachlan finally decided to show more of himself to

Lochguard? It was only a matter of time before her family or the MacKenzies would force it out anyway.

Or, so she thought. Lochguard had a reputation for helping people find their true selves.

However, before she could ask her sister for more details—to better prepare, Cat told herself—people filed into the large room.

First it was Finn and his mate, then Faye and Grant. And then right behind them was Lachlan, and Cat nearly did a double take.

He wore jeans and a button-down top, the sleeves rolled up to nearly his elbow, revealing the dark hair of his muscled forearms.

Between that and the peek of his chest where he had a few buttons undone at the top of his shirt, he seemed more male and less…DDA employee.

Even his gait seemed more relaxed.

Then he met her gaze from across the room. But while he'd relaxed his appearance, Lachlan's eyes were impassive as ever. He may be dressed casually, but that bloody façade was still in place.

Obviously the MacKenzies hadn't gotten to him yet.

And devil she was, she couldn't wait to see how he reacted when that lot finally turned their attention toward him.

She crossed the room to Lachlan and smiled. "I wasn't entirely sure you'd come."

He murmured, "I didn't really have a choice."

The tall, ginger-haired Fraser MacKenzie smacked Lachlan on the shoulder. "Aye, but you'll have a good time. It's my mission for the evening to make it happen."

Cat resisted a groan. She liked Fraser a lot, but he could get into trouble. Some of his dares over the years were legendary. He'd tamed a little since finding his mate, but not entirely. While she wanted the MacKenzies to rattle Lachlan a wee bit, Fraser would probably go overboard without the influence of his twin brother or his mate.

However, before Cat could look to either of the two calming influences for reassurance, Fraser's mate —a human female named Holly—spoke up. "Leave him be, Fraser."

Fraser's twin brother, Fergus, sighed and said, "Aye, he's our guest. Let the human decide how much fun he wants to have instead of trying to force it on him."

Chase McFarland—Grant's younger brother— jumped in. "Tell me your plan, Fraser. Maybe I can help you."

Chase kissed his pregnant mate, Layla, on the cheek, and the female merely laughed as Fraser and Chase went off to some corner to discuss who the hell knew what. However, Holly signaled she would keep Fraser and Chase in check—mostly because Layla was under orders to take it easy due to her pregnancy and had promised to sit down most of the night—and the human female motioned for Cat to take Lachlan away to somewhere safe.

Noticing the cheesecake in Lachlan's hands, Cat motioned toward the table. "Here, let's put your dessert with the rest of the food." Once they were away from the crowd, she stole a glance at Lachlan. And at the slight frown on his face, she laughed. "This is them being calm, so you may want to steel yourself for much worse."

As the music increased in volume—her brother did it on purpose to annoy their mother, she was sure of it—she took the cheesecake, laid it down, and turned toward Lachlan.

He stood there with his brows furrowed as he watched the growing group of Fraser, Chase, Holly, and Grant, and she wondered if all of this was too much too soon. She whispered just loud enough for him to hear over the music, "I tried to talk them out of it and suggested a smaller dinner first, but they were adamant about welcoming you properly."

Lachlan met her gaze again, and he shrugged. "I'll just watch and learn how things work here. Once I figure that out, I won't be so surprised."

She raised her brows. "I've lived here my whole life and I still don't have it all figured out. So good luck with that."

He almost smiled. "Aye, well, sometimes an observer notices things quicker."

When he relaxed, the Scot in Lachlan came out

more. However, she didn't want to spook him so didn't point it out. Instead, she handed him a plate. "Hurry and take whatever you want to eat. And don't be polite about it either. My brother Connor alone could eat half the food on this table." She took a plate as well. "I think we have about thirty seconds, maybe sixty, before they notice and come running. So, be quick about it."

And as she rushed from dish to dish, taking what she wanted, sure enough, the others made a beeline straight for the table.

Still, Lachlan waited off to the side. Oh well, he'd learn soon enough.

Smiling, Cat took the last of the food she wanted and waited at a safe distance from the table to see what happened.

LACHLAN PRIDED himself on watching a situation, gathering the facts, and making an informed decision.

But as most of the others in the room rushed over to the table, pushing him out of the way, he wondered if that kind of approach would work on Lochguard.

Especially as Faye shoved the ginger-haired twins —her brothers, if he remembered right—so hard they fell back on their arses.

One of the female dragons—the doctor?— stopped next to him and murmured, "And this is why we're in the great hall. Aunt Lorna's dining table isn't big enough anymore."

He glanced over at her, her hand on her barely noticeable pregnant belly—one of the dragon-shifters had mentioned her state to him coming in— and he frowned. "You should be going first."

Layla shook her head. "It's okay. Chase will get me a plate."

Still, the fact the others were piling their dishes full without letting the pregnant woman go first rankled him. So much so, he decided to screw being observant and restore some order. Manners weren't solely for humans, after all.

Lachlan shouted, "Stop!"

And, miraculously, everyone did and looked at him.

He may not be the most outgoing of people, but he was used to sometimes being the center of attention because of his job. So he cleared his throat and said, "Have some manners," before clearing a path to let Layla through.

Her mate instantly came to her side, murmuring questions if she were all right, and Lachlan let the dragonman take care of her. Still, Lachlan crossed his arms and glared around the room.

He didn't care if one of those people were the clan leader or that two of them were in charge of security. If they punished or lectured him for wanting to help a pregnant woman, then so be it.

Finn walked up to him and put out a hand. Lachlan barely resisted blinking at the gesture. Once he took it and they shook, Finn smiled at him. "Aye, you're going to do just fine here."

Lachlan had no bloody idea what that was supposed to mean, but he asked, "Was this some sort of test?"

Finn snorted. "I wish I were that clever, but my family is a bit wild at times. And we all know the MacKenzies will battle each other for food, so everyone usually just lets them sort it out amongst themselves. But you're right—Layla should've gone first." He slapped him on the shoulder. "But she's just about done, so now it's your turn. You're the guest, after all, aye?"

All eyes were on him again, and so he did as the clan leader asked. Once done, he scanned the room, and he hurried to the end of the lone, long table set up for the meal.

Between the wall on one side and one chair on the other, Lachlan at least minimized how many people sat around him.

It also gave him a better vantage point to watch how they all interacted with each other.

Regardless, he waited for the others to sit down before he began eating.

Since Cat had already filled her plate, she ignored the niggle of shame at not thinking of Layla first and walked toward the long table set up for the night.

She wasn't sure where to sit, but then Lachlan sat down at one end, the section nearest the wall, and she smiled. If she were new and didn't want to be in the middle of the madness, she would've picked the same spot.

And while she didn't mind her clan members, she quickly sat across from Lachlan and asked, "Were you a dragon-shifter in a former life?"

He frowned slightly, his fingers playing with the fork beside his plate. "What are you talking about?"

She shrugged. "I don't claim to be an expert on humans, especially human males, but I don't think many others would've done what you did just now, with Layla."

He grunted and laid down his fork. He murmured so quietly that if she didn't have supersensitive hearing, Cat might've missed it. "I spent too many years hurting others and disregarding everyone's feelings. I'm trying to make up for it."

As he began to play with the cutlery again, she tried to figure out his meaning. Lachlan may be uptight and not quick to laugh, but he'd never been mean or cruel to her. She should hold her tongue, but she blurted, "How did you hurt others?"

Their end of the table was still empty, although she didn't think for long since she saw Finn and Arabella heading their way. However, she wasn't entirely sure he'd answer until he said, "It's a long story. Maybe some other time."

She could tell by the set of his jaw that Lachlan wasn't going to change his mind this evening simply because she'd needled him.

Besides, as Finn and Arabella sat next to them, she noticed how Lachlan's face turned into the impassive front he usually wore.

Her dragon spoke up. *We need to figure out his secret.*
Since when do you care?

Her dragon huffed. *When doesn't a dragon want to discover a secret? It's a special kind of treasure, aye?*

Her inner beast was right, which could spell trouble for their working relationship with the human if her dragon decided to keep digging until Lachlan revealed his past.

Especially since she sensed it wouldn't be easy coaxing it from him. Her gut said Lachlan's truth was more than merely shouting at someone or getting into a fistfight in his youth. *He'll tell us when he's ready.*

Her dragon was about to reply when Cat noticed her mum quickly get up from the other end of the table and race from the room.

She saw Layla standing, but Cat jumped to her

feet and said to Layla, "I'll check on her, you sit down," and raced out of the room.

She entered the restroom and heard her mother vomit a few seconds before flushing the toilet. "Mum?"

For a few beats, nothing, then her mother emerged from the stall, her face pale and looking more tired than her forty-four years. "Mum?" she said again softly, more a question than anything else. "What's going on?"

Had her illness reached a critical stage? Was her mother dying?

She couldn't be; she just couldn't. Cat couldn't imagine her life without her mother.

But she needed to be strong for her mum, like she'd done right after Cat's father had died. So doing her best to push down her emotions, Cat kept a patient expression on her face and waited for her mother to answer.

Her mum went to the sink, rinsed out her mouth, and then placed her hands on the counter to steady herself. Leaning against it, she sighed. "This isn't how I imagined this conversation going."

She was at her mother's side and met her gaze in the mirror. Something about her mother's tone told her it was big news. She only hoped it wasn't about her illness being worse and that she was dying.

Pushing aside her fear once more, Cat said softly, "Just tell me."

Her mother closed her eyes a few beats, then opened them and said, "Oh, Cat. For better or worse, I'll just say it—you're going to be a big sister again."

Stunned, she merely blinked. Aye, Cat's mother had been barely eighteen when she'd had her and was still fairly young compared to the mothers of most of her friends, but she hadn't even known her mum had been seeing anyone.

Her dragon said softly, *You don't have to have a relationship to conceive a child.*

Ignoring her beast, she blurted, "How? Who? Is that why you've been so tired?"

Her mother finally turned to face her and gently touched her cheek. "Aye, and only the doctors knew. I made them promise not to tell anyone."

Something still niggled at the back of her mind. "But you've been ill for over a year." She gestured toward her mother's abdomen. "And yet you aren't even showing, so you can't have been pregnant the whole time."

Her mother replied, "I *was* ill for a while, which made me rather reckless for a few months." She placed a hand over her belly. "Which is how this happened."

More than the father's identity, Cat worried about the long-term consequences. She blurted, "Will the bairn kill you?"

Maybe it was blunt, and she should've been more tactful, but her mother's smile helped to ease her nerves a fraction. "Quite the opposite, love. I've been doing better, both in general, according to my lab results. The doctors are still trying to figure out why, but I don't care. All signs point to this pregnancy saving my life."

"So you won't be ill any longer?" she whispered.

Her mum squeezed her shoulder. "I don't think so, beyond the usual pregnancy things."

Relief washed over her at the news. Cat knew her mother couldn't live forever, but she wanted more time with her. And it seemed she'd have it.

After a beat, she said, "None of the others have guessed, have they?"

Even without mentioning it, her mother knew her meaning. "No, your siblings don't know. And promise me you won't tell them, Cat. I need to figure out a few things first." She looked away a second. "Especially concerning the father."

"Who is it?" she asked quietly.

Her mum looked back at her and smiled slightly. "I want to tell you, I do. But not yet. Please understand, aye?"

She nearly asked if the male in question knew she'd been sick.

Not to mention the lack of any male visitors to see her mother that Cat had noticed, which could mean he truly had abandoned her and the new bairn. If he had known about her mum's illness and had refused to help her with the bairn, he was an arsehole who should be punished.

So many questions, and yet for some reason, anger rolled in her belly. And not just about the mysterious male.

Part of Cat wanted to yell that they'd all been so worried about her and that she should've told them she was doing better instead of letting them think the worse.

To let them think she was dying.

And yet, at the pleading look in her mum's eyes, Cat knew she'd never betray her by telling her siblings without permission.

However, if it was going to keep the secret, she needed to leave and clear her head before she said something she'd regret. Her temper didn't strike often, but she was nearly at the tipping point.

Cat needed time to think. And figure out a way to keep her emotions from showing on her face around her siblings, which wasn't easy for her.

She took a step back. "I won't tell them, but I have to go."

"Cat—"

She put up a hand. "I'll be fine, Mum. Just give my apologies to the others, aye? Provided you're well enough to go back on your own."

Her mother bobbed her head. "Aye, I'll be fine. It's just the scent of the meat that did it."

Cat should be nice, and rational, and caring.

Guide her mother back to the table, return to Lachlan, and try to pretend her mother hadn't revealed to Cat how she would have a sibling more than twenty-six years her junior.

But Cat's feet had a mind of their own, and she exited the great hall, headed to a nearby landing area, and shifted into her dragon form.

Once she was in the air, she tried to sort through her thoughts and wondered why her mother's news bothered her so much. Maybe because she still thought her mother would die, or that Cat would have to take care of yet another sibling, especially if her mum fell ill again.

Or maybe, she just had wanted an easy few months with all the other artists, giving her a chance to focus on what fed her soul instead of trying to help keep her siblings in line and take care of everyone but herself.

But for whatever reason, the cool night air, the stars, and the pinpricks of light below from the few houses she passed held her full attention, and she merely focused on memorizing the scenes to use in future paintings.

She would be able to face everyone in the morning. But for now, the stars, the moon, and her dragon were her perfect companions.

Chapter Four

The next morning, Lachlan sat at his desk inside his new office on Lochguard and tried to focus on his laptop.

There was always paperwork and emails to do, more so than normal, given how he was orchestrating a months-long event starting in the autumn. He could spend all morning on them and still not finish everything.

And yet, he itched to forget about them for a while and go find Cat.

She'd left early the night before, her mother said something about an errand. But Lachlan noticed how once Cat's mother had returned to the table, she'd looked a little worried and maybe even a wee bit sad.

Something had happened between the two of them; he was sure of it.

However, everyone had taken Sylvia at her word and spend the evening trying to get him to talk.

And while he'd survived—it seemed when the dragonmen sat with their mates, they tended to behave a bit better—Lachlan had glanced at Cat's abandoned plate a few times and wondered what had happened to her.

He didn't doubt her family loved her—all of their banter and teasing proved it to him—but one of them should've gone after Cat to check on her.

But no one had.

Which meant no one knew if she was doing okay.

He let out a frustrated sigh and stood. Even though Lachlan was due to talk with Cat later in the afternoon, it was almost his duty to check on her sooner. After all, he needed her help with coordinating with the other clans and artists. And she certainly couldn't do that if she were missing or upset.

This is ridiculous. She's a grown woman and can sort out her own problems. Get back to work. He stared at the laptop again. But the words swam and he still couldn't concentrate.

So much for his iron-clad discipline.

Maybe once she smiled and teased him—maybe even threw a few swear words his way to try and make her point—then maybe he could bloody focus on his ever-growing to-do list.

Decision made, Lachlan walked to the door and

out of the cottage. On the day he'd arrived, the dragon-shifters had given him a tour of the dragon clan. And during it, they'd pointed out Cat's art studio. They said any time he couldn't find her elsewhere, she'd probably be there. So he was going to check.

A few people waved, and he returned the gesture, but kept walking. Once Lachlan had his mind set on something, he carried it out. Maybe the others would think him rude, but he didn't care at the moment.

Three dragons flew overhead, and he watched them disappear into the distance. He most definitely wasn't back home in Glasgow.

He finally approached Cat's studio—an addition added to a cottage—and knocked on the door. At first, silence. But just as he was about to knock again, the door opened, revealing Cat wearing a smock covered in more colors than he could count and several paint smudges on her face. She blinked. "Lachlan? I thought our meeting was in a few hours?"

He shrugged. "It was." Not wanting their conversation to be broadcast to anyone passing by, he motioned past her. "Can I come in?"

Her brows furrowed slightly. "I would say yes, but it's a mess, and I really need to finish what I'm doing before the paint dries."

"I can stand off to the side until you're done. But we need to talk as soon as you finish."

She studied him a second, and he couldn't blame her. There was nothing urgent for them to discuss. After all, there were almost two months until any of the events began, or artists arrived, and the nearest deadline wasn't for at least a week.

However, she finally stood back and waved inside. "Come in. Just be careful where you walk. I'm not the tidiest of painters."

His eyes darted to the paint on her face, her smock, and finally, her fingers. He smiled. "No, you're not."

She almost smiled back. "I can imagine you are, though. Pristine and perfect."

He shook his head. "I'm not a painter at all, lass. I just like to admire it."

Her smiled widened. "Well, maybe we'll have to get you to try your hand at it at least once." Before he could say that would be a waste of paint, she motioned again. "Let's go. I really need to finish what I'm doing."

He followed her down a small hallway and toward the door at the end. She gestured to the doors at either side of it. "One is storage, and one is a toilet. I'm telling you this because I get rather engrossed in my work, aye? So I don't want you to start dancing if you need to take a piss."

He nearly blinked at her words but then brushed his surprise aside. She probably did it to try and rile him up. And who the hell knew why, but he shot back, "I'm a man, which means I can just go find a bush somewhere."

She rolled her eyes. "Yes, one of the things males take pride in about their dicks."

"I'm not sure it's so much pride as convenience." She stuck out her tongue, and he snorted. "A very cogent argument, that."

"You clearly don't have any annoying siblings because it works well with them, especially if you want to rile them up as payback."

Lachlan had only the one, but rather than darken the mood with how he'd fucked up that relationship for years before fixing it—mostly—he pointed at the door. "Are we going in or staying here in the dark hallway?"

She put her hand on the doorknob. "Just be quiet whilst I work, aye?"

He nodded, and she opened the door. Lachlan followed on her heels.

The room was much bigger than he expected, each wall about fifteen feet long, with windows and sunlight coming in from three directions.

Even with it being overcast, light filled the room, making it almost cheerful.

But as his eyes glanced around the room, the bright colors of the paintings made it more so.

Cat watched him, but he waved toward the huge easel at one side, which had a cart and a stool in front of it. "Go finish what you're doing. Looking at all your work will distract me for a while."

She opened her mouth as if to ask something but then promptly closed it and nodded. "Aye, all right. I shouldn't need more than half an hour or so to finish this layer."

So as Cat focused on her piece, Lachlan slowly went from painting to painting, studying the subjects, colors, and tones. Art could tell quite a bit about a person, especially if you knew the artist behind it even a little.

And for some reason, he looked more closely than normal, almost as if Cat MacAllister was a puzzle he wished to solve.

CAT USUALLY HATED when someone was in her studio. Mostly because anyone who had come before tended to chat, or ask questions, or make a lot of noise. They didn't seem to understand that art took concentration, just like anything else.

However, Lachlan was quiet, didn't talk, and she barely noticed he was there as she focused on finishing her latest layer.

As she blended some green in one place and then some blue elsewhere, she once again became lost in her piece. Everything else melted away until it was just her and her art.

It could've been hours later for all she knew, but as Cat finished the last detail, she could tell from the daylight that it hadn't been too long. She took her palette and was about to go clean up when she glanced at the leftover paint and smiled. Turning toward Lachlan, who stared at a piece representing an ancient battle between the dragons and some human English soldiers centuries ago, she said, "Lachlan."

He took a few more beats to study the painting and then turned to her. "Are you finished?"

"Aye, I am. But before we go and have our meeting, there's something we're going to do first."

He raised a dark eyebrow. "I hope you're not going to suggest for us to tidy up together. Aye, I have a few ideas of how to make this space more efficient, but it'll take days."

She smiled. "I have a system in place, even if you can't tell. But no, that's not it." She motioned toward a smaller easel she had set up on a table. "Come over here a second."

As she placed a small canvas on the easel, she could feel the second he stood next to her. As silly as it sounded, heat radiated from his body, and he smelled faintly of some manly soap.

Her dragon yawned and woke up from her nap, which she always did when Cat painted, and said, *I smell more of the male than the soap. He smells better.*

Cat nearly took a deep inhalation to see if she

could notice it, but she quickly pushed that thought aside. This was Lachlan, after all. He'd probably call her mad and ask for someone else to be his co-coordinator, for someone who didn't randomly sniff other people.

Her dragon was about to reply, but Cat spoke aloud, silencing her beast. "I have a little paint leftover, so I thought you could try your hand at it."

She glanced at him, noticing the faint, dark stubble on his jaw. He was probably a male who had to shave twice a day if he wanted smooth skin.

Not that Cat minded a little roughness.

Willing her cheeks not to burn, she focused on grabbing a paintbrush and handing it to him. "And don't worry, we'll just try something abstract. That's just a shorthand way to say you can do whatever you want and call it art."

Adjusting his grip on the brush, he dabbed it into some blue paint and created a straight, diagonal line across the rectangular surface. "There. I'm done."

She rolled her eyes. "No, that was you being a cheeky bastard."

She wrapped her hand around his fingers. Her heart skipped a beat at the feel of his warm, rough skin under hers.

Maybe she had gone too long without sex. Because this was Lachlan, the opposite of everything she was.

Someone most definitely not for her.

Her dragon hummed. *But he's here, and his heart rate ticked up.*

Probably because he's nervous around dragon-shifters still.

Tell yourself that, but I think you're just a coward.

Ignoring her dragon, Cat cleared her throat and fell back on her art teacher persona. She moved his hand to dip the tip into the paint and put it back in front of the canvas. "Just put the brush on the surface and let it flow. Try to show a bit of yourself on the canvas. And don't say that you're a straight line. I know you well enough to call bullshit on that."

She saw him smile, the action making him less formal and, dare she say it, a wee bit more handsome. Lachlan replied, "One part of me is that straight line. But the other…"

He trailed off, and with her hand still on his, he moved it to one side, swiped up slowly, moved back, and created a curvy, complicated design out of blue paint.

He lifted the brush off the canvas, and Cat finally released his hand. She stared at the intricate pattern and then looked up at Lachlan. "That's more believable."

"What would your pattern look like?" he murmured.

"Probably not that different."

He turned the brush toward her. "Show me."

She took the brush, her fingers brushing against Lachlan's, and her heart thundered in her ears.

Part of her wanted to clear her throat and suggest they clean up. It'd be a lot easier to collect herself that way and reinforce that he was most definitely not worth the trouble.

But unlike how she grew tired of painting the same things repeatedly for art lessons or when she demonstrated painting stroke techniques, she actually wanted to show him her design.

So before she could talk herself out of it, Cat dabbed off as much blue as she could and then dipped it into the yellow. Putting her brush on the surface near the top, she moved in broader strokes, curving around and through some of Lachlan's, the paint turning green wherever they touched, until she lifted her brush off the canvas. "There."

He traced the design without touching it. "A bit more open than mine."

"Aye, but they complement each other, I think."

As soon as the words left her lips, she wanted to take them back. He'd probably interpret them wrong.

But he murmured, "Aye, I agree." Then he picked up a brush from the table, dipped it into a cup of water he must've gotten while she'd been painting, and did his best to blend where the two colors melted into one.

As the paint thinned and he spread it, she could do nothing but watch. When he finished blending every time their two lines intersected, he said, "And now you can't tell it wasn't meant to be painted this way."

She glanced up at his face. "For someone who says he's never painted, you seem to know quite a bit."

He smiled—a real one this time, not merely the corners of his mouth ticking up slightly—and her heart fluttered a second. When had Lachlan become so handsome?

He replied, "I'm a quick learner, and I learn from the best."

She snorted. "I highly doubt me telling you to draw a line constitutes the best teacher."

He shrugged. "Maybe not that, but I watched you as you painted earlier. So aye, you were my teacher."

He'd watched her paint? And she hadn't felt his gaze on her while she'd worked?

Her dragon spoke up. *You wouldn't notice a naked man standing in a corner whilst you painted. Especially since I always sleep when you do.*

Ignoring her beast, she studied Lachlan's blue eyes, surprised to see them full of heat and maybe even…mischief?

She wondered if this was who Lachlan truly was when he let his guard down.

And without thinking, her gaze dropped to his mouth, to the lips she'd had such a hard time painting in the past.

But as she stared at the plumper bottom one, she

didn't care about sketching him right now. She wondered if he became even freer, or at least a bit more open when he couldn't talk.

Such as when he kissed someone.

Her dragon all but shouted, *Yes, yes. Kiss him. Just once. It's been too long.*

Kissing him was a bad idea, aye, a very bad one.

And yet now that her dragon had mentioned it, she couldn't think of anything else but how he'd taste or how he'd groan into her mouth.

His husky voice filled her ears. "What does your dragon keep saying to you?"

Her eyes moved back to his gaze, and she nearly sucked in a breath at the intensity there. Gone was the cool composure, replaced with a warm, inviting one that looked as if he wanted to lick every inch of her body.

Which was wrong. They shouldn't do any of that. After all, they had an event to plan.

And yet, it was almost as if she needed to kiss him. Only then could she forget about him and focus on her work.

Before she could stop herself, she leaned closer toward him until their bodies were a scant inch apart. She replied, "You really don't want to know. Dragons are a randy bunch."

"Oh, aye?" he murmured. "Why do you say that?"

Her beast said, *Don't tell him, show him. Just kiss him*

already. For once, do something for yourself and not for other people.

If her beast had merely nagged her or said he would scratch an itch, or even guilt-tripped Cat into trying to kiss him, she might've been able to resist.

But Cat rarely did something because she wanted to, apart from her art. And maybe if she hadn't learned the night before about how she'd probably be helping her mother for many more years to come with yet another sibling, she might've resisted.

However, Cat was tired of never being spontaneous. That was something she used to be in her childhood, but never since.

So she placed a hand on his chest, and time stilled as they stared at one another, her heart thundering in her ears. She finally murmured, "I can show you what she's thinking about."

He took her chin in his fingers and leaned closer to her face, until she could feel his hot breath on her lips.

That was all the encouragement she needed to pull his head down to hers and kiss him.

LACHLAN HAD TRIED his best not to notice Cat's beautiful dark blue eyes or how wisps of her black hair swirled around her head, catching the light.

Not to mention her deep pink lips, ones she'd

licked, and he couldn't stop wondering about how they'd taste.

Then she had to go and place her hand on his chest, making it harder for him to breathe for a few beats.

When their fingers had touched during the little painting lesson, he'd brushed off the heat as nothing more than Lachlan going too long without getting laid.

But with her hand on his chest, her face so close he could feel her breath on his skin, and being surrounded by her light scent mixed with paint, desire surged through him.

He wanted her, plain and simple.

The thought scared him, and he'd been about to step back to regain his senses when she brought his lips down to hers. He groaned at how soft they were and barely teased them to open when she pushed him away, dashed to the other side of the room, and faced the wall, her shoulders hunched over as if in pain.

It was far more than mere regret at kissing him, of that Lachlan was certain.

He took a step toward her. "Cat? What's wrong?"

Her voice was strained. "Get my mother. She's at the restaurant."

He took another step toward her, but she moved even farther away, placed her forehead against the wall, and hugged her arms around her chest. She shouted, "Go and get my mother!"

It seemed wrong to leave her. Being as gentle as possible, he said, "Tell me what's wrong."

She glanced over her shoulder, her pupils flashing faster than he'd ever seen. She roared, "Go find her! Now!"

He didn't want to leave her. But then she crouched down on the floor, and her voice was even more strained as she said, "Please. Find her."

In that moment, Lachlan's stomach knotted with dread. He'd worked with the DDA long enough to know the basics of dragon-shifters. He had a feeling he knew what was wrong with her.

But he pushed it aside for the moment. He'd find her mother and then learn soon enough if he was right or not.

And if he was…he wasn't sure if he could help her.

No, don't think about it right now. Help Cat first. That's what's important. With that thought in mind, Lachlan ran out of the room, the cottage, and as fast as he could go to the restaurant called The Dragon's Delight.

Once there, he rushed inside and decided to hell with decorum. Cat was in pain. "Where's Sylvia?" When everyone just stared at him, he roared, "Where is she?"

The older dragonwoman walked out of a back door with a frown. "What's going on?"

He rushed over to her and whispered, "It's Cat. Something's wrong, and she needs you. She's in her studio."

She must've heard the fear in his voice because she nodded. Sylvia looked at someone and told them to watch the restaurant, and then walked briskly out the door.

Lachlan followed, wishing he could run, but he matched his steps to Sylvia's.

The slower pace allowed his brain to calm down and think, though, and he knew there was only one reason Cat would be in pain after kissing him.

He was her bloody true mate, and she was trying to resist the mate-claim frenzy.

It seemed like his one moment of weakness, of finally doing something outside of his schedule and plans, had backfired.

Because when it came to true mates, the dragon would keep demanding sex until the female was pregnant.

And if Lachlan refused and didn't give it to her, she'd be drugged at first, and then he'd be sent as far away as possible for years until her beast calmed down.

Which would still mean months and months of hell for her.

After all the years of him trying to be better, to

avoid hurting others, it looked like he'd caused chaos yet again.

And Cat was suffering because of it.

Then finally Sylvia said, "Tell me what happened."

Once he recounted it, she took a second before saying, "I suspect you know what's happened, aye? Being with the DDA for as long as you have."

"Aye," he murmured.

The studio came into view. Sylvia pointed toward a road going off to the left. "Go to Finn's house, tell him Cat's fighting the frenzy, and have him send a doctor."

Lachlan felt as if he should say something, do something, but Sylvia gestured down the road. "Go. Right now, focus on helping Cat. The rest can wait."

And so he did what she asked, and while not his strong suit, he waited.

Chapter Five

Cat lay on her side, curled into a ball, using every bit of energy she had to stay where she was.

Her dragon kept trying to take control of their mind, wanting to run after Lachlan.

And when she didn't let her, her dragon kept roaring, *Find him and fuck him. He is ours. Why do you resist it? I won't. I'm going to find him, claim him, and take what I want.*

At some point, the demands to find and fuck Lachlan became a low hum, one she could barely make out as she did her best to keep her dragon in the back of her mind.

She barely noticed her mother finding her, only that she could hear her muffled voice, as if coming through water. "Shh, Catherine. The doctor is coming."

She had no bloody idea how long she lay there, trying to fight her dragon—who had always been her best friend up until that point—until suddenly, her dragon fell silent. Almost as if she'd disappeared completely.

Then she heard a familiar voice, that of Dr. Alex Campbell, Lochguard's junior doctor. "It's okay, Cat. Your dragon will only be gone a few days. She'll be back when you're ready."

Cat's entire body felt like it was weighed down with stones. She'd never been so tired in her life. But somehow, she managed to open her eyes. Her mother's face came into view. She was the one person Cat ever let her guard down around, the only one she didn't always have to be strong for.

And so she broke down into tears.

Her mother managed to get her sitting upright and hugged her close.

Maybe some people would be embarrassed crying into their mother's shoulder, but Cat didn't care if she were in her twenties. No, she took strength from her mother, and eventually, she calmed down.

Her mum said softly, "It's just you and me, Cat. The doctor's gone. So tell me why you're crying, aye?"

She looked into her mother's eyes, and a mixture of guilt and comfort rushed through her. Guilt at yelling at her mother the night before, but comfort from the one thing that had been constant in her life the longest. "I've ruined everything."

Her mum raised her brows. "Did you force yourself on Lachlan, or him you?"

She murmured, "No."

"Aye, well, then it takes two people to kiss, doesn't it?"

Cat sighed and looked off to the side. "I shouldn't have kissed him in the first place. I was given a huge responsibility. Finn even convinced the DDA to hold their event on Lochguard instead of in Glasgow or London, and I shirked it all for a kiss. Even if I didn't know he was my true mate, it was always a possibility. I should've been stronger, more responsible, and even a wee bit less selfish."

Her mother laid her cheek against the top of Cat's head. "You couldn't have known, love. And you're not the first one to get lost in the heat of the moment."

She shook her head. "That doesn't matter. I still screwed up."

For a beat, her mother said nothing. And then she finally replied, "You've always been the responsible one, taking on more than you should, especially once your father died. And I don't think I've ever told you, but your desire to help me even when you were still young yourself, well, aye, that is what pulled me out of my despair in the end."

At that, Cat moved so she could look her mother in the eye. "What do you mean?"

Her mum smiled, and it turned bittersweet. "I was sad, so very sad when your father was killed. As you know, he was my true mate, my best friend, and the love of my life. All of a sudden, he was gone without warning, and I was left with five children all on my own. I knew I needed to be there for you all. And still, it was so hard to get out of bed, let alone be what a mum should be." Her mother brushed some hair off Cat's face. "Then one morning, you came in with a breakfast tray, standing tall and far too mature for your fifteen years, and told me that the restaurant invoices were due. You'd convinced your siblings to help you carry me out of the bedroom to deal with them, if need be. And whilst it was ridiculous, it was exactly what I needed to hear."

Cat remembered how worried and yet determined she'd been back then. "I always wondered about that. Why did it work?"

Her mother stroked Cat's hair. "I realized that if you, at fifteen, were so determined to put our lives back together and order your mother to get out of bed, then I should try harder. Because if I didn't, you'd probably try to pick up the pieces. And that was selfish, unfair, and not at all what your father would've wanted." She finally smiled warmly. "Thank you, Cat, for that. But just know that it's okay to mess up sometimes to discover who you truly are. I think from that moment, you were determined to be the perfect daughter, the perfect sister, and the perfect everything. But we're the most interesting when we're a little less perfect, love. So rather than punish yourself for slipping up, do what you did with me— pick yourself up and think of your next move. It's your life, Cat. And you need to think of which way you want it to go."

She didn't pretend to misunderstand. "Bairn, or no bairn."

Her mum nodded. "I think Lachlan is a factor in there, too, aye?"

She frowned. "I barely know him."

Her mother shrugged one shoulder. "Maybe not, but he relaxes around you. I noticed it last night. And you light up, too, when talking with him. You almost seem a bit more like a young female than someone who's had to help take care of a family for a decade. And while it's not undying love, it's a start. You can use the next three or so days to see if it's enough."

Even if no one had told her, Cat knew her dragon was only quiet because of the shot to keep her dragon silent. Sometimes it was necessary when mate-claim frenzies kicked off unexpectedly.

Which meant she had approximately three days before her dragon woke up again to decide if she wanted a child or not.

Her first reaction was no. She'd barely finished raising her siblings with her mother.

And yet, if she had a true partner and male who cared for her by her side to help with it all, it might be okay. Despite her grumblings, she loved having a big family. Some people never had a sibling, and she couldn't imagine being alone so often.

Of course it wasn't solely her decision to make.

Before she could think better of it, she blurted, "Did Lachlan leave Lochguard already?"

"I don't know for certain if he's still here, but I wager he's probably waiting at Finn's house. He was really worried about you, Cat. I don't think he'd leave without a word. He seems the type of male to face things and handle them directly."

She thought so too. Although she could easily be wrong.

After all, she knew so little about him.

Still, she wasn't going to be a coward. That wasn't her way. "If you can help me get to Finn's place, I want to see Lachlan right away."

Her mum searched her eyes, her brows drawn a fraction. "Now? But you're exhausted, love. Maybe you should take a nap first so you can have a clear mind."

Cat shook her head. "No. I wouldn't be able to sleep anyway. Besides, I don't have a lot of time to spend with him. If he doesn't flee, that is."

Three days. Cat had three days to figure out if she wanted to have the frenzy and become a mum in the process or suffer a few years of strain and stress until her dragon's need finally calmed down.

And as her mother helped her up and lent her strength the whole way to Finn's place, Cat wasn't sure if three days would be enough.

LACHLAN DIDN'T USUALLY pace since the action was all but broadcasting how he wasn't in complete control.

However, as he waited for word of how Cat was doing, he couldn't help himself. Especially since Finn had been in a meeting and hadn't talked to him yet.

For all the Department of Dragon Affairs liked to think it knew about dragon-shifters, each clan—hell, each individual—acted in their own way. Would Lochguard merely send him on his way, thinking it was better for Cat to suffer and push aside the frenzy rather than get involved with a DDA employee and all the headaches that would follow?

And why did Lachlan want to stay and at least talk with Cat—if he could, that is, without her jumping him and ripping his clothes off—and try to make her understand why he didn't think he could go through with the frenzy. Not because he didn't want her—fuck, he was honest enough to say she was beautiful and her touch was addictive—but Lachlan wasn't exactly father material.

Hell, it wasn't even just his fear of losing control and drinking again that worried him. Although, aye, that was a struggle he'd face for the rest of his life.

No, there was something much worse possibly lurking in the background, waiting to come out. Something that scared him.

Lachlan could end up like his father.

Not that he wanted to, especially since the idea of hitting his wife or child made his stomach roll, but his father's father had done the same, as he'd often heard as a young lad. It was how the MacKintoshs handled their families and kept their wives and children in line.

Lachlan didn't agree. He'd stood up to his dad when he'd been old enough to try and protect his mother and sister. But he always carried that fear— the one of him drinking, losing his temper, and hitting someone he should be protecting.

Like father, like son.

No. He didn't want to be that way. It was part of the reason he kept to himself. Isolation was safer for everyone.

Finn entered the room, and Lachlan forced himself to push away his deepest fears. Dragon-shifters sometimes had a second sense about things, and he wasn't going to risk the dragonman noticing.

Lochguard's clan leader stopped a few feet away from him, placed his hands on his hips, and asked,

"You know what happened, aye?" Lachlan nodded. "Right, then we're going to have a wee chat."

Impatient to get it over with, Lachlan jumped in. "If you're going to send me away, I won't go until I get the chance to talk with Cat. Even if it's through a video chat, to keep her from me, that's fine. But I need to talk with her."

Finn searched his gaze a second, the teasing man from the night before all but gone.

In the abstract, Lachlan had known how much responsibility lay on a clan leader's shoulders. But for some reason, right then and there, with Finn's face more serious than he'd ever seen, it became a hell of a lot more concrete.

Finn finally replied, "I had no plans to send you away without a word. But is that what you plan to do —have a wee chat and run back to the city?"

He could lie and make up an excuse to make it easier for himself. However, his actions were going to hurt Cat one way or the other, and he needed to be honest with all involved. It was one of the things he'd vowed to try and do ever since he'd become sober. "I'm not what she needs. I think we both know that."

Finn raised an eyebrow. "Is that so?"

"Aye, she deserves better."

She deserves someone who can be as carefree as she is. Someone who might not turn into a monster one day and destroy her life, break her soul, and make her cry.

Finn said, "Let me tell you something about how true-mate pairings work, aye?"

"I know the basics," he gritted out. "All DDA employees do."

The dragonman waved a hand in dismissal. "They give you the fairy-tale version, I'm sure. But I'm about to give you more of the truth. Now, sit down."

He recognized the dominance threaded into Finn's voice—it was one often used by dragon clan leaders.

And while Lachlan didn't have an inner dragon who wanted to obey that dominance, he did sit on the sofa.

As soon as he did, Finn sat in the chair opposite him. "The DDA will tell you that when a dragon finds their true mate, that person is their best chance at happiness. And, aye, often that's the case. But it doesn't always work out. Sometimes, it ends in pain. And even for those of us who find the love of our lives, it takes work. You have no idea how long it took for me to convince my own mate to give me a chance."

He blinked. Finn and his mate, Arabella, were always touching each other, kissing, and teasing each other. Sure, sometimes it was dry humor or even a wee bit of bickering. But he'd be hard-pressed to use any other word to describe them but besotted.

Finn shrugged. "It's true. There are many people

who now live on Lochguard who are happy with their mates but had to work hard to achieve that happiness. You're not the only one with a less than perfect past, or even a bastard father."

Lachlan frowned at that. He wondered how Finn knew more about Lachlan than what was public knowledge.

Finn added, "I've seen shadows lurking in your eyes when you think no one is looking. Call it a clan's leader perceptiveness. At any rate, I'm not saying everything will be perfect or even easy, but sometimes a dragon's choice is the right one. It may take some fight and stubbornness, but I can tell you from experience that when you finally do get everything you want, it's like nothing else."

As he struggled with how to reply to that, Finn stood and added, "You also have to ask yourself if you're going to let your past ruin your future. Because there are a few who almost let that happen here. And if they had, they would've ended up a lot less happy, in my opinion."

Lachlan knew he wasn't the only one with problems, but he doubted many of the others Finn talked about had the fucked up past he did.

However, Finn continued before Lachlan could say anything. "I sense strength in you, MacKintosh. The only question is—will you draw on it to at least attempt a good future, or will you take the easy path and run away to avoid any sort of pain?"

Lachlan wasn't used to such bluntness, and yet, it made him wonder if he could be strong enough to face the future instead of letting his past keep it from him.

Was he really going to think about this? He barely knew Cat. Surely he couldn't face the monumental task of dealing with his childhood, his fears, and even his coping mechanisms to keep him sober simply because she made him smile more than anyone else?

Finn's voice filled the room. "Just think about it, aye? That's all I ask."

His mate, Arabella, knocked and poked her head into the room. She glanced at Lachlan before looking at her mate. "Cat and Sylvia are here. Cat wants to talk with Lachlan." She looked at Lachlan. "Her dragon is temporarily silent, which means she's in control again, in case you were wondering."

Finn met his gaze again. "Well?"

He stood, straightened his sleeves to help pull himself together, and nodded. "I'll see her."

Finn made a gesture for him to stay. "I'll bring her here."

Once he was alone again, Lachlan took a deep breath and let it out.

For a man who had lived the past ten years following a routine and strict schedule, the chaos he was about to face was almost too much.

But at the very least, he owed Cat a conversation

to try and warn her of why he was the wrong choice to be a partner, or a father, or to be anything more than an acquaintance.

Not to mention how he knew she could do a hell of a lot better than him.

So he waited, still unsure of what he'd say or do when he saw Cat again but ready to face her all the same.

Chapter Six

Cat hadn't wanted to keep Lachlan waiting, but as she stood outside the door of the living room, a wee bit fortified from a quick cup of tea and a few biscuits, she was glad she'd listened to her mother and Arabella's advice about needing caffeine and sugar to get through the upcoming conversation. She no longer felt as if she'd topple over.

Normally her dragon would've said something to tease her, but there was only silence.

It was still hard to believe she'd spend the next three days without her inner beast.

And yet, she had bigger things to worry about—namely, the human male waiting for her.

Taking a deep breath, she knocked and opened the door.

Lachlan stood near the window, his hands behind his back and looking over his shoulder at her.

She couldn't read his expression. But at least he was still on Lochguard, which was something.

He took a step toward her but then stilled. He said, "I would offer to help you to a chair, but I don't want to make things worse by touching you."

At his concern, her nervousness faded a fraction. "Touching won't matter this soon after the shot, although kissing will. So just try to resist me, aye? Otherwise my dragon might come back."

Without another word, he was at her side. He wrapped an arm around her waist and guided her to the chair.

True, she could've made it on her own. She might be weak, but she could bloody well walk to a chair.

However, his solid presence at her side, the heat of his body, and even just his scent reminded her of why she'd kissed him in the first place.

Attraction wasn't the problem. No, just the wee hiccup of a frenzy and child at the end of it.

Once she sat down, he moved back toward the window, except he faced her rather than the glass. She didn't like the distance but understood how it might help make it easier for him.

He stared at her for a few seconds. Just as she said, "I'm—" he said, "I'm—" and then they both stopped. She smiled, but he cleared his throat.

Since it had to be harder for him than her in that moment—Cat had at least grown up with the constant knowledge and reminder of true mates and frenzies—she waved for him. "You go first."

He cleared his throat again. "I'm sorry to have caused you pain."

That wasn't exactly what she wanted to hear. Maybe she'd bemoaned the start of the frenzy to her mother, but it was a done deal, and she'd melted when she'd kissed him.

She may not like the choice she now faced, but she wouldn't apologize to Lachlan for the kiss. Did he regret it that much?

Remember he's human, Cat. He's in way over his head. Trying to remain calm, she replied, "I hope you mean for the frenzy part and not the kiss itself."

He blinked, clearly not expecting her words. "Er, yes."

He was being bloody formal again. Too tired to be polite any longer, she blurted, "Just tell me what you're thinking, Lachlan. Ask your questions. Shout at me for drawing you into this. Anything but that bloody politeness you use as a shield. And aye, you do, so don't deny it."

He straightened. "Are you sure you can handle it? You look exhausted and what I need to tell you isn't full of rainbows and roses, Cat. Getting to know me will only cause you even more pain."

That piqued her interest. "How, exactly?" He hesitated and she sighed. "I'm stronger than you think. My father was murdered by dragon hunters when I was fifteen. I survived that, so I bloody well can handle whatever you think is so awful."

Irritation flared in his eyes. Maybe some would try to smooth things over, but not her. He only seemed to drop his façade when he felt strong emotions. And she wanted to get this bloody conversation going already.

Because she still didn't know what she wanted to do, and probably wouldn't, until Lachlan stopped being so damn cryptic and started being truthful with her.

He took a few steps toward her, his voice less controlled when he replied, "You want the truth? Aye, then I'll give it to you." He moved even closer and crouched until he was at eye level, his eyes full of some emotion she couldn't pin down. He continued, "I'm a recovering alcoholic, Cat. I spent years getting lost in a bottle, raging out at my family and friends, and driving just about everyone away. One slip up, and that puts you in danger. Especially given my family history."

She'd known about him being a recovering alcoholic. That didn't shock her. However, his last sentence did. "What family history?"

He leaned closer, narrowing his eyes. "My father beat me. Not only me but my mother and sister too. And my grandfather did the same to his family before that. It's in my blood to be an abusive bastard. And that's why you should stay as far away from me as possible."

Her heart squeezed as she stared at him, trying to picture him as a defenseless boy at the mercy of his father.

She suspected the abuse had probably led to the drinking as well.

The mere notion of a parent hurting their child and causing a lifetime of pain made her angry. Even without her dragon, she wanted to find the male, corner him in her dragon form, and show him what it felt like to be the weaker one.

But Lachlan looked away from her, breaking her revenge fantasy, and she focused on the male in the room. He needed her. And she decided instead of anger, a little humor might help him more.

"I'm sorry that happened to you. But I think you're forgetting one very important fact."

His gaze found hers. "Which is?"

She smiled. "I can shift into a very large, very powerful dragon with extremely sharp teeth and talons."

He shook his head. "Maybe it could save you physically, but I hurt my sister emotionally when I was drinking. Of all the men in the world, I'm toward the bottom of the list of who you should want a child with."

Some would prickle at Lachlan's repeated dismissal. But she sensed his scars ran deep, to the point he didn't believe he could have anything resembling a happy future.

And she remembered when Arabella had first come to Lochguard, reclusive and prickly, and then how she'd changed into a loving mother, mate, and friend because of one male's belief in her.

Not to mention Cat had seen progress with Aimee King as well.

She knew comfort, support, and even caring could help someone realize they were worthy of love and affection.

The only question was whether she wanted to take up that task.

On the one hand, she could end up like Finn and Arabella, with a loving family and a mate who was her best friend and meant the world to her.

On the other, it could also end in disaster and maybe even heartbreak, especially if Lachlan kept trying to make up excuses or did his best to remain distant in an effort to protect her.

At any rate, she needed a little more information from him before she made any sort of decision. So she leaned forward, took his hand to keep him from fleeing, and said, "I wouldn't put up with anyone treating me badly. And I'm not saying tomorrow you're going to wake up and instantly think everything will be fine and rosy. However, knowing how I can take care of myself and have an entire dragon clan to back me up if need be, maybe you can forget for a second about all of your family history. What do *you* want, Lachlan? Do you want to spend your life alone, always insulating yourself from others just in case you slip up? Or do you want a chance at being part of a community, one that will do their best to support you in case you need it and carve out the life you want for yourself?" She leaned a little closer to him. "Just tell me what you want, Lachlan. Be honest with me. That's all I ask."

And as hard as it was not to push him further, she waited. She had a feeling his answer would give Cat her own about the whole frenzy and resulting child.

LACHLAN COULDN'T TEAR his eyes from Cat's because of the way she spoke with fire and determination, not allowing him to brush things aside.

He'd known she was responsible and kind, and even occasionally funny. But right here, right now, he saw just how strong she was too.

He believed her words that she wouldn't allow him to treat her badly, and not just because she could change into a dragon either.

Cat had a confidence his mother never had possessed, an inner fire that she wouldn't let anyone extinguish.

While, of course, he'd loved his mother despite her flaws, she'd been broken a long time. Even once his father had died a few years ago, the last of his mother's strength had faded away, and she'd barely lasted a year before dying herself.

So when Cat asked what he wanted, truly wanted, for himself, Lachlan didn't use his usual excuses. No, instead, he imagined a life where he didn't have an abusive father, or one when he didn't lose himself in drink to cope with his mother refusing to leave her husband, even when Lachlan and his sister were old enough to support her.

Stripped bare, he was just a man who wanted love and comfort. To belong somewhere, with someone who made him forget about the worst parts of his life.

He could see a future with a strong woman like Cat, one who would keep him on his toes but also be there if he ever needed support.

But he also knew that was a lot to ask for. So he finally answered truthfully, to give her the best information about him to make her decision. "When I was a child, all I dreamed and wished for was a normal family. One where the parents might argue, but my mother didn't end up in the hospital with yet another 'fall.' To merely tease my sister and not worry about if our bickering caused my father to reach for a belt to keep us quiet. I wanted laughter and love, and all those things I saw my friends take for granted." He paused, trying to gauge her expression, and failing. So he continued, "But I just can't pretend my past isn't there, Cat. It'll shadow me for the rest of my life, and it'll take a massive amount of work to overcome. You mentioned once how you helped raise your siblings. And whilst you didn't complain outright, I could tell how much of a burden it'd been to you. Just having a child with me and us living separately will be even more work, on top of everything you already do. And if there's one thing I can't tolerate, it's being a burden to anyone. At least, no more than I already have been in the past."

By the end, his voice had grown scratchy. While he'd shared his fears before in addiction recovery meetings, it was different here with Cat. She was so happy and carefree and the opposite of dark and twisted.

Speaking the truth and spreading some of his darkness was fucking hard. But he owed it to her. He didn't know why, but he felt he did.

She finally replied, "Aye, it was hard with my siblings after my dad died. But after speaking with my mum today, I realized how rewarding it felt when she told me how much I'd helped her. I guess I'm saying I may complain, but when someone tells you how important you are to them, it almost makes up for everything."

She searched his eyes, and Lachlan stopped

breathing. Was she saying she wouldn't mind his problems or the fact she'd have to help him?

And why did that matter so much all of the sudden?

However, she spoke again before he could say anything. "And you might not have realized it at the time, but even you just ensuring Layla could be served first last night tells me you're not like your father." She squeezed his hand before adding, "I can't promise anything, but I think you may be worth a try, Lachlan MacKintosh. And that when push comes to shove, you'd stand up for me or any child we had instead of turning your anger at us, aye?"

The words fell from his lips before he could stop them, "I'd kill myself before hurting you."

She smiled slightly. "I think so too. So I guess that brings up one last question—do you want the frenzy with me? If not, you can leave, and I won't hate you. Maybe curse you a few times over the next few years, but not hate. It was my choice, after all, to kiss you despite the risks."

He didn't like Cat shouldering all of the blame. "I knew it could happen as well, even if it didn't cross my mind in the moment. But deciding blame is pointless. No, what's more important is what you want. Do you want a bairn, Cat? All of this was just as sudden for you as for me, and I have no idea what you want for your future."

She reached for his other hand and squeezed them both gently. "At first, I cried at the thought."

The idea of Cat crying did something to his heart, to the point he wanted to rub his chest over the tightness.

She shrugged. "But I think it was more the fear of the unknown, of some male I barely knew giving me a child. However, after this conversation, I'm not so scared anymore. A wee bit nervous, of course, but not scared. I wouldn't mind it. But you have to know it will probably cost you your job."

DDA employees weren't supposed to fraternize with dragon-shifters. A few had in the past, of course. The leader of the English dragon clan in the north— Stonefire—had mated a former DDA employee named Evie Marshall. But she'd been forced to resign.

Most likely Lachlan would as well.

The DDA had been his rock, his foundation around which he structured his life, the one thing that had kept his life together over the past decade. Could he give it up so easily?

As he stared into Cat's blue eyes, he wondered if maybe he could have it all. She'd put the idea into his head about working toward a future he wanted. And for the first time, he itched to do just that.

He said, "I plan to make my case to keep my job, at least through the event this autumn. It'll give me time to find a way to convince them as to why having employees who live with dragon-shifters is a good idea. After all, the books and secondhand accounts only go so far."

She nodded. "I'm sure Finn will help you any way he can, provided you work toward earning his trust."

He murmured, "Aye, maybe. But I'd rather earn your trust first."

Her eyes widened a fraction before she squeezed his hands again. "You can start by spending time with my family. We have a few days before my dragon returns from the drug-induced coma, and we have to fully commit to the frenzy. So I think it's best for you to learn what life would be like if you stay. Not to mention you can get used to the idea of my dragon sometimes taking control and being a bit rough during the frenzy."

He'd heard stories of mate-claim frenzies before, of course. However, the thought of Cat above him, riding his cock as she dug her nails into his chest, sent a rush of heat through his body.

He somehow didn't think dealing with her dragon would be a burden.

Needing to keep his cock in check, he focused on Cat and what she'd proposed. "But I'd get to spend time with you as well, aye? I'm sure your dragon is great, but if I'm honest, I'm more looking forward to sleeping with you." He removed one of his hands from hers and dared to brush some hair off her face. "The kiss, especially, has me curious."

She murmured, "Me as well."

As she stared up at him, her eyes full of heat, he stopped breathing. She was so fucking beautiful.

Although it was more than beauty that drew him to her. It had only been one deep conversation, but he already felt closer to her. Before, he would've suppressed the feeling and pretended it was merely attraction.

However, Cat had dangled something in front of him—hope for a future—and he wanted to know her inside and out.

Maybe she could be his new addiction, but in a good way.

She released his hand and cupped his face instead. Her soft fingers against his skin sent another thread of heat through his body. Never before had he been so aware of another woman's touch.

It took everything he had to focus on her words and not try to kiss her again. "Aye, you'll get me during the frenzy too. But my dragon is a part of me, so the bargain is two for one. I know that's sometimes strange for humans to understand, but it's essential you understand this now. Because if we have the frenzy and I go back to having my dragon around, you'll have to give attention to her as well. If you ignore her, you're ignoring me too." She paused and leaned closer, to the point he felt her breath on his lips. "Do you think you can handle us both?"

He knew he couldn't kiss Cat right then and

there, or it could wake her dragon up. But fuck, he'd never burned to kiss anyone so desperately before. Almost like he needed to do it, or he'd have trouble breathing.

He truly wanted her, more than anything.

And that scared him a little.

You can't have her yet. He focused on her question, placed his hand over her, and answered, "Aye, I could handle you both. I'll need some instruction, but to truly know you, I'll try."

She smiled, which lit up her eyes. When had he started noticing all the changes of her face and expression so well?

Cat said, "You could take lessons with the students. They have classes about inner dragons and what to do. I'm not sure you'll fit in the desks, but the teachers can think of something."

He grunted. "I'm not sitting at a bloody tiny desk. I'd prefer private lessons, maybe with a certain beautiful dragonwoman."

She laughed, the sound soothing his soul. He wanted her to laugh more often around him.

Was that even possible?

Fuck, he was getting too damn romantic.

She rubbed his cheek with her thumb. "You'd never be able to concentrate around me. Besides, the students could learn a lot from you too. In case you haven't noticed, the only human adult male living on Lochguard is Ross, who's a wee bit on in years. I imagine the students have all sorts of questions to ask of a younger male."

Lachlan didn't always do well with groups of children. But he'd face that hurdle when the time came. "We'll see. For now, my focus is on you, Cat. So what do we do now?"

She released his cheeks and gestured toward the door. "We'll tell Finn our plan. Then I'll need a wee nap before dinner with my family. Will you come tonight?"

He nodded. "Of course."

She hesitated a second but then put up a hand. "I'm exhausted and need some help getting home. Will you help me?"

He instantly stood, pulled her up, and drew her against his side. They stood a second like that, hip to hip, staring at one another, and Lachlan felt more relaxed than he had in a while.

He'd never have thought it before, but maybe this one dragonwoman was what he needed to be whole.

Which was crazy given how he barely knew her.

Not that he wanted to dwell on that. So he helped her out of the room, briefly told Finn what they planned to do, and escorted her home.

When he finally said goodbye to Cat, Lachlan smiled, not even bothering to put his usual mask on.

He'd never have imagined that he'd look forward to dinner with a close family. Even a week ago, the thought would've been too painful for him, a mere reminder of what he'd never had.

But he was eager to see Cat again, rested and teasing like usual. And that overrode any hesitation he had about a close family dinner.

Chapter Seven

Later that day, Cat watched as her brother Connor pinned their youngest brother Jamie to the ground and resisted sighing.

They knew Lachlan was coming to dinner. Hell, they even knew about the frenzy and her currently silent dragon.

And still they acted like wee beasts.

She sighed louder than normal to maybe get their attention, but no one noticed. Aye, well, if they were going to act twelve, then she'd treat them that way. She stomped over, took Connor by the collar, and yanked. Hard.

"Ow, stop it, Cat."

She speared him with her best big-sister glare. "Leave Jamie alone. You can try to kill him later; I don't care. But not until after dinner."

Connor shook his head and stood. "I wasn't

killing him, but merely showing him how to pin someone down."

She eyed Jamie on the ground, rubbing his shoulder, and raised her brows. "Why don't I believe you?"

Connor shrugged before offering Jamie a hand up, saying, "Don't worry, we'll be on mostly good behavior. I thought it best to get it out now, aye? Maybe Jamie will be a wee bit less annoying during dinner."

Jamie growled at his brother as his pupils flashed. "I'm not annoying."

Connor snorted. "Tell yourself that, lad. But if I have to hear one more time about that legend of Loch Naver, or how you've seen the spirit, I'll pin you right back to the ground."

Jamie said, "It's true, I did see her. I can't help it if you're too stupid to understand how important that is."

Connor brushed his sleeve. "Not stupid, Jamie, just grown-up."

As Jamie moved to launch himself at Connor, her middle brother, Ian, rolled his eyes and quickly moved between them. He shoved Connor one way and Jamie the other as he spoke. "Go to that side and you to that. Cat looks about ready to explode, and I'd rather not have to hear it from Mum about how we're upsetting her. Did you two idiots forget that her dragon is gone right now? She clearly doesn't have the strength to deal with your shite."

She mouthed, "Thank you," to Ian as the other two grumbled and moved across the room from each other.

Cat was just about to check in on her mother in the kitchen when the doorbell rang. It had to be Lachlan.

She hissed at her siblings, "Behave," before she went to answer it.

Smoothing her hair, she opened the door and did her best not to let her jaw drop.

Lachlan was in a dark blue top that made his eyes all but glow, and his jeans, well, they were fairly snug, and she could see his muscled thighs.

But it was more his face that surprised her. The usual mask of indifference was gone, replaced with a nervousness mixed with amusement. He murmured, "Hello to you too."

She frowned at the change in him, but then Lachlan handed her a box of chocolates, noting they were her favorite—chocolate-covered almonds.

There was no way he'd just happened to guess her favorite type. She studied him and asked, "Who told you?"

He smiled, and her heart skipped a beat again. Damn, he was far too attractive when he smiled.

Good thing her dragon wasn't around, or they'd

be off to some dark corner of Lochguard to do more than talk.

Realizing where her thoughts were heading, she did her best not to blush and focused on his answer. "Arabella let it slip."

Arabella most definitely didn't let things slip. Just what else has she told Lachlan?

Brushing the question aside, Cat gestured for him to come in. "So you saw Finn and Ara again?"

"Aye, for a wee bit, but we can talk about that later." He straightened his sleeves—a habit she noticed that he did when he was about to tackle something—and added, "I'm here to get to know your family."

Once he was inside, she shut the door and chuckled. "Good luck with that. Connor and Jamie have already had a wrestling match of sorts. And once they do that, they're at each other for the rest of the night. I'm not sure you're going to be able to get a word in edgewise until they form yet another temporary truce."

He looked at her, his eyes intense as he murmured, "I don't mind. It'd be lovely to see a family who likes each other."

For all his tough ways, all his pretense of appearing controlled and content, Lachlan was a wee bit lonely, she thought.

Her family might not be the best to ease into

anything, but in for a penny, in for a pound, or so the saying went.

She took his hand and tugged. "Come on then. But don't say I didn't warn you about them. No doubt they'll interrogate you, or my brothers will try some sort of male initiation ceremony that will seem like complete madness to me, but somehow is supposed to make you like each other in the end."

He squeezed her hand, and she swore he said, "They are important to you, so I'll try." But even with her supersensitive hearing, she couldn't be sure.

So she did what worked best for the MacAllisters and marched into the living room to face them all head-on.

Lachlan had spent the entire walk to Cat's mother's cottage replaying the bit of advice Arabella had given him: *Be your true self and not the version you want people to believe is you. If you can't do that—or at least try—save yourself time and just leave now because inner dragons don't like deception.*

It had been a rather strange conversation. Finn and Arabella had shared more than he thought anybody should with a stranger about their own courtship and marriage—no, mating, he reminded himself—but he wasn't stupid and knew their intent.

They wanted him to try to make Cat happy.

He wasn't entirely sure he could do that yet. Did he want to try? Aye, of course. His earlier conversation with Cat had been one of the most honest—and surprisingly easy considering the topic —of his life. Apart from his own sister or mother, he'd never revealed so much about himself so freely.

But one day did not make him a whole, healed individual worthy of caring for someone else, let alone a child.

Still, he was going to try to be the man he thought he could be.

So he'd bought her favorite chocolate and did his best to not retreat behind his mask when she opened the door.

And the expression on her face, one where her jaw dropped, told him all the effort was worth it.

Although when she dragged him into the living room, and he was suddenly faced with three rather tall dragonmen, all standing with their arms crossed and looking down their noses at him, he blinked.

If they weren't dragon-shifters, the sight would've been ridiculous. He was at least a decade older than the youngest one.

But as their pupils flashed between round and slits, he knew that age didn't matter. They would always be stronger than him, a mere human.

Still, he stood tall and didn't look away from them.

That was when Cat dropped his hand and

walked up to her brothers. She poked each one in the chest and murmured something he couldn't hear. The oldest one—he thought it was Connor?—merely looked at Lachlan and said, "If you hurt my sister, I won't hesitate to drop you into the loch from the greatest height I can manage without killing you."

"Connor," Cat scolded.

However, Lachlan sensed this was important. If he couldn't stand up to her brothers, he didn't deserve a chance with Cat anyway. He may only be human, but he would no doubt be challenged by many more on Lochguard. He needed to set the standard now.

He replied, "I don't plan on hurting her, if I can help it."

The youngest one tried to stand taller—he was about an inch shorter than the other two—and stated, "Try harder. Because if Connor drops you once, then I'll scoop you up and do it again."

The middle one rolled his eyes. "That'll surely kill him, you idiot. You should suggest something like scooping him up and abandoning him in the wilds somewhere. At least he'd be alive when you left him."

The shortest one growled, "Unlike you, I don't spend time thinking of how to punish people who cross you."

The middle one spoke again, "I don't spend time doing that. It's called being quick-witted. Which you aren't, apparently."

The shortest one growled and launched himself at the middle one. "I'm going to kill you, Ian."

As Ian—and the last one had to be Jamie, Lachlan noted—easily flipped his brother onto his back and put a foot against his throat, Cat turned her back on her brothers and faced him. "Come on. This could take a while, and I rather hope one of them ends up with a black eye. They'll come once Mum has the food ready anyway."

He smiled. Irritated as she appeared, he could tell she loved them.

And in a flash, an image of Cat sighing over three small boys as they wrestled on the ground, with Lachlan at her side, flashed into his mind.

A yearning he hadn't known he had rushed forth. He'd never even allowed himself to think of wanting children.

But with Cat, aye, well, maybe he could.

Not wanting to get stuck in his own head, he placed a hand on her lower back—loving how she leaned into his touch—and murmured, "Leave them to it. I still need to meet your sister anyway."

She smiled. "Emma's better than that lot, but not by much. She has a tendency to be blunt to a degree that'll make you uncomfortable."

After so many years of deceiving not only others, but himself, Lachlan actually looked forward to that sort of honesty, which would probably keep him honest as well.

He nearly froze at that thought. Since when did he want people to get to know the real him?

However, he didn't have time to think about it as Cat guided them into the kitchen and toward her mum and sister.

CAT WOULD GIVE her brothers an earful later, when they were alone. Clearly her idea of being nice and well-behaved in front of Lachlan and theirs was vastly different.

But then she introduced him to her sister and mother, and before her mum could do anything but smile, Emma blurted, "You look a wee bit more relaxed. Usually, I'd say it's because you shagged my sister, but I know that's not true. So maybe my granddad dropped off some of his 'happy brownies' earlier. Did he?"

Both Cat and her mum yelled, "Emma!"

Emma shrugged. "Well, something's changed. I'm just trying to figure out what."

Cat thought she was used to her sister's manner, but still, her cheeks burned. How, exactly, was she supposed to transition from "oh, you didn't sleep with my sister but did my grandfather give you some weed-laced treats?"

Maybe having a close-knit family was overrated.

Lachlan laughed, and the sound wiped away her

embarrassment. He looked so much younger when he laughed—the strain eased around his eyes, and his cheeks flushed slightly.

Which made him that much more handsome. Now, if only she could make him laugh herself instead of her sister.

Lachlan replied to Emma, "I don't mind the bluntness. Besides, maybe you'll finally tell me the truth about your grandfather. No one seems to want to explain him and the other two to me."

Emma lit up. "It's been so long since someone asked about Grandda Archie. He's one of the most interesting people I know." Her sister all but yanked Lachlan away from Cat's side. "You can sit next to me at dinner. Then I can tell you all about it."

Her first instinct was to reach out and drag Lachlan back to her side.

But Emma already had him sitting at the table. Her sister whispered to him—no doubt to keep her and their mum from scolding her again—but Lachlan met Cat's gaze.

The amusement there made her belly flutter in a good way.

It was hard to believe she'd thought him cool and detached not even a week ago.

Not that Cat thought he was suddenly going to be open and sunny all the time. No, she had a feeling he'd barely touched on the darkness of his past with his father.

Still, she wasn't going to press him about it in front of her family. This meal was simply a chance for him to get to know the MacAllisters, and maybe even have a good time in the process.

Cat sat across from him and did her best not to roll her eyes at Emma's recounting of Grandda Archie's escapades.

Her mother said, "Supper," and all three of her brothers raced into the room and slid into their seats. Jamie's chair stopped a foot away from the table from the effort.

She wondered if merely mentioning a meal would get all the males—and a few females, at that— in the clan running. It'd be fun to try.

Usually her dragon would've made a remark about that, but the silence in her mind was deafening. She missed her other half more than she ever would've guessed.

Which helped her better understand Aimee King and the other dragon-shifters who had lost their beasts.

However, she pushed aside her sadness. Cat was lucky—her silent dragon was temporary.

Once everyone was seated with full plates, her mother turned to Lachlan and asked, "How long have you worked with the DDA?"

While Cat knew it was an ordinary question to ask about one's job, she did her best to focus on her food and not Lachlan's face. He was probably going to have to give up his career if they went through with the frenzy.

And she hated the thought of making anyone give up something for her.

Lachlan answered, "Just over ten years this past January. I started as an administrative assistant and worked my way up to head events coordinator."

Emma jumped in. "But how are you going to do that now? You can't exactly plan this big art event if you're busy trying to get my sister pregnant."

Cat choked on her food a second before she managed to swallow it. She glared at Emma, but her sister ignored her.

Lachlan met her gaze and raised his brows, asking if she was all right. She nodded and took a sip of water.

Emma pushed, "So? Cat's good at multitasking, but not *that* good."

Cat growled. "Emma, I swear, if you don't stop, I'm going to hide all your electronics some place where you'll never find them."

Her sister grinned. "I have spares everywhere." She looked back at Lachlan. "So?"

Bloody hell, had her sister always been so tenacious?

Aye, she had. But it had never involved talking about one of her siblings' sex lives before.

Lachlan cleared his throat and said, "I discussed

this with Finn earlier. Someone from Seahaven is going to come help if, er, we become indisposed."

Cat bit back a laugh. It seemed when Lachlan was uncomfortable, he became formal again.

Not that the change in tone would deter Emma in the least. Her sister leaned forward. "Oooh, who's coming? None of the males my age on Lochguard are worth my time. Maybe my own true mate will show up, and wouldn't that be brilliant, Cat? Our bairns will be almost the same age."

She rolled her eyes. "The odds of that happening are astronomical."

"Still, it could happen. And then you can watch my bairn when I have to do some big security upgrade. It'll work out brilliantly."

Cat shook her head. "I'm not going to become your de facto babysitter, Emma."

"But I do really important work. Ian's good, but I'm better. The clan will need my skills."

Since stating Cat had work as well would do nothing to stop her sister, she turned toward Lachlan and explained, "Ian and Emma are some sort of computer geniuses. Don't ask me how my sister can concentrate long enough to do that sort of thing, but it works."

Emma huffed. "I can concentrate longer than Jamie."

Jamie let out a grunt of protest, but Cat spoke before he could. "Do you really want to start an argument with Jamie, or do you want to find out an answer from Lachlan about who's coming to help?"

Emma glanced at her younger brother—the only one younger than her since Ian had been born a few minutes before her—and then waved a hand in dismissal. "He's not worth it. Who's coming from Seahaven, Lachlan?"

Cat saw Ian pass more food to Jamie, which seemed to keep him from exploding. But once Lachlan spoke, she focused back on him. "Some dragonman named Adam Keith."

She knew who that was. "Aye, that makes sense. He and I have collaborated on a few things before, mostly for the student lessons on Seahaven. Adam's more into photography, but sometimes he does mixed media too." Since none of her siblings were artistically inclined, they merely stared blankly. She explained, "It means he sometimes uses his pictures and something like paint or ink to make a piece. That's not important, though. He's quieter than any of us, but he seems nice."

Emma raised her fork into the air. "Quieter, aye? I like that. That should mean he's good at listening, and he should know all the best gossip to share with me. People tend to talk around the quiet ones." She leaned forward. "And the quiet ones can also be surprising in bed, too, aye? Or so I've heard."

It took everything Cat had to not bang her head

against the table. If Lachlan dashed out the door at any second, it wouldn't surprise her in the least.

Her mother finally jumped in and said calmly, "Emma, that's enough."

Since their mother didn't warn them often anymore—she believed her adult children should be able to sort things out among themselves—they all knew to heed it when she did. So Emma sighed and speared some potatoes on her plate. "Fine. Although it was just getting interesting."

Ian, being the most diplomatic of any of them, cleared his throat and asked Lachlan, "So when will Adam arrive?"

Lachlan shrugged. "Probably tomorrow."

Silence fell a beat, and then Jamie asked, "Have you heard the legend about Loch Naver, Lachlan?"

Everyone groaned, but Lachlan barely paid it any heed and shook his head. "No."

"Then let me tell you about it…"

And as Jamie explained the blasted legend for what had to be the ten-thousandth time, Cat ignored her brother and watched Lachlan. His expression was a little less open than when she'd greeted him at the door. But he didn't seem overly strained or nervous.

Her brother distracting him gave Cat a chance to better study his profile—his firm lips, his strong jaw, the way his hair was a touch too long around his ears.

She hadn't sketched him for a few days and itched to do it again.

Maybe she could even get him to model for her.

Not that she'd have the chance any time soon. The absence of her dragon commenting on how they should strip and ride him was a stark reminder that while the evening seemed almost normal, it wouldn't last.

Within days, she'd have to make a decision. Well, she and Lachlan would both have to make a decision.

Which meant her time was precious. And so after dinner, she was going to force him to go for a walk with her.

Aye, well, force might be too strong of a word, but while she was glad he'd met her family and knew what he could be getting into, she wanted some time alone with him.

When dinner was done, the dishes washed, and her mother distracted her siblings for a few beats, she murmured for Lachlan to follow her as she took his hand and guided him out of the house.

Chapter Eight

L achlan had never eaten dinner with anyone like Cat's family before.

Conversation moved quickly, the family lovingly needled each other, and not once had someone yelled or barked an order that caused a flash of fear or shame to fill their eyes.

In other words, it was the complete opposite of any family meal Lachlan had ever experienced as a child.

But while all of that was fascinating to him, Lachlan liked watching Cat roll her eyes or how she threatened to spear a sibling with her fork.

And he especially liked it when her cheeks flushed from something her sister said.

She was so bloody open with her feelings.

And that had been the only thing to scare him during the meal. He had tried—and still planned to try—to answer whatever questions she had, but he'd never be so open and free as her or anyone in her family.

Which made him worry a little. He was trying so bloody hard to be who he thought he was, but it wasn't easy. At some point, he was bound to fuck up and make Cat angry.

And for the millionth time, he wondered if he'd be the best fit for her, let alone what she needed from the father of her child.

However, as she snatched his hand and half dragged him out the door and down a barely visible path, he forgot all about his worries and concerns. Her warm skin against his was like a soothing balm. And he decided that for *at least* for this evening, he would try to be his best self for her and not repeatedly drown in his doubts.

Once they were a fair bit from her home, she slowed down and smiled up at him. "Ready to run yet?"

He frowned. "Run from what?"

"You can't be serious." She waved behind them in the direction of the cottage. "From them. Emma's never been quite that blunt before. I guess you're just special that way."

He shrugged one shoulder. "The possible frenzy is why I was there. So her behavior wasn't that unexpected."

"Right, because everyone just casually mentions

how someone can't have sex at the same time as planning an art exhibition."

He smiled. "Aye, well, maybe not that exact scenario." He paused a beat and then added, "I'm sure living with them can be a wee bit irritating at times, but they're wonderful, Cat. You're lucky to have a family like that."

She sobered and said quietly, "I know."

Fuck. He hadn't meant to drag his past into it all. "What I'm trying to say is thank you for inviting me. What you read and hear about in the DDA versus what happens inside a dragon family itself are two different things. I'm guessing that a fair few humans would give their left arm to be a part of that family."

Cat's lips twitched. "Anyone who joins my family is going to need both of their arms to survive. Trust me."

He chuckled, the sound unfamiliar to even himself.

But he had a feeling Cat would keep making him do it, if he stayed.

Wanting to keep it light, he said, "Okay, then how about offering a toe? Or a finger? Something to show how much they want to be there."

She snorted. "Knowing Emma, she'd keep the collection in jars or something to use as conversation starters."

He blinked and she laughed. "I'm joking, Lachlan. Emma can't stand the sight of blood to begin with. She'd probably be too busy chasing all the males to see if one is her true mate or not. She's determined on that front, although I'm not exactly sure why since she's still fairly young and thinks motherhood consists of pawning off her child on me whenever she feels like it."

Her words made Lachlan wonder if Cat had wanted to wait a little longer before looking for her own true mate.

Before he could ask her, though, they reached a line of trees, one that instantly opened into an enclosed clearing. Once they were in the middle of it, she stopped and faced him.

The moonlight highlighted her face, her neck, and even the curves of her collarbones peeking out from her top.

She looked ethereal, almost too pretty to be true. And he had to touch her, if even just for a moment.

He reached a hand up to cup her cheek. She leaned into his touch, and he nearly groaned at the softness of her skin. He whispered, "I wish I could kiss you right now."

She put a hand on his chest, her touch searing his skin through the fabric, and murmured, "As long as you don't kiss me on the lips, we should be okay."

He leaned closer. "I'm not sure I like the 'should' part of that statement."

"I'd say I'm 95 percent certain. The silent drug works better on female dragons than males."

The 5 percent made him hesitate, but then she moved until her body was only an inch from his, her heat making his heart pound and blood rush south.

And suddenly, he focused more on the 95 percent effectiveness.

Lachlan rubbed his thumb against her skin, and he couldn't help but say, "You're so beautiful, Cat. So bloody beautiful."

Her smile widened. "You're not too bad yourself."

Needing to touch more of her, he moved his mouth to her jaw and said, "I want to kiss your skin. Tell me I can."

"Aye, of course."

No hesitation or reminding him to be careful. Just, "Aye, of course," as if she trusted him.

Maybe to some that wouldn't seem such a big deal. But he'd broken so many people's trust during the darkest period of his life. And while his sister forgave him, she still didn't quite trust him.

But Cat did, at least with this.

Needing her more than ever, he moved his lips against her jaw, her neck, and down to where her neck met her shoulder. As he licked, nibbled, and worshiped her skin there, she grabbed his shoulders and moaned.

The sound turned his cock instantly hard, and he suddenly needed to taste more of her, much more.

He moved down to her collarbone and then to the neckline of her top. As he traced her skin along the blasted fabric, wishing she were bare, he moved a hand to her waist and slid it under the material to her skin.

When his hand touched her soft side, a mixture of desire and something almost primal rushed through him.

He wanted her more than anything in his life.

He didn't care if it was some sort of dragon-shifter magic he didn't understand when it came to true mates. He wanted this woman to be his.

Not only to help her with the frenzy or even to give her a child.

No, he wanted her laughter, her scowls, and so much more.

For her, he thought he could be better.

Needing to see her eyes, he lifted his head as he continued to glide his hand up her ribcage, stopping just below her bra. As he rubbed her skin with his thumb, she sucked in a breath.

"Do you know what I want to do next?"

She never looked away from his gaze. "What?" She breathed.

He moved his fingers to the bottom edge of her bra, tracing the line as he replied, "I want to take this off."

Her gaze turned even more heated. "And then do what?"

"Study you for a beat as I decide the best way to torture your breasts."

She swallowed, her cheeks turning pinker. "Aye?"

He leaned over and nuzzled her cheek with his. "Aye. Should I be more specific?"

She clutched his shoulders tighter. "Yes."

He smiled against her cheek and said, "I would roll and pinch your nipples until they were hard peaks, begging to be suckled. And then I'd torture you with my tongue, then my teeth, and then figure out what you like best until you were moaning my name."

She sucked in a breath, the sound making his cock even harder.

Who knew words could be so powerful?

Cat moved her head until she could meet his gaze. "Then do it."

He wanted to, oh how he wanted to, but he had to ask, "Are you sure? Won't it wake up your dragon early?"

"I don't think so." She shook her head. "No, it should be fine. Tomorrow, it might be risky. But today should be fine since I only had the shot this morning."

Had it really only been a day?

She ran a hand up to the base of his neck, her nails lightly scratching his skin. "If you want to wait, I understand. I know how you like to be cautious."

Aye, he was that. It was the only way he'd been able to piece his life back together after he'd become sober.

But right there, with Cat looking up at him, the moonlight making her skin glow, he wanted to throw some of that caution to the wind. He murmured, "Promise me you'll tell me if I need to stop, aye? I don't want to cause you any more pain."

She searched his gaze, her fingers stilling on his neck. "Maybe this is the wrong time to ask you, but why do you keep mentioning hurting someone or causing me pain? This isn't the first time."

And just like that, his control slipped back into place. Although he did let his hand linger on her skin, under her top. Partly because he craved the heat, but also because touching her seemed to ground him. "Maybe it's the perfect time because you should know me a wee bit better before any sort of intimacy."

He knew he was becoming formal again, but it helped him to keep it together. Especially when he needed to talk about things he wished he could forget.

Of course, if he ever forgot what he'd done, then Lachlan might end up back at his low point, waking up in some bloody alley somewhere, unsure of how he'd gotten there. His face bruised and bloody, and his memory hazy.

She murmured, "Tell me, Lachlan. Unlike my sister, I can listen."

Her words made his lips twitch. And just like that, his nervousness faded a fraction.

He looked over her shoulder at some undefined

bunch of trees and said, "I hurt a lot of people when all I could think about was my next drink. But the worst of it was when I finally reached a tipping point of either I got help, or I lost the last few people I loved forever."

The breeze blew, and he watched a leaf tumble across the clearing. He knew Cat needed to hear the rest, but it wasn't easy for him.

Then her fingers lightly massaged his neck, and he met her gaze again. Even without speaking, her eyes urged him to carry on. And so he did. "After nearly two years of constantly drinking to excess, I had pushed just about every friend and acquaintance of mine away. It's hard to explain addiction, but nothing ever seemed as important as the next fix. It wasn't that I liked alcohol so much as I *needed* it. As my tolerance increased, so did my amount consumed per night.

"My sister, Sarah, tried to keep me in her life the longest. For all intents and purposes, we didn't have a father, even though he was alive at the time. And our mother refused to leave him to live with either of us, no matter that he kept beating her. In a strange way, Sarah and I were our own little team. We'd always looked out for each other growing up and somehow always knew when the other needed cheering up.

"But the more I was consumed with drinking, the less I returned her calls. I even missed her engagement party and forgot to RSVP for her wedding.

"The day before her wedding, she found me in a pub and dragged me home to talk. She said my behavior needed to stop, that I needed help, and that if I couldn't realize it, then maybe she should stop trying."

He paused, the blurry image of his sister pleading with him to listen flitting through his mind.

He'd made it right—mostly—over the last ten years, but it still hurt to remember what came next.

He closed his eyes, embracing the shame and regret that coursed through him. He'd never shared this memory with anyone outside of his recovery meetings. There he'd felt safe sharing with others who had their own pain and regrets.

But Cat was so much purer and kinder, and the opposite of him in just about every way.

And he craved to have that sort of peace and happiness in his life.

However, the truth might drive her away.

Still, he had to finish telling her this. He owed it to her, and more importantly, he needed to be strong enough to face it all again. Otherwise, he wasn't in a good enough place to become a father or try for a relationship.

He finally whispered, "I don't remember exactly what I said to my sister that night, but I remember the instant fear filled my sister's eyes as her gaze darted from my face to something at the side. And it was in that moment I realized I'd raised my hand as if to slap her."

His throat choked up, but he forced himself to keep going. "I became my father that night. I was about to hurt someone I love for saying something I needed to hear, or maybe didn't want to hear."

"Oh, Lachlan."

Not wanting to break down, he kept his eyes closed so he couldn't see Cat's face and said, "I still don't know how I managed it, but I turned away and braced myself against the wall as I told her I was sorry. And when she asked one last time if I'd get help, I finally said yes."

He opened his eyes again, but Lachlan looked at some point in the distance rather than Cat's gaze. He wasn't quite ready for the pity, or anger, or disgust. He wanted to finish first.

"And I did get help, and I've been clean for just over ten years. But to this day, my sister still won't let me watch my nephews for more than a few hours. She's forgiven me, but I broke our relationship, our little team, back on that day I nearly hit her. And I live every single day fearing I'll become that monster again."

He finally met her eyes, wondering why it was free of disgust or pity. Cat was usually such an open book, but in that moment, he couldn't judge her expression.

Regardless, he wanted to give her an out. "This is who I am, Cat, and why I keep saying I don't want to hurt you. Because given my track record, I might do exactly that. And even though it'd kill me inside if I ever did, you need to know why I'm so careful all the time."

As she studied his face, Lachlan's heart beat double-time.

It was one of those rare moments in life, one that would change everything.

So he waited to see which way it'd go.

IT'D TAKEN everything Cat had to not start crying as Lachlan shared his story. The disgust, and pain, and self-loathing as he recounted the memory was evident in his voice.

When he finished and looked at her again, he all but said she shouldn't bother with him. Well, maybe not quite in those terms, but he clearly wasn't expecting her to fight for him.

And even though they'd only started to become close in the last few days, she wanted to be there when he laughed more freely, when he let go a little to tease her, or even maybe to teach any child of theirs how to ride a bicycle.

He was a male who'd grown up in a broken

home, had tried to deal with it, and failed until he faced his greatest fear—becoming his father.

The descent was easy, but coming back from it, fighting tooth and nail to be better, was so much harder. He had great strength within him, and somehow she didn't think Lachlan realized it.

She moved her hand from his neck to his jaw and gently traced it. She murmured, "I think you're careful because you want to stay sober, aye. But I also think it's because you've isolated yourself and have so much time to dwell on what you could become again." He opened his mouth, but she beat him to it. "I'm not saying you'll wake up one day and instantly forget about what you've done, or not ever fight the urge to drink again. However, if you had someone—or someones—in your life constantly, helping to make new memories to replace the old, you might dwell on your fear less and focus more on what you have in the present."

She could tell from the confusion on his face that he hadn't expected her to answer like that. Still, Cat wasn't quite done, and she pushed onward. "In the last few days, I've seen a side of you that I don't think you share with many people, a side that is also who you are. And he can sometimes be funny, and brave, and even gentle. That is the male I like enough to be the father of my bairn. And if he comes with some flaws? Aye, well, we all have them. I'm sure I'll lose my temper or close myself off for a bit to avoid a fight, but does that make you want to just give up because I'm not perfect?"

"Of course not, but—"

"No buts. I may not know every horrible memory from your childhood, or even what you did whilst you lost yourself in drink all those years ago, but I've listened to all you've told me, and I'm still here, Lachlan. So are you going to run and give up? Or will you include me in your struggles and try to fight for the best future you can for the sake of our child?"

Or, for us. But she didn't say that part. It was far too soon to mention it. Although the more he told her, the more she wanted to know him. Maybe even better than any other person alive, crazy as it was.

She didn't want him to be so heartbreakingly lonely anymore.

For a second, he merely stared down at her, as if trying to make a decision. Then he moved both of his hands to her face and cupped her cheeks as he laid his forehead against hers. "How are you this bloody wonderful?"

Wanting to make him smile, she whispered, "It comes naturally. Just wait until my dragon comes back, then I'll be doubly so."

His smile reached his eyes, and it did something to Cat's heart.

She didn't know when, but his happiness was starting to mean an awful bloody lot to her.

He replied, "I would say I don't deserve you, but

I'm a wee bit selfish and want you too much, Cat. So, aye, I'm going to stick around. Not even if your sister Emma starts asking me about the inches of my dick will I run for the hills."

She laughed. "I bloody well hope she doesn't. If she does, then my dragon will have some words for her. You don't mess with someone's true mate and hope to remain unscathed."

He leaned back and tucked some hairs behind her ear. "Is that why you're doing this? Giving me a chance because of the true mate thing?"

She shook her head. "No. Whilst it can become painful to resist a frenzy, I still have free will. I'm doing this because I like you, Lachlan. And I'd like to get to know you even better."

He took her hand, and she threaded her fingers through his, the action the most natural thing in the world in that moment.

And as she asked him random questions about his likes and dislikes—steering away from anything dark since they'd had enough of that for one evening—she found herself laughing and smiling most of the time.

With time, Lachlan could easily win her heart. But Cat pushed that aside, not wanting to break the magic of one of the few dates she had with him before her dragon came out, and he'd have to endure a mate-claim frenzy.

Chapter Nine

The next morning, Lachlan woke up with a smile on his face, the first time he could remember doing that in years.

No, usually he ran through everything he needed to do for the day, creating a detailed schedule, before finally rolling out of bed.

However, when he slid off the mattress this morning, he barely gave his daily schedule a thought. Aye, he'd have to visit with the Seahaven dragonman and try to get things settled enough for the duration of the mate-claim frenzy.

But the rest of his thoughts were filled with Cat. Her laughter, her warm skin, and every memory of her fingers brushing against him.

Maybe she'd been right about how isolating himself had made him worry every second of every day about straying again.

Smiling like a fool, he went about eating and getting ready. He had just about finished up when there was a knock on his door. He opened it, revealing two of Cat's brothers—Ian and Connor.

He did his best to ignore their flashing dragon eyes and said, "Yes?"

Connor spoke up. "Come with us."

He raised an eyebrow. "Why, exactly?"

Connor shrugged. "Before you think of living here, you need to prove you can defend yourself."

He raised his other brow too. "Against what, or should I say whom? You two?"

Ian answered, "We won't beat you to a bloody pulp for Cat's sake, so aye, you'd best spar with us."

Leading up to his time on Lochguard, Lachlan had trained extensively. Dragon-shifters were always stronger than humans, no matter if it were a male or female. However, there were still certain maneuvers and tactics that could give him a chance to win.

And he rather wanted to win against at least one of Cat's brothers. The two lads might be younger, but they were Cat's family and were obviously protective of their sister. Besting at least one of them would go a long way toward their acceptance of him being with Cat.

Besides, it could be fun. Their surprise at him winning even once would be worth it.

He shrugged. "Aye, well, let's go then. I have a meeting in a few hours, so it'll have to be now."

Ian studied him a second, but it was Connor who motioned down the path. "Then come on. We have the perfect place to practice."

The slightly evil glint in Connor's eye told Lachlan how it wasn't going to be somewhere private, most likely.

Which suited him fine. The more people who saw he could handle himself, the easier it should be to gain their approval with at least their dragon halves.

As he followed the pair, he asked, "Cat doesn't know about this, does she?"

Connor shrugged yet again. "No, but this is between us. You want our sister, you have to earn her."

"I'm not sure she'd like to be 'earned' and bartered like some sort of chattel," Lachlan said dryly.

Ian muttered, "Great, Connor. Now Cat will yell at us even if we don't end up bruising him at all."

Connor replied, "We don't have a dad, so it's up to us. She knows our inner dragons want to protect her."

"I don't think that will make a difference," Ian stated.

Connor grunted. "Just shut it, Ian. We have a job to do."

Lachlan watched the younger men with amusement and wondered if their bravado was a result of their youth or something all dragonmen did.

He added it to his list of things to ask Cat later and followed them into a large open area he thought was the landing and takeoff space.

A makeshift stage had been set up, and a small crowd filled the edges of the area. It was mostly men, with a few women. He even spotted the ginger-haired MacKenzie twins.

Aye, well, this looked to be a test for him. And Lachlan wasn't about to fail.

So he removed his shoes, socks, and top like the other two lads did and waited to hear the rules.

WHEN CAT HEARD from Jamie what her other two brothers had planned for the morning, she'd cursed and run out of the house.

Stupid Ian and Connor, out to pummel Lachlan in front of who knew how many clan members.

It wasn't that she thought Lachlan was weak, but he was human and her brothers were dragon-shifters. Maybe if it were in private, she would've brushed it off as some sort of male-bonding experience. However, Jamie had said it was to be held on a fucking stage inside the landing area.

She was most definitely going to kill Ian and Connor when she had the chance.

When the main landing area came into view, she swore a few more times. There had to be at least forty people standing around something she imagined was the stage.

After she sorted out her brothers, she would have a word with Finn. She somehow didn't think he'd approved of the ad hoc event. After all, it wasn't as if any of the human females had to put on such a public display merely for a chance at staying.

She heard grunting but couldn't see over the heads of the taller dragon males. Somehow she pushed and elbowed others aside, attempting to make her way. Once people realized it was her and murmured the news through the crowd, they finally cleared a path. She reached the front just as Lachlan flipped Connor onto his back and put a foot against his windpipe. Lachlan stated, "Cede."

But then Connor extended a talon from one of his fingers and pressed it against Lachlan's foot. Even from several feet away, she smelled the faint whiff of blood.

She wished she could extend a talon, too, and see how Connor liked it. Stupid silent dragon meant she couldn't, though.

And her brothers had probably counted on that.

They would most definitely be dead by the time she finished with them.

Lachlan then kicked up his foot and thrust it against Connor's talon, bending it the wrong way.

Her brother yelped, and Lachlan took the split-second distraction to grab the lower part of Connor's talon, flip him over, and yanked both of her brother's hands behind his back. Lachlan growled, "Cede."

Aye, her brother could merely shift into a dragon, and then Lachlan wouldn't stand a chance. However, not even her idiotic brother was going to risk that and a lecture from Finn. So Connor mumbled, "I cede."

Lachlan released him and helped her brother up as everyone clapped around her.

She was a wee bit proud but far more furious. So Cat jumped onto the stage and shouted, "What the bloody hell did you think you were doing, Connor? If you killed him, you know what it would do to me."

Connor rolled his eyes. "I wouldn't kill him. Bruise him a little, aye, but not kill him."

The smell of blood was stronger on the stage, and Cat felt a slight stirring at the back of her mind.

Fuck. It was her dragon.

Her brother's stunt had made her inner beast angry enough to weaken the drug still in her system.

She dared a glance at Lachlan, and the stirring strengthened. "Connor, you bastard, now you've done it."

Not wanting to risk her beast waking up in front of a crowd, with Lachlan only a few feet from her, Cat turned on her heel and fled, the rumblings in her mind growing stronger with each step.

Thanks to her idiotic brother threatening her true mate and drawing blood, her dragon was fighting to wake up. The need to protect wasn't just a male dragon prerogative; no, females were just as fierce.

And now she couldn't be near Lachlan unless he was ready for the frenzy.

Heading toward her mother's restaurant, Cat would have to tell her mother and Finn everything. Then she'd have to hide in the cottage they would use for the frenzy until Lachlan was ready.

A thread of nervousness rushed through her. Not because sex with Lachlan would be a bad thing. But she'd wanted another day with him, to know him, to better prepare him for when her dragon came out.

And her brothers had stolen it from her.

Aye, as soon as she was able, she would kill them both.

Lachlan watched Cat run into the distance and wondered if he'd been mistaken.

Because he swore he'd seen her pupils flash once before she left.

A female voice cut through his thoughts, one he recognized as Faye MacKenzie. "You fucked up, Connor. You've provoked her dragon enough to want to protect him."

Lachlan turned, blinked at the sleeping bairn strapped to Faye's front—did she really bring the wee thing everywhere?—and asked, "What are you talking about?"

Faye sighed as she switched her gaze to him. "I told everyone this was a bad idea, but all the males said it was just good fun. And that a female dragon wouldn't be so protective if her mate was losing a fight. Bullshit, for sure. But of course no one listened."

Faye's pupils flashed rapidly before she spoke again, "Come with me, Lachlan. Connor, clean up this mess and make sure Cat is okay."

Lachlan blurted, "But Cat said the silent drug worked better on female dragons."

Faye nodded. "Aye, they do. However, when one's mate looks about to be stabbed by a talon—not to mention the fact Connor drew blood—it'll wake up the most docile of dragons." She glared at Connor. "The rules were no shifting *any* part of your body."

Connor shrugged. "I knew he could handle it."

Under normal circumstances, Lachlan would acknowledge how Connor's words were all but an endorsement of his skills. However, he wanted to know more about Cat's situation. "Is Cat in pain now?"

Faye took his hand and guided him off the stage —she glared at her older brothers for good measure along the way—and finally replied, "I'm not sure. If it's not magical dick time now, it'll be soon. So I hope you're ready." She glanced over at him. "My gut says you're going to go through the frenzy."

"Aye," he murmured.

She nodded. "Good. Whilst I'm happy for Cat, it also means I can train you on the side once you've finished it and watch with glee as you best some of the dragon males."

He blinked. It wasn't as if he was going to wrestle every week in front of an audience.

However, he pushed her comments aside to focus on what was important.

Of course, that meant asking a near stranger something Cat had promised to explain in more detail today.

Still, he'd rather have Faye explain it than her mate or the clan leader. She seemed blunt and to the point, and he could use that right now.

Not to mention he didn't have to try and impress her to the same degree as he did with the clan leader.

So he cleared his throat and asked, "Cat was going to explain more about what happens when her dragon takes over today."

"And now she can't." She muttered a curse. "Aye, well, I guess that means I get to give you the dragon side of the birds and the bees."

Maybe he'd be wrong to ask Faye after all.

She grinned over at him. "Oh, don't worry. We don't have talon-lined vaginas or anything. It's more that the dragon will take over our human form and demand sex. Rough and hard most of the time." Her gaze turned soft. "It's quite good, actually."

Not wanting her to regale him with her own sexcapades, he steered the conversation toward something much tamer. "But will her dragon be out the whole time? I know it can take weeks sometimes before the frenzy stops."

Faye shook her head. "No, usually the human and dragon half take turns, sharing the experience like they do with almost everything in life. And her dragon can sense when you need sleep or food, and will give some breaks. But if you try to leave, her beast won't allow it. So you have to be doubly sure about this." She pierced him with a fierce look. "Are you?"

He didn't hesitate to answer, "Aye, I am."

"Good. Cat's my friend, so whilst I know her brothers would've issued warnings, I'll do it too. Hurt her and you'll have to deal with me."

He looked at the baby girl sleeping against Faye's chest and murmured, "Hopefully you'll leave the bairn at home. It'll be easier to fight me then."

Faye snorted. "Why, Lachlan MacKintosh, are you trying to be funny? Who knew. I thought you were stuffy and too serious, actually."

He wasn't sure how to respond to that, but it didn't seem as if Faye needed a reply. She shrugged and then stared down fondly at her child. "Isla is special to me. I lost her twin during my pregnancy and had a hard time giving birth to her. So I want to treasure her." Her voice turned soft. "She might be my only one."

He had no idea why Faye had shared something so personal, but he felt the urge to say something. "I wish my own parents had cared as much for me as you do her. Your daughter is lucky to have you as her mum."

Faye's eyes turned wet, and he wondered what the hell was going on now. Cat seemed so easy to understand, but other women? He had no bloody idea.

Faye wiped her eyes with her free hand and said, "You'll do, Lachlan MacKintosh. You'll do." She tugged his hand. "Now, come on. There's a lot to set up and get ready before Cat's dragon wakes up fully. There's no time to lose."

And so the next few hours went—everyone asking him questions and educating him about what was to come. Not to mention he had to type out some notes for the Seahaven dragonman about what needed to be done for the exhibition while he was stuck in the frenzy.

The only thing he didn't do was explain the truth to the DDA and instead had said he needed a quick holiday for a family emergency. He hadn't had a chance to discuss his future with them. He'd just have to do it once he was free.

Aye, well, not exactly free. He'd have a child on the way by then.

Which was something that both frightened and excited him.

Once everything was finished, he sought out Finn. He was as ready as he'd ever be, and Lachlan was eager to get started.

Chapter Ten

Lachlan stood at the door of the cottage where he'd be spending the next however many days, took a deep breath, and entered.

Finn had told him that Cat should be waiting in an upstairs bedroom, and to be very sure he was ready. Because as soon as he entered the house, Cat's dragon would know, and there would be little chance of escape.

And yet, the mobile phone in his trouser pocket seemed like a giant weight. Apparently, he did have an escape, but only if he truly needed it. Finn had made it clear that once he called to be extracted, that was it. He was done and would be asked to leave Lochguard.

Not that he was going to.

He removed his shoes and socks and walked up

the stairs slowly, listening for Cat. With each step, his body burned a little hotter in anticipation.

Aye, he'd enjoy the sex. But he wanted to kiss her, and hold her, and feel her skin against his.

And maybe during the brief moments when her dragon would let him eat, he could talk to her too.

It seemed that after so many years alone, he craved company, especially with someone as bright and upbeat as Cat MacAllister.

The dragonwoman appeared at the end of the hall, her body tense, her fingers clenched into fists. "Lachlan?"

Her voice was weak and strained, and he didn't like it. He rushed toward her, but she said, "Wait." He froze, and she added, "Are you sure? I can hold her back long enough for you to run if you want."

"I'm not going to bloody run, woman." He charged toward her, scooped her into his arms, and walked through the open doorway. "I want you. Now."

Her pupils flashed once, and she shut her eyes for a second before opening them, no sign of her dragon in charge. She murmured, "As long as it's quick, my dragon will let me have the first time." She put a hand on his neck and leaned more against him. "So hurry up and kiss me, Lachlan. Whilst we still have the chance."

The responsible thing to do would be to place her

on the bed first, make her comfortable, and then kiss her.

But he crushed his lips against hers, his tongue sliding into her mouth, needing to taste this woman more than anything he'd wanted in his life.

She deepened the kiss, her tongue stroking against his, sending heat through his body and down to his cock.

As much as he loved her mouth, he needed to feel more of her against him, much more.

Lachlan adjusted her in his arms until she could wrap her legs around his waist, and he crushed her to his body. Her hard nipples pressed against his chest, and he groaned.

One hand threaded through her hair, tugging her head to the side for better access. The other went to her arse and pressed her against his cock. He hissed at the pressure, and it spurred Cat on. Her tongue became more insistent as her nails dug into his scalp, and she rubbed her hips against him, her movements making him harder than he'd ever been in his life.

And as his cock let out some precum, Lachlan knew that if he wasn't careful, he'd come with his clothes still on.

No bloody way he was going to let that happen.

Somehow he managed to tear his lips away and say, "Fuck, woman. I won't last if you do that. And I don't want your dragon to count me coming in my trousers as the first time."

He loved the humor in her eyes. "So logical, even now." She pressed her breasts against his chest again, and even through both of their clothes, the points of her nipples made him moan. "I think it's time to add a little dragon-shifter flavor to this."

In the next second, she extended a talon, sliced it through the back of his shirt, and the fabric sagged apart. He barely noticed the cool air since her fingers traced a line down his spine, fire spreading through his body at her touch.

She murmured, "Put me down so I can finish taking off your shirt."

He slowly slid her to the ground, loving her softness against his front. The second her feet touched the floor, she ripped his shirt off and placed a hand on his chest. "So warm, and hard, and yet still soft."

As she ran her nail across his flat nipple, Lachlan growled. "My turn."

He may not have talons, but Cat was merely wearing a robe. He tugged the tie, and the fabric instantly parted. He sucked in a breath at her pale, slightly flushed skin. "You're so fucking beautiful."

Her cheeks flushed a deeper pink, as did the upper part of her chest. He slowly slid the fabric over her shoulders, paused a second to stare into Cat's eyes, and then let it fall.

For a beat, he couldn't tear his gaze from the heat in her eyes. Then they flashed, and she said,

"Please, Lachlan. Go faster, or my dragon will come out."

He cupped her cheek and nodded. "But as soon as this whole frenzy is over, I'm going to show you just how thorough I can be."

She shivered, and the act broke his control. He kissed her as his other hand moved down her body, stopping to cup her breast and tweak her nipple before doing the same to the other one, and then headed toward her belly. He traced just above her thatch of hair, loving how she swayed toward the touch before he finally reached between her thighs. He parted her hot, swollen lips and groaned. "So fucking wet for me already."

Her voice was husky. "Don't sound surprised. I want you, Lachlan, and I have for a while. Now, hurry up and fuck me before my dragon takes control."

Her words shot straight to his cock. A beautiful, dirty-talking woman wanted him; it was as if he'd won the lottery.

When he slipped a finger into her pussy, she gripped his digit so tightly he nearly lost his mind. All he wanted to do was pound in the wet, warm center of her until she cried out his name.

But somehow, he managed to hold back, smile at her words, and say, "Patience isn't necessarily a bad thing, Cat."

She growled, and he laughed before taking her

lips again as he continued to tease her opening with light thrusts, needing her to be as desperate as he was, with his cock already hard as granite.

As she moved on his finger, he walked them back toward the bed. When they reached it, he broke the kiss, took his hand away from her cunt, and stepped back.

She cried out, but he chuckled as he quickly took off his trousers and boxers. "I don't know if dragons have spearlike cocks that can cut through fabric, but I don't."

She opened her mouth to say something, but he didn't wait, taking her lips as he quickly guided her back on the bed.

The second he lay on her, every inch of her front against his, he growled and took the kiss deeper, licking, stroking, needing to taste more of her.

He'd never get enough.

Not wanting to think of how she could be his next addiction, he pushed her thighs apart and ground his cock against her, moaning as her heat and wetness moved against his flesh. She cried out into his mouth as he rubbed his cock faster against her clit, but he didn't stop kissing her.

Then he felt her nails in his arse, pressing forward. And as much as he wanted to take his time, kiss down her body, and worship her sweet pussy with his mouth until she shouted his name, he didn't want to risk her dragon.

The first time, he wanted Cat all to himself.

So he slowed the kiss until he could pull away. He positioned his cock and murmured, "Ready?"

She stroked some of his hair behind his ear. "If that's not obvious by now, then I worry about your observation skills."

"Little minx," he muttered as he slightly pushed into her. Cat sucked in a breath, and he stopped.

She shook her head. "No, don't stop. You're so big and hard, and I want more." She dug her nails into his arse harder. "Much more."

Bloody hell, she was like a sex fantasy come to life.

Lachlan wanted to slam into her, but he moved a little more forward and then pulled until he was almost out. She frowned. "You're too slow."

He took her lips in a kiss as he slowly deepened his thrusts, doing his best to not spill like a green teenager. "You're so fucking tight, Cat. I have to go slow right now, or I'll lose my mind."

She smiled slowly, approval flashing in her eyes at his words. "Coming as many times as possible is rather the point to a frenzy." She arched her hips until he was inside her to the hilt.

The feel of her hot, wet pussy all around him, gripping him, hell, possessing him, was almost too much. To distract her and give him a minute, he moved a hand to her clit and flicked it with his fingernail. Cat jumped a little. "Do that again."

He did, kissing her as he did so, loving how her tongue didn't hesitate to meet him stroke for stroke.

Once he wasn't about to explode, he broke the kiss and met her gaze. At the lust there, he decided to hell with restraint. He growled, "Now, let's see if I have a little dragon in me too."

He lifted her hips a little so she was at an angle, put a pillow underneath, and then began to move.

Each thrust was harder than the last, making her squirm to meet him, the sound of flesh against flesh filling the room, making his cock even harder.

But feeling the grip of her wet pussy wasn't enough. He needed to taste more of her. Leaning down, he drew one of her nipples into his mouth, loving how she seemed to grow even wetter when he bit her lightly.

A need coursed through him, primal and demanding. Almost as if he didn't claim her now, he'd lose her.

And he'd be damned if that happened.

He released her nipple to hold her in place as he pistoned his hips, loving how she cried out each time he slammed in.

Over and over he thrust, trying to reach deeper, harder, until he knew he was close. The pressure at the base of his spine was near breaking point, so he moved a hand to her clit and rubbed hard in fast circles. Cat cried out and then stilled, her pussy milking his dick in quick spasms, coating his dick with her honey.

With a growl, he let go, joining her in pure bliss, as he released and shot his hot seed into her, each jet marking her as his and no one else's.

When she'd wrung every last drop from him, he collapsed on top of her, his legs moving behind him.

But barely a second passed since he laid his head against her shoulder before he found himself on his back, Cat looming over him with slitted pupils.

Her voice was slightly deeper as she said, "Now, you're mine. All mine."

And Lachlan knew Cat's dragon was in charge.

CAT HAD KNOWN since she was thirteen how mate-claim frenzies worked, but as soon as her dragon pushed to the forefront of her mind, she wished she had the strength to tell her beast to wait a minute so she could enjoy some post-orgasmic bliss with Lachlan half laying on her chest.

However, her dragon didn't care about romantic notions or silly "human moments," as her beast often called them. He was their true mate, he would give them a child, and there was no time to waste.

Which was why her dragon now had Lachlan on his back, straddling him, his cock in hand.

She tried to reason with her beast. *He's human, dragon. He needs more time to recover.*

I'll just stroke him until he's hard again. Then I want him. It's my turn. He's ours. I need him.

Her dragon did exactly as planned, gripping Lachlan's cock and stroking him repeatedly as she said, "Hurry. Mine. I want you, need to fuck you. Many times over. I want a child."

She half expected Lachlan to blink in confusion, or frown, or even to look afraid.

But he merely groaned and then murmured firmly, "You can have me, but I want Cat too."

Lachlan was standing up to her dragon. Cat didn't know whether she should be pleased or annoyed.

A challenged dragon only became more obstinate.

Her dragon growled, "You're too slow with her. I should keep you to myself, riding your dick until you give me what I want."

Cat noticed Lachlan suppress a moan when her beast squeezed the base of his dick, but somehow the male found the strength to reply, "No, that's not going to happen. You share her. Understand?"

Her beast paused at the dominance in Lachlan's voice. If Cat had been in charge, she would've blinked.

It seemed their human could act a wee bit like a dragon-shifter when he wished.

Her dragon never stopped stroking Lachlan's cock and then started to fondle his balls.

She could see him trying not to moan, which made her want to smile.

Her dragon growled, "You promise to fuck quickly, and I share."

Way to bring out the romance, she mentally drawled.

Of course her dragon ignored her.

Lachlan's cock started to harden again, and it was only a matter of seconds before her dragon would ride him.

But he put a hand on her wrist. "You want my seed? Then you share her, end of story."

Her dragon hissed, "For a human, you're either very brave or very stupid."

Cat mentally laughed. Her dragon had expected Lachlan to do her every bidding.

He quirked an eyebrow, and her dragon grunted. "Fine. But if you take too long with her, you sleep less."

He released her. "Agreed."

Then her dragon positioned his dick and sank down.

Lachlan never moved his gaze from her dragon's as he gripped her hips and helped her move.

As much as Cat wanted to lean down and kiss him, she merely let her beast ride him, digging their nails into Lachlan's chest.

He guided, caressed, and all but worshiped the

parts of her he could reach. Cat may not be in charge of their mind, but she felt every brush of his fingers, wanting to be able to touch her fill too.

But her beast only moved their hips faster, not caring about touches, or kisses, or whispers of breath against her skin.

And even though her dragon only cared about his orgasm in that moment more than anything, he still reached up and played with her clit.

Her human really did embrace both sides of her, wanting to pleasure them both.

Something shifted in Cat, but she barely had time to think on it before Lachlan growled and stilled. Even as he came, he still pinched their clit until pleasure coursed through her body.

Once her inner muscles stilled, her dragon murmured, *I like him.*

Me too, dragon. Me too. Can I have him for a bit?

A short while. But only so I can nap.

It seemed that an orgasm with her dragon in charge made the beast sleepy. Cat needed to remember that.

As her dragon moved to the back of their mind and curled into a ball to sleep, Cat took charge again and moved to lay to Lachlan's side. She brushed some of his hair off his face, noticing the sweat on his brow, and she smiled. "I think we're working you too hard."

He moved his head, although she could see how much effort it took. "Cat?"

Stilling her hand on his jaw, she nodded. "For now. My dragon needs a nap."

He was still catching his breath as he said, "If she keeps up this pace, I think she's going to kill me."

Cat laughed. "She won't. But she's quite determined. Reasoning won't help you with her, just to let you know."

He took her hand on his face, moved it, and kissed her palm.

The action made her heart flip. Under the cool, logical exterior, Lachlan was a wee bit romantic.

He said, "As long as she doesn't fuck my dick off, I don't care. This is a way I can help you, and I'll do it."

She kissed him gently and pulled away a few inches from his mouth. "You've helped already." She ran a hand down his body, to his cock. He was semi-hard, and Cat lazily swirled her finger on the tip.

Lachlan sucked in a breath. "You do something to me, woman. I've never been hard again so fast in my life."

She continued teasing his dick. "Dragon-shifter magic, aye?"

He rolled until she was on her back, he half on top of her, with her wrists pinned over her head. "Aye, must be." He kissed her, thoroughly exploring her mouth and making her breathless before he pulled away again. "But I don't bloody care. I have some magic of my own."

And as he took her again, slower this time, Cat forgot everything but the man above her, inside her, claiming her with the sheer determination as if he were a dragon-shifter himself.

Chapter Eleven

Lachlan had tried to keep track of the days during the frenzy, but since he hadn't carved notches in the wall to keep count, he had no bloody idea what the date was.

However, as Cat slept curled against him, nestled against his chest with his arm over her waist, he didn't think it was important.

The snippets of time he'd been able to rest and talk with Cat had been some of the best in his life. She was funny and smart and playful.

The complete opposite of everything he'd known his entire life.

As she murmured and settled again, he smiled. It would be easy to love this woman. Even without a child, he wanted a future with Cat.

However, Lachlan still didn't know if stressful situations might wipe away his ease and replace it with a burning desire to run and lose himself in drink again.

Having a randy dragon want constant sex was one thing. Forming an actual relationship and eventually raising a child was another.

She murmured again, but this time she moved her hand against his chest and lightly ran her fingers through his chest hair.

Despite the fact he was sore, Lachlan's cock stirred again. He had a feeling that after the frenzy, one small touch from this dragonwoman would always turn him hard in an instant.

Cat spoke in a sleepy voice. "Morning, I think."

He glanced out the window and then back at her face. "Aye, I think so." Her eyes opened, the now familiar deep blue, but with round pupils instead of slitted. He brushed her hair from her face as he added, "Usually your dragon is up when you are and then makes some sort of demand. Is she actually tired for a change?"

Her pupils flashed a few beats but then returned to round. Cat smiled slowly, looked up at him, and touched his cheek. "She said she deserves some rest and that we can do some boring human things again."

He frowned. "I didn't think it was possible to wear out an inner dragon during a frenzy."

She hitched her leg over his hip and murmured, "You can't. The frenzy is done." She took his hand

and moved it to her lower abdomen. "You're going to be a dad, Lachlan."

He stared down at his hand on her belly for a good minute.

Him. A father.

As the initial shock faded, a mixture of happiness and worry coursed through him. He was going to be a dad in roughly nine months' time.

And he was terrified of fucking it up.

She kissed his cheek, and he finally met her gaze again. Once he did, she said, "Say something. Despite all my dragon-shifter abilities, I can't read minds."

"I—" He wanted to say he was happy, but he blurted, "I'm a wee bit scared."

She didn't frown or roll her eyes or tell him he was being silly. She merely nodded. "I am too. I think it comes with the territory."

"Aye, but—"

She placed a finger on his lips. "You aren't your father, Lachlan. You might be a bit protective, and I daresay cautious, but so are many of the other parents on Lochguard." She moved her hand to his hair and lightly played with the strands at the back of his neck, the action soothing him. "I think you have so much more love to give than you realize. Between that and my family, our bairn will be extremely spoiled, I'm sure."

No one had ever believed in him so completely. Her faith in him did something to his heart.

While he'd worry plenty later, for the moment, he pushed aside his doubts and kissed her slowly, taking time to merely worship her mouth for no other reason than he wanted to.

When he finally pulled away, he traced down her neck, to her shoulder, and then lightly circled her nipple. "So what now?"

She grinned. "Now, we have fun." She jumped off the bed and rushed to the doorway of the bathroom. "I've always wanted someone to make me come in the shower. Up for it?"

His cock may be hurting, but Lachlan rolled off the bed and slowly walked toward her. "Aye, it's time to make you come on my tongue."

Her pupils flashed a second before she ran and threw over her shoulder, "Let me get the water ready. I want to be clean first."

As he stood in the doorway, watching Cat fiddle with the shower, he had a hard time believing this was his life now—a beautiful woman, a child on the way, and more laughter in the last couple of weeks than in the last ten years.

Lachlan wasn't usually the optimistic sort, but for once, he thought maybe he could be.

As soon as Cat was in the shower and started washing her body, he followed her and did exactly as he'd promised.

Twice.

SEVERAL HOURS LATER, Cat was clean, sated, and walking as slowly as possible toward her mother's house.

Her dragon snorted. *You know they're going to make a big deal out of it. Delaying it a few minutes won't change that fact.*

You can say that as you'll just laugh from the back of my mind. I'll be the one trying to keep them a wee bit tame with their comments whilst also protecting Lachlan.

After the last couple of weeks, I think he can protect himself.

She glanced over at the male in question. He had her hand in his and was doing his best to scroll through the DDA emails he'd missed during the frenzy.

She knew why he had to do it now instead of talking with her. After all, he'd told the DDA only that he'd be gone a few days. But she wished he didn't have to worry about the future of his job.

And not just because it was her fault that it was in jeopardy either. She'd experienced his event planning skills firsthand the year before, and he was bloody good at it.

Not even an eccentric archaeologist running off

into the night had flustered him. Well, at least not much.

Her dragon sighed. *He's clever. I'm sure he'll figure some way to make it work.*

Before she could reply, her friend Faye's voice came from off to the side. "Cat!"

She turned, and Faye—for once without her daughter—ran toward her and skidded to a halt to hug her. "Finn said you two were done." She leaned back so she could see Cat's face. "This is brilliant, like I told Grant. Our kids won't be too far apart in age. They can get into mischief together."

"Aye, that was exactly my first thought," she drawled.

Faye released her and rolled her eyes. "Come on, it's definitely a perk." Faye glanced at Lachlan and winked. "I guess her dragon didn't break you in the end, aye?"

Lachlan squeezed Cat's hand but kept his gaze on Faye. "She tried, but I'm fairly stubborn."

Faye snorted. "You might be human, but you act like a dragonman sometimes, that's for sure. If I wasn't so devoted to my mate, I would've liked to try out a human male first, just to compare."

Cat's cheeks heated. "Faye MacKenzie, what would Grant say?"

She shrugged. "He'd just grunt and ignore it because he knows I'm happy." Faye took another step backward.

"Speaking of which, Grant is with my mum and daughter, and whilst he's patient, he could probably do with some rescuing." She waved. "Congrats, you two."

As Faye ran off, Cat looked up at Lachlan. His lips twitched at the edges. "Faye's growing on you, isn't she?"

"A wee bit." He gently tugged her hand. "But we should hurry. Otherwise, your brothers might show up, tell us we're too slow, and carry us to your mum's place."

She snorted. "I'd like to see them try. I think they could only manage it if they shifted."

Lachlan raised an eyebrow. "Seeing as they mentioned dropping me into a loch at one point, I'd rather not tempt them."

Cat laughed. "It's not too bad, as long you're fairly close to the water when they let go."

He raised an eyebrow. "Why do I feel as if you speak from experience?"

She shrugged. "I do. Let's just say that teenage dragon-shifters have their own brand of fun."

Lachlan muttered, "Remind me to learn what they all are before our child is old enough to try them."

The image of Lachlan keeping a detailed list of all the ways their child could get into trouble made her smile.

They soon stood on the front porch of her

mother's house. Cat could hear muffled sounds inside the cottage.

A lot of them, meaning it was more than just her immediate family.

Her dragon laughed. *This is going to be brilliant. I want to see if Lachlan will actually blush.*

Ignoring her beast, she glanced up at Lachlan's gaze. "Ready?"

He leaned down, kissed her gently, and murmured, "Now I am."

She nearly sighed. Lachlan was really quite a romantic at heart.

Her dragon yawned. *Aye, aye, he is. Now, hurry up. We need to get this done so we can free up time for me to shift. I want him to scratch behind my ears.*

I'm not sure we'll get to it today.

It better be soon. I want some attention too.

Cat bit her lip at her dragon's petulant tone and opened the door.

Squeals at their entrance made her wince, and soon they were inside the cottage, surrounded by her family, her cousins, and even her grandfather and the other two partners of his thruple.

Cat could easily push aside and dodge her family's innuendos and eyebrow waggles.

However, she worried about Lachlan. He was open and sweet and honest with her. How would he do with so many people focusing on him this time around?

And why did it seem so strange to worry about him still?

Her dragon growled, *Because he's ours now.*

Everyone thought male dragon-shifters were protective and territorial, but female ones were just as bad.

Cat replied to her beast, *Aye, but let's not overstep just yet. He's strong, as you know, and let's watch how he does first.*

Her beast huffed. *I suppose. But if Connor tries to challenge him to a fight again, I'm going to take charge and toss him outside on his arse.*

She tried not to smile. *He'll deserve it, but let's save that as a last resort, aye?*

And so Cat did her best to watch Lachlan as he interacted with her family and not step in too soon.

LACHLAN WENT from holding Cat's hand to being forced apart and instantly surrounded by a bunch of men.

Correction, a bunch of dragonmen.

Some he recognized—her brothers, for example —but there were quite a few he'd never seen before. Or if he had, he hadn't taken much notice.

Connor slapped him on the back. "Survived the frenzy, aye? Female dragons have been known to break a cock or two, so you're a wee bit ahead of some dragonmen."

An older man Lachlan only recognized from pictures as Cat's grandfather, elbowed him in the ribs. "If he couldn't handle a wee female dragon, then he wouldn't be worth Cat's time."

Some unknown woman said, "I heard that, Archie MacAllister."

Archie flashed a grin toward the woman with gray hair. "Except for you, love. Not even two of us is enough to satisfy your hungry beast."

Lachlan nearly groaned, but quite a few others did. Connor spoke. "Stop it, Granddad. It's embarrassing."

"Why, lad? It's the truth. The stories I could tell you…you'd be redder than a beet in no time."

A middle-aged man Lachlan didn't know put an arm around Archie's shoulder. "Come on, Dad. Save your stories for another time."

Archie grunted as the man led him away. "You always say that."

Once Archie was gone, Ian murmured, "Remind me to thank Uncle Seamus later."

Lachlan glanced around the room. "Just how much family do you have?"

Ian shrugged. "Heaps. A few distant relatives moved to Seahaven decades ago. If they were here, we'd have to hold the party outside." He motioned toward a table loaded with food. "Come, have a bite, and you can tell me a bit more about your family. I never got to interrogate you properly, what with

Connor trying to kick your arse and waking up Cat's dragon."

Connor shrugged. "It turned out all right in the end, aye? That's all that matters."

Ian rolled his eyes. "One of these days, that attitude is going to bite you in the arse."

Lachlan didn't have a brother, but even if he had, he probably wouldn't have been as close as this pair. Not even he and his sister had been able to joke so freely.

Ian handed him a plate and asked, "What's your family like? We'll need to have them over. Maybe you'll have a sibling for me too."

He blinked. "What?"

Ian gave him a strange look. "I'm joking, aye? There's no dragon-shifter pattern of siblings mating siblings. Well, rarely so. Sometimes twins will hook up with twins. But that's all I've heard."

Lachlan wasn't entirely sure how to respond to Ian. The dragonman jumped from topic to topic with no clear path.

However, as he found Cat's gaze across the room, she raised her brows in question, with a silent *Are you okay?*

And Lachlan realized, aye, he was. This was her family, and he needed to get to know them.

Even if they were bloody mad half the time.

He decided to steer the conversation back to something more reasonable and focused back on Ian and Connor. "I only have one sister, and she's married."

Not that Lachlan knew much about Sarah's husband. His sister didn't talk about her marriage and only ever stayed on the topic of her sons whenever they chatted during his visits with his nephews.

However, being surrounded by Cat's family, with all of them being nosey with one another, he decided he needed to fix that and get to know his sister again.

Well, once he sorted everything out with the DDA first, both for his job and permission for Sarah and her boys to visit.

Ian finished swallowing whatever was in his mouth and replied, "Pity she's married. She'd probably be older than me, but there's something to be said for that. No blushing virgin for me, thank you."

Connor snorted. "Which is exactly why you'll end up with one."

Ian shot his brother a look. "Which means you'll end up with a shy one, for sure."

Curious, Lachlan blurted, "Do true mates work like that then? Are they always opposites?"

Connor shrugged. "Sometimes. You and Cat seem to be like that—she's outgoing and sunny, whereas you're extremely reserved. No offense, but at least so far, that's my impression."

He said quietly, "I'm lucky to have your sister. She's what I never knew I needed."

The two males blinked at him a moment, unsure of how to respond to his serious statement, but then went back to ribbing each other.

Lachlan couldn't believe he'd said that, but it was the truth. And one of his top priorities going forward was to be truthful with those Cat cared about.

And especially with Cat herself.

So he tried his best to answer questions from her family. Whenever he thought it was too much, he'd seek out Cat's eyes again and recharge.

Aye, he was indeed lucky to have her. And he was going to do everything he could to try to fit into her life.

Chapter Twelve

The next morning, Cat watched as Lachlan slept and debated slipping out of bed to get a sketchpad and a pencil.

The early morning light created wonderful highlights and shadows, accentuating his jaw, his nose, and even his brow.

She didn't like the lines etched into his forehead —no doubt from worry or stress—and yet they were a part of him that she wanted to include as well.

The lines were probably something she never would've noticed so clearly if not for her artistic eye.

Her dragon's sleepy voice said, *Just draw him already. He wouldn't say no, or care if you did.*

She didn't think so. But with the frenzy over, the ease of their own little bubble had popped, and she was still trying to figure out how they worked together.

Sex and attraction weren't a problem. But matings and love required a lot more than that.

Her beast sighed, but before she could say anything, Lachlan spoke with his eyes still closed. "I can feel you staring at me."

She smiled. "Now who's the one with supersensitive senses?"

He blinked open his eyes and his blue gaze found her own. "Unless I was deaf, your little sighs would've let anyone know you were nearby."

She frowned. "I wasn't sighing."

His lips curled upward slightly. "Aye, you were. At least five times that I heard. Who knows how many before that, when I was still sleeping."

"Well, you snore a wee bit."

"And that doesn't embarrass me at all." Before she could think of what to say to that, he reached over and touched her cheek. "I love your wee sighs, and your growls, and even your snorts. You give your emotions so freely. Don't ever change that, lass."

And just like that, her irritation faded. "I always wished I could hide them when I was younger."

"Aye?"

She laid her head on his shoulder and snuggled against his side. "You've met my siblings. Ian was always the best at hiding things, although Connor can when he wants to as well. I love them all now, but we're really close in age, the lot of us, and when we were younger, we all tried to find weaknesses to torment each other. Needless to say, Emma and I were the easiest targets."

He played with her hair. "What about Jamie?"

"Jamie was the youngest, and even if we're all close in age, he's still a good five years younger than me. By the time he could come up with ways to get back at us, I was a teenager."

"And not long after, you couldn't be a child any longer."

Maybe it should surprise her that Lachlan pieced it all together so quickly. But her human was clever and observant, and she rather admired him for it. "Aye. Once my dad died, I couldn't think like a sister any longer. I was more a guardian, of sorts. At least until my mother finally came out of her depression, then it was more like a partnership to raise them."

He continued to stroke her hair a few seconds before asking, "What happened between you and your mother that night of the get-together in the great hall? You never did tell me."

She battled between sharing and keeping the secret. Her dragon spoke up. *He's not just anyone—he's our true mate. Just tell him. I think he can keep a secret.*

As she looked up at his face, she found his eyes studying her. If she was to ever want more than sex and a tentative friendship with Lachlan, she needed to trust him. And so she whispered, "I found out my mum's pregnant."

She expected him to blink in surprise, but he merely nodded. "It was one of my theories."

Propping her chin up on his chest to better see him, she asked, "One of your theories?"

"Oh, aye. I always like to think of what the cause of something is or what action comes next. It's why I'm so good at event planning." He took one of her hands and threaded his fingers through hers. "Will she be okay?"

"I think so, especially since her pregnancy seemed to chase away her illness—at least according to her test results, which showed improvement for certain stats—meaning she should live longer."

He squeezed her fingers. "But? There's something else bothering you, aye?"

She nodded. "She won't tell me about the father. I have no idea if he's right here on the clan, or from somewhere else and she doesn't want him to find her again. Or if she's just nervous about telling the male he's going to be a father."

"Give her time, Cat. Sometimes secrets are difficult to share, even when it's your own family."

She sighed and laid her head back on his chest. "You're too reasonable sometimes."

He chuckled, the sound echoing beneath her ear. "I think your family could use some caution and reason. I would never want to change them, but you have to admit your grandfather could use some taming."

She snorted. "If he hasn't been tamed by now, he never will be."

They remained quiet for a few minutes, the silence comfortable as Lachlan continued to touch her skin, stroke her hair, and in general, soothe her with his hands.

Her dragon grumbled, *When will it be my turn to get some stroking?*

Today, I promise.

Cat slowly sat up. The morning light was even better now, and she decided to just ask him. "Will you let me sketch you? Right now, before we do anything else?"

"Aye, if that's what you want. Go ahead, lass."

It was the second time he'd called her lass. With most people—apart from her grandfather—it annoyed her. But with Lachlan…it felt almost like a special endearment, just for her.

Probably because it revealed how relaxed he was. No more Mr. Formal Speech with her, it seemed.

She released his hand, jumped from the bed and went to a drawer in her dresser, took out a sketchpad and a pencil, and headed back to the bed.

She bent over to pick up the large shirt she usually slept in—although it seemed pointless to keep doing it anymore with Lachlan around—and her human said, "No, don't put it on. If you want me naked, you remain that way too."

"Don't be silly. It's chilly."

She tossed the shirt over her head. And as soon as her head popped out of the opening, Lachlan covered himself with the blanket up to his chin.

Her dragon laughed, but Cat ignored her beast and narrowed her eyes. "I'm being practical and you're being absurd."

He grinned, and Cat did her best to ignore how her heart skipped a beat. The bloody male was too handsome for his own good.

Lachlan said, "I guess the tables turn every once in a while, aye?" He snuggled deeper into the blanket. "I rather like being the illogical one for a change."

She almost asked who was this male.

But the question was stupid, of course. Lachlan was becoming more and more the male he should've been, if his family had been different.

If he'd been loved.

She had a feeling he would only be this way with her, at least for a while. And there was no way she was going to scold him at his first signs of trust in her.

However, since she wasn't going to freeze to death as she sketched—irrationally ignoring how it was nearly August and not exactly that cold—she decided to do what worked best with any difficult person she knew on Lochguard.

Which was to bargain. "Let me sketch you naked,

with me still dressed, and after breakfast, I'll show you my dragon."

"Weren't you going to do that anyway?" She sighed, but he continued before she could say anything. "Connor mentioned something about a painting or two you've done of me. Show me one of those, lass, and I'll gladly lay here and let you sketch to your heart's content, even if my balls retreat into my belly from the cold."

She growled, "The list of reasons to kill Connor is getting longer by the day."

Her dragon spoke up. *Just show him. He's revealed so much about himself to us. We should do the same.*

Her beast was right, of course. *But one painting in particular is a wee bit embarrassing. I'm not sure I can show that one.*

It doesn't matter. If he can tell us about the lowest point of his life, we should be able to share a painting or two.

When her beast put it that way, Cat felt about two inches tall.

She nodded at Lachlan. "Aye, I'll show you. As long as you promise not to laugh."

"I'll try my best, but until I see it, I can't promise that."

She shook her head. "Well, at least you're honest."

"With you, Cat, always."

The certainty of his words took her breath away.

It would be so easy to fall in love with Lachlan MacKintosh.

However, she didn't want him to guess her thoughts. At least, not yet. He was a male that clearly needed time to accept anything happy or positive, given his past. And she didn't want to spook him.

So she nodded toward the blanket. "If you'd disrobe, fine sir, I can get started."

He snorted as he tossed back the blanket. "If you think formal words will make this more clinical, you're in for a surprise."

Once the blankets settled, she took in his body. The morning light bathed over every inch of him, including the heavy, swollen length of his cock resting against his belly. As much as she wanted to lightly tease him with the tip of her eraser, she focused instead on capturing the erotic image on paper.

Not just his hard cock, but the heated gaze, full of longing. The casual way he had an arm behind his head and one of his knees splayed to the side.

It was almost as if he lay there, merely waiting for her.

Ignoring the impulse to toss the sketchbook aside and climb atop him, she focused on drawing him. It was most definitely one of the harder things she'd done, but the second she had her sketch finished to her satisfaction, she tugged off her shirt, crawled over him, and claimed him as her own.

LACHLAN HAD SOMEHOW MANAGED to shower, dress, and eat breakfast without pinning Cat against a wall and making love to her yet again.

After the frenzy, he should want a wee break from so much sex.

And yet, with Cat, he would never have enough.

Just remembering her eyes caressing him as she drew him naked made his cock twitch.

But somehow, he contained the lust and instead focused on Cat unlocking the storage door inside her little studio space. Ever since Connor had mentioned the paintings of him, Lachlan had been waiting for the right time to ask Cat to show him.

Maybe someone would say it was no big deal that she'd agreed to do so, but he'd worked with a number of artists over the years. And even if they were confident and proud of their work, sometimes they still had doubts, like anyone. Certain pieces were more personal than others and should only be shared when the artist was ready.

Although he had to admit that knowing Cat had painted him before their fateful kiss and ensuing frenzy made him stand a little bit taller.

She flipped on the lights, revealing various shelves lined with stacked paintings, as well as some hanging on the wall, while others were on the ground propped against walls and furniture. As he surveyed the room, he asked, "Were you saving all of this for the exhibition show?"

"Some, aye. But in recent months, I've painted more than I have in the past and I've been too absorbed to do the finishing touches like varnish, take pictures, and put them up for sale online or take them to the shops that offer to sell them for me."

As he glanced over the various paintings depicting mostly bits of history, some myths, and others he couldn't place into either category, he asked, "Have you ever considered putting together a book? Not just of the paintings themselves, but the stories that went with them? There's a fair bit of dragon-human history and magic in this room that I'm sure many would love to discover."

She looked up from the stack of paintings she'd been sorting through. "As brilliant as that'd be, writing isn't my strong suit. Not to mention I don't have the time to do the research required."

He smiled. "I'm good with both counts, although Kiyana Boyd is better at research and combing through dusty tomes than me. I'm sure the three of us could make it work. And depending on if you trust that Adam Keith bloke from Seahaven, you could even outsource the photography bits to him."

Lachlan hoped she didn't think he wanted to take charge of her art or force her into anything. But ideas were his strong suit, and he couldn't help but share them.

However, as soon as Cat walked up to him, brought his head down, and kissed him, his worries faded away. She whispered, "I love how without a thought, you just come up with a strategy to try and make an idea into a real possibility. Once everything settles down, let's talk to Kiyana and Adam and see if they're interested."

He ran a hand down her back and kissed her again. "Good, that'll give me time to come up with more of the specifics."

She laughed, kissed him, and stepped away to return to the shelf she'd been near before. "I'll leave the details to you. Although you may want to keep the extent of your brilliant planning skills a secret, or everyone will be asking for your help."

If the DDA didn't allow him to keep his job, he might just need the work.

But Lachlan didn't want to think of that right now. So he gestured toward the shelf. "Are any of the ones with me in there, or are you just stalling?"

She stuck her tongue out at him, and he grinned. Cat pulled out a canvas but kept the painted side toward her. "I did this one not long after we first met, back when you still had long hair."

He frowned. "You've been painting me for that long?"

She bobbed her head. "I was a wee bit obsessed in the beginning. But this is definitely one of the better ones."

Before he could say she was always talented, she turned the canvas around, and Lachlan took a step closer.

He stood bare-chested, wearing only jeans and boots, his long hair blowing in the wind. Behind him was a dark purple dragon who had one forelimb wrapped possessively around his middle, their wings outstretched behind.

They stood on a ledge above a loch, with Lochguard in the distance. Upon closer inspection, he could tell the buildings started out crude and simple on one side, slowly morphing into the more modern-day layout of the dragon clan on the other.

He must've studied it a long time because Cat cleared her throat and asked, "So? What do you think?"

Rather than empty praise, he was honest. "I rather like how you showed the passage of time in the background, almost as if you wanted Lochguard of the past to merge with that of the present."

He chanced a glance, and Cat nodded. "I thought it fit the main subject since in times long past, no dragon-shifter female and human male would ever be allowed together."

Standing upright again, Lachlan never broke her gaze. He had a feeling he knew the answer to his question, but he wanted to make doubly sure. "Who's the purple dragon, lass?"

She murmured, "Me."

He'd been right, as hard as it was to believe. Cat had wanted him all this time, which seemed impossible. "I was rude and cold to you back then, though. Why would you paint us together?"

She shrugged. "It was just a painting. Besides, there are loads of purple dragons on Lochguard. No one knew it was me except, well, me. And it was just a painting, and in it, we could be whoever I wanted us to be."

He took a step closer. "Am I what you wanted, lass?"

"Better."

Lachlan gingerly took the painting, placed it on the ground, and hauled Cat against his front. "Don't ever sell that one. When you feel ready, I want it hanging in our home."

As he cupped her cheek, she leaned into his touch and said, "I won't sell it. But there are others where I used you for inspiration, so maybe you should wait to pick the best one. I'll allow one or two, but not all of them. Because then my siblings would tease us endlessly about how I'm turning our cottage into a Lachlan shrine."

He smiled. "For now, at least, that's the painting I want."

She gestured toward the other pieces. "Let me get the other ones and show you first. They're all here."

He threaded the fingers of one hand into her hair

and guided her head closer. "Right now, I don't care about the other paintings."

She smiled, mischief dancing in her eyes. "Oh, aye? Then what are you thinking?"

He pressed her closer against his front, doing his best not to hiss at her soft stomach against his erection. "I'm thinking it's time to make some art of our own, in your studio, with us both naked."

She raised an eyebrow. "If you're suggesting we paint our bodies and have sex on top of some canvas, let me stop you right now because cleanup would be ridiculous. Paint would get *everywhere*."

He chuckled. "No, lass, not that. I'm thinking of a more live-action sort of piece." He moved to her ear and whispered, "The exploration of Cat MacAllister." He nipped her earlobe and added, "Directed, produced, and performed by one Lachlan MacKintosh."

She snorted. "That sounds a wee bit ridiculous."

"The title or the production?"

Leaning more against him, her voice turned husky, "Definitely the title. I'm rather curious about the production and performance."

"Then let's have a rehearsal, and you can tell me what you think after, aye?"

Her pupils flashed, only emphasizing the desire in her gaze.

It took everything he had not to kiss her right then and there. But the storage closet was small, and he wanted to see her naked, bathed in the sunlight of her studio.

Taking her hand in his, Lachlan tugged her from the storage closet and into her studio space.

Since there wasn't any furniture beyond the table, stools, and chair, he motioned for her to stay put. "Don't move."

He grabbed the blanket he'd seen in a chair, laid it on the ground, and then stood in front of Cat. She reached for him, but he shook his head. "My production, remember?"

Her pupils flashed again. "Then start directing, or I may take over."

The corner of his mouth ticked up at the impatience on her face. "Then let's begin, lass."

He moved behind her, brushed her hair off her neck, and kissed the soft skin. Cat's body instinctively swayed toward him. However, Lachlan drew upon his years of learning patience so he could resist her, knowing the reward would be sweeter at the end. And so he murmured, "Stay still."

"Surely you can't expect me to—"

He took her earlobe between his teeth and lightly worried it. She sucked in a breath, and he whispered, "Aye, I do. You've taught me how to have a wee bit of fun. Now it's my turn to teach you some patience." He kissed down her neck and lightly bit where it met her shoulder. After laving the bite, he added, "Now, raise your arms."

She did so, and he traced her side, across her belly, and toyed with the hem of her top. When his fingers finally brushed her soft skin, Cat sucked in a breath.

He bit his lip to keep from chuckling. Lachlan honestly didn't know how long Cat would play his game, and he wasn't going to risk irritating her.

He loved her fire, but he liked playing with her like this too.

Slowly, he dragged the fabric of her top up her abdomen, even slower over her breasts, taking care to rub across her peaked nipples. When she shivered, he finally tugged it up and over, tossing it somewhere behind him.

Lachlan moved in front of her and met her gaze. Her eyes were flashing, her cheeks flushed. He raised his brows. "Enjoying it so far?"

"The verdict's still out."

His little dragon minx. Lachlan stood closer and lightly pinched one of the nipples through her lace bra. "Then I'll just have to try harder, lass." He released her and nodded. "Take it off."

She took down one strap and then the other. As she turned it around to undo the clasp, she revealed her beautiful breasts, her pointed nipples making his cock hard and his mouth water.

When she finally tossed her bra behind her, Cat stood tall. With a knowing gleam in her eye, she rolled her shoulders and made her tits bounce.

Lachlan's dick let out a drop of precum, and he wondered if he'd have the patience needed to draw this out for his woman or not.

No. He could do this. Hell, he wanted to.

Not only because he was bloody aroused, but because it was also…fun.

Something Cat always brought to the table.

He stalked closer until he could circle her, lightly running his hand over her bare skin as he moved, until he stood in front of her again. Tweaking one of her nipples, he leaned to her ear. "Take off the rest."

She began to undo her jeans when Lachlan leaned down and took her nipple into his mouth.

He laved the tight bud with his tongue, swirling, making her groan.

He'd learned during the frenzy how sensitive her nipples were. He suckled, and she placed a hand on his shoulder for support.

Releasing her taut peak with a pop, he looked down to see her jeans unbuttoned but still on.

Lachlan licked her nipple one last time before helping her out of her clothes and then her underwear.

When she was naked, he ran a finger through her pussy and groaned. "You're so fucking wet for me, lass."

She opened her mouth to reply, but he picked her up by the waist and sat her on the table. Spreading her thighs, he kneeled down before her and rubbed his hands along her inner thighs, back and forth, loving how she moved her pussy even closer to him.

Somehow resisting her addicting scent and glistening center, he forced himself to look up and met Cat's scorching gaze. "What do you think? Should I keep going or scrap the whole production?"

Even though her cheeks were flushed, she still raised her brows and stated, "Stop now and you'll regret it, Lachlan MacKintosh."

He was tempted to see what she'd do, but with her dripping pussy mere inches from his face, her musky scent filling his nose, Lachlan's own restraint was fading. It took everything he had not to merely lap and feast until she screamed.

However, he wanted to drive her madder for his tongue first.

When he blew through her folds, Cat bucked her hips toward his face, begging for more.

"You're so fucking beautiful, lass." He teased the lips of her cunt. "Even here."

When she became even wetter for him, Lachlan's restraint fractured. Keeping her thighs spread wide, he leaned down and licked her slit slowly, teasing her opening before continuing upward, taking care to circle around her clit but never touching it.

Cat's hips jumped, but he kept her in place as he continued to lick, lap, thrust, and tease her pussy, loving her taste, feasting as if he'd never get enough of her sweet honey.

Her fingers threaded through his hair and pushed forward slightly, trying to tell him what she needed.

When he flicked her clit once with his finger, she moaned.

Meeting her eyes, he teased her sensitive bud, loving Cat's heavy-lidded gaze as she watched him.

She was so beautiful, so perfect. And his. Most definitely his.

He needed to show her with actions what he was far from admitting with words.

Teasing her bud, he gently thrust a finger into her core, loving how she instinctively moved her hips to meet his thrusts, her tits bouncing as she did so.

Adding another finger, he stopped teasing her hard nub and took her swollen little clit between his lips. He suckled and teased with his tongue, taking care to curve his fingers even more. Her cries let him know he'd found that secret spot inside her.

Cat threw her head back, but Lachlan released her long enough to say, "Look at me."

She did, and he rewarded her by lightly nibbling her clit the way he knew she liked it, and Cat arched her back as she came, crying out his name.

Once she slumped slightly, Lachlan removed his fingers and gave one more, possessive lick, groaning at the taste of her orgasm.

He'd never tire of her taste. Never.

Finally moving his head back, he ran a finger through her wet, swollen center, loving her sigh at the touch. "What do you think? Is this a good place to stop?"

Her pupils flashed to slits as she growled and tried to get up. But his hand on her leg kept her in place. She said, "I've been patient, but if you don't fuck me soon, Lachlan, then me and my dragon are going to take over."

He smiled as he rose, standing between her thighs.

She looked about to say something again. But Lachlan had other ideas for her mouth. Closing the distance, he kissed her, their tongues twining, licking, trying to dominate each other.

Not a shy one, his Cat.

And that was perfect for him.

Between her sucking his tongue and her taste still lingering in his mouth, his cock let out a few more drops of liquid.

Fuck, he needed to be inside her. He'd always want to be inside her.

He somehow broke the kiss and tore off his clothes. When he moved back between her legs, his cock in hand, Cat smiled. "What happened to teaching me patience?"

As he ran the tip of his dick through her core, loving how her sweet honey coated his cock, he murmured, "This is just the rehearsal. I'll fix my mistake next time."

She laughed, the sound breaking any semblance of self-control he had left.

Lachlan positioned his cock and thrust to the hilt. Cat's laugh morphed into a groan.

He moved her closer to the edge of the table, crushed his lips to hers, and held her close, needing to feel her skin against his, even if just for a moment.

Then his cock pulsed, telling him to do more than stand there. Cat arched her hips upward, saying the same, and he finally moved his hips.

Slowly at first, but with each thrust, he moved faster, to the point the table started to move, and things crashed to the floor.

But Cat didn't seem to care, instead digging her nails in his back, pulling him closer, meeting each of his thrusts with her hips, her tongue also stroking his own.

Even with things falling to the floor, the sound of flesh pounding against flesh reached his ears, making him harder.

He was so, so close.

But he wouldn't go it alone. Moving a hand between them, he pressed and rubbed Cat's clit hard, the way she liked.

With a growl, she dug her nails into his arse, the slight pain sending him over the edge. He stilled as his orgasm hit, Cat's pussy spasming around him, drawing every drop out of him as if necessary for life.

As he spent inside her, a sense of rightness settled over him as he claimed Cat as his yet again.

It was almost as if he'd been waiting his whole life for this woman.

When her cunt had milked every last drop, he released her lips and held her close, pressing his mouth to where her neck met her shoulder, and inhaled the combination of female musk, sweat, and the unique scent that was his Cat.

He was content to merely hold her, the woman who was growing to mean so much to him already, her warmth seeping into his skin, making him want a future he'd never thought to want so damn much before.

It was Cat who spoke first and broke the silence. "So if that was the rehearsal, I wonder what we can improve upon for the final version."

He chuckled before kissing her neck. "Oh, give me a day or so, and I'll come up with something even better."

"Maybe we should practice certain scenes at home first. You know, just to make sure they're perfect."

He moved his head back until he could see her eyes. With sunlight coming in from three sides, she almost glowed, as if a sort of beacon for him. One he'd always be able to find no matter what darkness tried to consume him.

But could a beacon light the way forever? That he didn't know.

Before further doubts could seep in, he replied, "We can practice as much as you like, lass."

Although he couldn't bring himself to say for the rest of their lives.

He wanted Cat more than anything, but he had been cautious for more than a decade, and he couldn't shrug that off so easily.

No, he'd need to make sure that once the almost honeymoon-like period wore off, she still wanted him before allowing himself to hope for the future.

However, as she snuggled against him, he pushed his worries aside and merely held the dragonwoman he wanted to one day call his own.

Chapter Thirteen

The next day, Cat shucked her clothes at the side of one of Lochguard's landing areas and tried her best not to be nervous.

No, it wasn't the fact she was going to be naked that did it. Dragon-shifters grew up treating nudity as just another normal state. Rather, it was because she was about to show Lachlan her dragon form for the first time since the frenzy.

Her beast snorted. *He saw our dragon form over a year ago, during the exhibition he ran. Being nervous is silly.*

I know, but this time it's different. He's embraced you taking over when we're human, but this is something else entirely, seeing the mother of his child changing into a dragon. It might be weird for him, and I don't think I could bear that.

It's strange for most humans, although I think he'll be fine. Besides, it'll be good to show him our dragon form since it'll remind him that we're stronger than him. Not that I think he'll hurt us, but he keeps thinking he can and will someday.

Not wanting to waste time debating with her beast, Cat merely tucked her clothes into one of the cubbies at the side of the landing area and strode toward the center.

Once there, she met Lachlan's gaze. Even from this distance, she could see his clenched jaw and slowly narrowed eyes. He didn't like her naked in public.

He was still jealous of others seeing her, apparently, no matter how many times she'd stated it was as normal as shaking hands with someone inside Lochguard.

Her dragon sighed. *He'll learn eventually. At any rate, now's all the more reason to shift quickly.*

Not needing any more prodding, Cat imagined her wings sprouting from her back, her arms and legs extending into fore and hind legs, and her nose extending into a snout until she finally stood in her tall, purple dragon form.

Lachlan's gaze trailed from her head, down to her feet, and back again.

Leave it to her male to make a thorough study of her other form.

Her dragon snorted, but then Lachlan walked toward them and Cat's heart beat double-time, her nerves on edge as she waited for their human to touch her.

For all the stories and legends told of fierce dragons with few—if any—weaknesses, many of her kind relished being scratched behind the ears, or stroked along the side.

It would be another way for Lachlan to show he accepted her, all of her.

Her dragon sighed. *Stop being silly.*

Lachlan finally stood in front of her and Cat lowered her head. As soon as his hand caressed her snout, her dragon hummed. The sound made Lachlan smile.

He said, "The dragon purrs much like when the human does—when's she's happy, aye?"

She lightly butted his shoulder and he chuckled. Even though he did it more often, Cat still treasured each and every time he did so.

He kept his hand near her nose and murmured, "You're beautiful in any form, Cat. I love how your scales sparkle a little, even when it's overcast."

His words made both female and beast sigh.

Her dragon said inside their mind, *He still needs to scratch behind our ears.*

He will. But maybe we should have some fun with him first. He's due for it, given his lesson in "patience" yesterday.

Aye, but I think we both rather enjoyed that.

Not wanting to remember Lachlan worshiping her inside her studio and get lost in the delicious memory, she pushed it aside for the moment.

No, she was determined to have her turn with him. Maybe even make him squeal a wee bit.

True, it wasn't the mostly dignified or macho of things, but Cat didn't care. She had a feeling they would be trading "lessons" for many years to come.

Or so she hoped.

Lachlan patted her cheek and then reached up to scratch behind her ear. Her dragon hummed louder and Cat did her best to focus on what came next. Her dragon was getting her ear scratches, so next it'd be her turn to have fun with their human.

ONCE CAT finally stood in her tall dragon form, Lachlan forgot all about his points to convince Cat to at least toss a towel or sheet around her naked body when shifting.

He couldn't resist her glinting scales or eyes that were both the same and yet foreign to him, and he instantly went to her.

However, when she started humming at his touch, he couldn't help but smile and revel in this side of his dragonwoman.

He'd barely had a chance to compliment her, though, before she gently used her snout to guide him toward her tail.

Not that he minded. Running his hand along her

side, he loved how her scales were hard and smooth, and slightly warmer than he would've expected.

Between the teeth she'd flashed and the solidness of her scales, it only reinforced that she was indeed a woman who could take care of herself.

And that was before his gaze fixated on the talons of her hind feet.

Aye, his lass was strong in many ways.

He reached her tail and was about to ask her what now when it wrapped around his middle and he was suddenly up in the air, a foot or so away from Cat's snout.

He didn't know if dragons could smile, but her open, toothy mouth surely looked like one. He asked, "What're you doing?"

She showed more of her teeth, ensured she was standing on all fours, and then deposited him on her back, in between the wings resting on her sides.

Lachlan was now at least ten feet off the ground.

Not that he cared much about that. No, he was more worried about what Cat might do. "Don't even think of jumping into the air, lass. If anyone reports you carrying a human in the air, then you'll be in trouble."

She flicked a wing out to the side and back, almost in a shrug.

Lachlan tried to think of what he could say to change her mind—Cat was stubborn, but usually not quite so reckless—however, her tail tapped her side, garnering his attention.

It moved down her flank, back to where he sat, and down again.

He raised his brows. "You want me to slide down your side?" She nodded and he eyed the distance. "That's almost straight down."

As if she'd known the argument was coming, she moved a leg out to the side, making the angle less severe. Then her tail repeated the earlier motion.

Given that Lachlan was in his thirties, he couldn't even remember the last time he'd gone down a slide.

Part of him wanted to, but the more rational part knew it was not only dangerous, but it could also lessen the respect others had for him within the clan. Because surely adults didn't go sliding down one another's sides for fun.

It was then he noticed a ginger-haired woman standing next to a double pram, another woman at her side balancing a toddler on her hip.

Bloody fantastic. They now had an audience.

Lachlan recognized the ginger-haired woman from the meal in the great hall when he'd first arrived. She was human and named Gina MacDonald-MacKenzie; she was mated to the dragon-shifter named Fergus. She shouted, her American accent readily apparent, "You may as well just do it. Trust me, my mate did the same thing in the beginning. I was scared at first, but actually it's pretty fun."

The other woman grinned. She also had an American accent too as she said, "It really is. I convinced Fergus to let me slide down his side too. I think it's a rite of passage for any human living on Lochguard."

Even though he'd never met her, the accent told him the other woman was Kaylee MacDonald, Gina's sister.

He grunted and shouted back, "It seems bloody dangerous to me."

Gina said, "Cat won't let you fall."

Even without Gina saying it, he knew that as well.

He stole a glance at Cat and she tilted her head, almost in challenge. Surely if the two women could slide down a dragon's side, he could as well.

Of course neither of them worked for the DDA or hoped to remain employed with them.

But then it hit him that if he refused to do this, then maybe Cat would construe it to mean he didn't value her dragon form as much as her human form.

That was all it took for him to take a deep breath, scoot into a better position, and propel himself forward.

He slid down, her smooth scales making it easy, and Lachlan just managed to get to his feet at the bottom without a problem.

Kaylee asked, "Well?"

He met Cat's gaze. "Maybe I should try it again."

Cat bared even more teeth—the dragon equivalent of a grin—and placed him on her back again. As soon as he was back on the ground, Kaylee had somehow convinced Cat to let her have a go as well.

Eventually Gina convinced her sister they needed to get the children home and he was left alone with Cat. She motioned for him to stand back and he watched as she slowly shrank back into her human form.

He wasted no time unbuttoning his shirt, walking up to her, and putting it around her shoulders.

Amusement danced in her eyes as she said, "Well, that went well. I'm sure Kaylee will share your adventures far and wide within the day."

He sighed. "Which means others are going to tease me, aren't they?"

She placed a hand on his cheek. "Don't worry about it, aye? Everyone slides down a dragon at some point." Her lips twitched. "Although to be fair, it's usually as an older child."

He lightly slapped her arse. "Minx."

She laughed, and the sound made him forget about everything else but the fact he had a beautiful female in his arms.

Cat was his, and that was all that mattered.

He lowered his head closer to her lips. "I think maybe it's my turn to play with you for a wee while."

"Oh? And how, exactly?"

He scooped her into his arms as she squeaked. "It requires somewhere far more private."

She put her arms around his neck, leaned against him and replied, "There's an empty shed not far from here. True, it only has a table inside it, but we both know how much you like those."

Memories of the day before, with him taking Cat inside her art studio, flashed into his mind, making his cock turn to stone.

With a growl, he said, "Tell me how to get there."

She did. And in less than five minutes, he had his woman spread on the table and showed her what his version of playtime entailed.

Chapter Fourteen

Over the next few days, Cat and Lachlan fell into a routine. The early mornings and evenings were filled with teasing, conversation, and plenty of sex.

During the day, however, they'd both had to face reality. Not only were the various artists due to arrive in about six weeks' time, but Lachlan was also still trying to find a way to convince the DDA to let him keep his job.

For the time being, the DDA didn't know about the frenzy, which of course, meant no mating ceremony.

Although Cat wasn't entirely sure if Lachlan was ready for one anyway. He still worried about failing her—and probably even hurting her—and it would take time to convince him otherwise.

And while she wasn't always patient, she could be

in this. Lachlan's scars ran deep, and she had to give him time to heal.

Well, she could give him at least until after the art collective project was finished. Because if they weren't mated by then, Lachlan wouldn't be allowed to stay on Lochguard.

And just thinking of him leaving made her throat tighten, her dragon unable to comfort her because they were sitting with Aimee King at the moment.

There was too much bloody uncertainty in her future, apart from having a bairn of her own in a little less than nine months' time. Almost everyone else with human mates on Lochguard seemed to have had everything settled so quickly. But apparently not her.

And yet, as Cat watched Aimee fill in her latest paint project, she decided to be grateful for all that she did have. Aye, she didn't like the fact Lachlan could lose his career for simply choosing her, but she had no right to complain when compared with Aimee.

The brown-haired lass had been imprisoned and drugged as a teenager. Cat suspected there was more to that story, perhaps even torture, but she wasn't about to ask. The female would share when she was ready.

Regardless, Aimee's situation did put things in perspective.

Usually her dragon would comment, but she was trying to stay quiet with Aimee.

Instead, Cat thought about how Lachlan might know more about the whole Clan Skyhunter upheaval—how Aimee, her brother, and so many others had become prisoners in the first place—when something lightly hit the window.

Their art therapy session was in Aimee's room today, at a different time than usual since their normal spot had been temporarily claimed for storage.

The tiny clacking sound happened again. However, before she could stand to check out the sound, Aimee asked, "What time is it?"

She checked her phone. "Half ten."

The lass jumped up and rushed to the window. After a beat, she gave a wave.

Her dragon's voice was sleepy as she said, *Go see who it is.*

I don't know if we should.

If there's someone she's waving to, wouldn't Finn and Ara like to know? The lass could do with a friend.

Her dragon was right. So Cat rose slowly and did her best to walk as quietly as possible to the window.

Aimee was so engrossed in watching whatever was happening, she didn't acknowledge Cat at all.

Interesting. Usually the female reacted to everything.

Cat finally reached the side of the window and

peeked out, just in time to see her brother Connor doing some sort of somersault.

She glanced over and barely stopped herself from gasping—the lass smiled. It was small and almost hesitant, but she smiled.

Because of Cat's brother.

Her dragon spoke up. *Now* that *is interesting.*

Not wanting to take away the small bit of joy from Aimee, Cat slowly moved back to her chair and sat down. *Aimee asked us about the time. Does he do this every day?*

If not every day, then semi-regularly.

She watched as the female stayed at the window a few minutes longer before she waved again and headed back to the table, careful to avoid Cat's eyes.

Maybe she should drop it. After all, the lass had made tremendous progress since first setting foot on Lochguard, and Cat didn't want to ruin it.

But she couldn't let it go. She'd never seen Aimee smile. Never. Not until today, at any rate.

Aimee had picked up her paintbrush when Cat asked softly, "Are you friends with my brother?"

The female's hand stilled a beat before she dipped the brush into some white paint. "I've only seen him through the window and for a second when he barged into that one session we had. I don't even know his name."

"It's Connor. Connor MacAllister, my younger brother."

Aimee nodded and went back to painting a cloud in the sky.

Cat had a feeling that was all the female would say on the topic.

It took everything she had not to drum her fingers on the table until their session was over. She wanted to find out more right away, corner Connor, and get some answers. However, she had more lessons and a meeting with Lachlan before she could do that.

However, once she finished her appointments, she didn't care if Connor was dead tired at the end of his shift at the restaurant, she was going to take him aside and get to the bottom of it.

As CONNOR MACALLISTER finished serving up his latest order, he moved on to the next.

His other siblings all hated working at his mother's restaurant, but he loved it.

He loved the bustle, the chaos, and how a good meal could make someone smile or improve their day.

He'd tried explaining it to his brothers before, but they'd said it was too monotonous, too boring, too "insert excuse here." His brother Ian had tried to lay out how finding out a new way into a computer security system or designing some new program, was so much more interesting.

But he had no desire to sit in front of a computer all day. He'd go mad.

No, Connor preferred keeping busy, moving, doing something.

And as one of the head cooks—humans used some fancy term he didn't remember, but dragons liked things simple—he was usually too busy to think about much else but getting his next meal finished quickly.

However, as he chopped some onions on autopilot, he took a second to try to think of a new way to make Aimee King smile.

The whole thing with the female had started out by chance, of course. On his way to work, when he'd seen her staring from her window, he'd had the cheek to wave, and she'd run away.

He'd walked the same way to work the next few days until he saw her again, and for reasons he couldn't comprehend, Connor had suddenly done a backflip.

She'd stayed to watch him do a few more.

Which had made him want to try even harder the next time. Maybe it was because he hated the thought of anyone being so sad all the time. Or maybe it was just that all the Lochguard females were used to his antics, and it'd been a long time since he'd made someone smile instead of roll their eyes.

But regardless, Connor had this driving need to come up with new routines to one day make her laugh.

His dragon yawned inside his mind. *Are you done with your shift yet?*

His beast had no interest in food beyond eating it. *No, just prepping some ingredients.*

And yet, you were thinking about her again. You should just go say hello. It's strange for you to be shy.

Shy was probably the last word Connor would use to describe himself. His family would say the same.

He replied, *Maybe when she's ready.*

And when will that be? When she finally opens the window, tosses down a rope ladder, and shouts for you to come on up?

Don't be ridiculous, dragon. But she almost never leaves her home. So I'll wait until she can at least handle that.

His dragon huffed. *Fine. You know I can't tell she's ours or not until we meet her in person and talk with her. The few seconds when we barged in on her session with Cat wasn't enough.*

Meaning there was a wee chance Aimee King was his true mate.

Which would be wrong on so many levels. Not the least of which was the fact her dragon was silent, and it would be cruel to subject her to a mate-claim frenzy. If she ever grew strong enough for one, that

220   JESSIE DONOVAN

was. *We're young still, so there's no need to rush and find our true mate.*

Unless someone else snatches her away first.

He didn't like the thought of another male making Aimee King smile, but he quickly pushed aside the thought as he added vegetables to the hot oil on the cooker. *We'll talk about this later. I have to focus on my job.*

His beast curled up and went back to sleep.

Somehow Connor managed to get through the rest of his shift without thinking about Aimee again. However, as soon as he washed up, changed clothes, and went to the back exit to start thinking of a few new tricks, he came face-to-face with his sister Cat.

And she had that look—furrowed brows and a stare.

Meaning she wanted some answers.

He sighed. "Now what did I do?"

She took his arm and moved until they were a fair distance away from the restaurant. "What is going on between you and Aimee?"

He blinked. "What are you talking about?"

"Don't play coy with me, Connor Archibald. I was with Aimee today when you stopped in front of her window and did some tricks."

He nearly blurted that it wasn't the right day for Aimee's art therapy, but he held his tongue. It was best to be as vague as possible with his sister. He loved her, but she could be like a dog with a bone when the mood struck her.

And he liked to think that what went on between him and Aimee was theirs and no one else's.

He shrugged. "I walk that way to work. I noticed her staring from the window and decided to make it interesting. That's not a crime."

She searched his gaze, but he didn't squirm in the least.

Finally, Cat sighed. "Just be careful, aye? She's delicate."

He murmured, "I know."

She nodded. "Aye, well, you can walk me home and update me about Mum. She keeps saying she's fine, but I sense she's not."

At the mention of their mother, his irritation faded. "She has more energy than before, but she's far too quiet, even for her."

Cat nodded and glanced to the side. She usually only did that when she was hiding something. "I noticed that too."

Since it was merely his sister, he blurted, "Do you know something about Mum that I don't?"

She turned toward him and scowled. He knew that look as well—I'm not going to answer. She said, "Just watch her, aye? If she starts slipping into depression again, like after Dad died and when the doctors said she was dying, ring me straightaway, and I'll talk with her."

Aye, his sister was most definitely hiding something. "Anything else?"

"Ensure she eats enough and doesn't work too hard. That should help her loads."

Both man and beast wondered if their mother was sicker than before or not. Connor had never been good at emotion-filled conversations, though.

But he probably would have to find a time to ask her.

His dragon grunted. *I have my own suspicions, but I'm waiting to see if she tells you first.*

Wait, what? Now you're keeping secrets from me?

Mum is a far more private person than anyone else in the family. Unless it threatens her life, I'm going to let her determine when to share.

Now his bloody dragon was trying to protect him. *I'm nearly twenty-five years old. I can handle whatever it is.*

Just be patient. We and our siblings bulldoze to get information. That doesn't work with everyone. You should know that, given how Aimee is.

He did, but it didn't mean he liked it when it came to his own mother.

However, his dragon fell silent, and he finally replied to Cat, "I'll watch her. But if anything bad is about to happen, tell me, aye?"

Cat nodded. "Of course I will."

Rather than think about how strange it was not to have Cat at home and taking charge when needed, he decided to change the subject and focus on his sister and her human to lighten the mood. He elbowed her in the side. "Broken any more beds lately?"

Her cheeks turned red. "How did you hear about that?"

He grinned. "I'm friends with the bloke who carted off the old one and replaced it."

She looked up toward the sky with a sigh. "I swear, Lochguard is one big gossip mill."

He shrugged. "Just try not to make it a habit, or not only will everyone tease you about your dragon trying to break your human, you two will go broke fairly quickly from buying so many new beds."

She glared, and he laughed, the tension clearly broken.

It's what Connor loved to do—lighten the mood and make people laugh.

And he was determined to hear Aimee laugh at least once if it killed him.

Chapter Fifteen

It was the week before the human and dragon-shifter artists were due to arrive when Cat first jumped out of bed in the morning and raced to the bathroom.

At first, Lachlan had wondered what was wrong. But as the sounds of vomiting filled his ears, he grimaced.

Since they'd eaten the same meal the night before —not to mention he'd shared Cat's late-night snack —he had a feeling it was morning sickness.

Which was, of course, his fault.

He rose and knocked at the door.

Cat shouted, "Go away."

He knocked again. "Not until you tell me if there's anything I can do."

"You've done enough already," she got out before

some more heaving sounds came from the other side of the door.

He fully expected shame and guilt to wash through him. But unlike with the damage he'd caused with his friends and family more than ten years ago, this was different.

Aye, she wouldn't be pregnant without him, but he couldn't be sorry about her carrying his child.

Over the weeks, Lachlan had grown used to the idea. And as he'd watched the other parents with young children on Lochguard, he'd started to wonder if he could make silly noises and faces or play peekaboo with the same joy as the others.

And while it was still hard for him to hope he could be a good father, he didn't instantly dismiss the notion anymore.

He waited until Cat eventually emerged. Before she could do more than glare, he took her hand and kissed her fingers. "I'm sorry but not sorry at the same time."

Her glare slipped, and she leaned against his chest. Lachlan's arms instantly went around her.

They stood like that for a few beats before Cat finally said, "I know. I'm not sorry either. But I still get to blame you for all pregnancy-related matters. It's only fair."

He laid his cheek against the top of her head. "Blame away. I owe you so much already, and I'll do anything to repay it."

She leaned back and frowned. "What are you talking about?"

He brushed some of her hair behind her ear. "If not for you, I would be in a cottage by myself, keeping my distance and obsessing over the past. Instead, I'm here with a beautiful woman in my arms who carries my child, making me think I can have more than I ever imagined."

She placed a hand on his cheek. "Lachlan."

"It's true. Maybe some would think the last weeks were boring, what with us both getting things ready for the collective, not to mention helping your family and the other tasks we do for the clan. But to me, it's been heaven, Cat. You've made a lonely man not so lonely anymore."

She shook her head. "It's not just me. We're a team, so we help each other. Having you to lean on whenever I get frustrated, or irritated, or any multitude of adjectives I use about my family has been a lifesaver."

As he stared into her eyes, he knew he loved this woman with his whole heart.

But Lachlan being Lachlan, he was far too cautious to say it until he was more certain things would go right. Maybe it was selfish or unfair to Cat, but so much could still go wrong, and he didn't want to hurt her even a little if they did.

So instead of words, he leaned down and kissed her cheek. He murmured something he never would've dared before meeting Cat. "I'd kiss you, but I'm not sure if you brushed your teeth."

She lightly hit his chest. "Of course I did, although maybe I shouldn't next time just to keep you guessing."

He smiled against her cheek. "That just means you'll have to deal with the nasty taste yourself, and you'd hate that."

She sighed. "You're right. I'll just have to come up with something else."

"And I look forward to it."

He kissed her, taking his time to tease her lips and the corners of her mouth before he slid his tongue inside.

She groaned into his mouth and pressed her breasts against his bare chest.

And even though he'd had her more times than he could count by now, his cock hardened, and he needed to claim her again.

Lachlan broke the kiss to scoop her into his arms. However, he'd barely taken a step when Cat said, "Put me down."

Her face was pale, and he did as she asked.

Cat took a second, steadying herself against him, before murmuring, "I think sex is going to have to wait this morning."

He took her hand and held it over his heart. "Do you want to lie down? Or try eating or drinking something simple to settle your stomach?"

She smiled at him, and it was as if the sun broke through the clouds.

Cat motioned toward the door. "Some toast might help. Just walk slowly, aye? No sudden movements right now. Even if my stomach's empty, I'd rather not dry heave if I can help it."

They made their way to the kitchen, and as Lachlan went about making some hot chocolate and toast for Cat, he hummed the whole time. When he'd been a child, he'd hated being forced to take care of his mother and sister. Because each time, it only reminded him of the power his father had over them all.

With Cat, it was different. Taking care of her wasn't a chore. No, it made him happy.

And maybe, despite it all, he could have the loving, stable family he'd always dreamed of.

SEVERAL HOURS LATER, when Lachlan was told his sister was waiting for him inside the Protector's main building, he began to doubt everything again.

Oh, aye, he'd called Sarah a few times since arriving on Lochguard. Once simply because he wanted to check in on her, but the other two times because Cat had asked him about how his sister was doing.

Not that the calls had ever been long or overly

involved. He and Sarah weren't anywhere near as close as they'd been as children.

And while he'd secured permission for Sarah and her boys to visit, it wasn't supposed to be for a few weeks yet.

Which meant something had to be wrong.

As soon as he entered the Protector building, he went to the reception desk and said, "Where's my sister?"

The young dragonman said, "In the visiting room."

He didn't know the layout of the Protector building well, but he'd been to the visiting room before. It was where non-clan members conducted business with Lochguard, and Lachlan had held some of his event-related meetings there.

Reaching the correct door, he stopped, took a deep breath, and knocked before entering.

Sarah had her back to him as she stared into the long mirror along one side. "Sarah?"

At his voice, she turned around, and his stomach dropped at the fear in her eyes, the same blue as his own.

He walked over. "What's wrong?"

She glanced at the mirror. "Are we alone?"

"I don't know. But if anyone's there, you can trust them. I promise."

His sister didn't trust easily, much like Lachlan

until he'd found Cat. So his words might not be enough.

He almost put a hand on her shoulder to try to comfort his sister, but resisted. She looked about ready to jump out of her skin. He softened his voice. "I can't help you if I don't know what's wrong."

She studied him a second before murmuring, "You seem different."

"I *am* different." Thanks largely to one dragonwoman. He added, "Now, tell me what's going on."

She took out an envelope and handed it to him. He noticed it merely had her name on the front of it, nothing else.

Before he asked where she'd found it, he opened it and read it:

Your two sons would be great recruits for the dragon hunters. Tell your brother to stop the event, or we'll take your boys when you least expect it. Talk to no one but your brother. If you try to contact the police or the DDA, then your husband may have a fatal work accident no one can explain.

As soon as Lachlan finished, a mixture of fear and rage rolled through him. "When did you get this?"

She bit the nail on her thumb before answering,

"Last night. Someone put it through the mail slot on the front door."

A million questions raced through his head, but he couldn't do anything until he knew who she'd told. "Am I the only other one to see this?"

She nodded. "Rob's working on a job site over in Falkirk and won't be home for several days. And I didn't think it was something I should risk discussing over the phone."

Rob Carter was her husband, and for once, Lachlan was grateful for the bloke working away from home so much. Rob had pretty much always avoided Lachlan, which hadn't been hard to do in the beginning since Lachlan had been drunk and self-absorbed when his sister had met and dated the man before marrying him.

But from what little of the man Lachlan knew, he was rash and often acted without thinking. He also tended to blame either Sarah or their sons for any sort of failing.

While he'd often wondered if he could've stepped in and protected his sister back then, Lachlan couldn't change the past. All he could do was focus on the present. "And what about your boys? Where are they?"

"At school for now, but they're going to stay with Rob's parents afterward." She took a step toward him. "Will you cancel the event, Lachlan? Tell me you will."

He wanted to say yes, but he needed more information. And to talk with Finn. "I know the letter says not to talk with anyone but me. However, I really need to discuss this with Lochguard's clan leader. He needs to know what's going on."

The fear returned to her eyes. "But Lachlan, my boys. You can't risk it."

He moved closer and finally took her hand. "Remember how you trusted me when we were younger? Can you do that again, Sarah? Just for this? I've been working with the Department of Dragon Affairs for a long time, and I can tell you that the dragon hunters aren't the most trustworthy lot. There might be another way to protect your family, but I can't assume anything until I talk with Lochguard's leader. And, to be technical, the letter didn't mention anything about the dragon-shifters."

She stared at him for a few beats, and it took everything he had not to order her to trust him.

He was one of the main reasons she was so hesitant, after all; their father was the other. But if she said no, he'd have to do something to convince her because doing what the dragon hunters demanded probably wouldn't end well.

The hunters may have been quieter the last year or two as the Dragon Knights had stolen most of the headlines. But the Knights had been taken down for good and were no longer causing trouble.

As a result, the dragon hunters probably felt they

needed to step up their game again or the dragon-shifters might succeed in swaying public opinion more to their side.

And given the years the hunters had lain in wait, planning their next moves, he didn't think whatever was coming would be good.

His sister finally spoke again. "You mentioned that you have a bairn on the way now, aye?" He nodded. "Would you risk his or her life by talking with the clan leader if the situation was reversed?"

He didn't miss a beat. "Aye, I would."

He'd gotten to know Finn through their meetings every week. The dragonman could be annoying at times, but he loved his clan dearly. If there was a way to help family, Finn would do it.

She nodded. "Okay. But promise me you'll find a way to protect my boys, Lachlan. Please."

He gently squeezed his sister's hand. "I promise. I won't let anything happen to them."

After a few beats, Sarah nodded. "I'm going to try trusting you. Just don't let me down again, Lachlan. If anything happens to my sons, I won't survive it."

His sister's uncertainty was like a knife to the heart.

But he understood her hesitancy.

No matter what it took, Lachlan was bloody well going to make his promise a reality, whatever it took. He hadn't been there when his sister had needed him, back when she'd dated the arsehole Rob, and he'd been too drunk to notice before she married him, and he refused to flake out again.

So once he told his sister to stay in the room and ordered some tea and biscuits for her while she waited, he went to find Finn.

Chapter Sixteen

A short time later, Lachlan waited for Finn to finish reading the note to Sarah before asking, "What should I do?"

Finn sat back in his chair. "Aye, well, there are only two real choices here. The first is to cancel the event, but I'm guessing you don't want to do that if you can avoid it?"

Lachlan shook his head. "Not if there's a way to keep it going and still protect my sister's family."

Finn paused a beat, his pupils flashing, before he asked, "Why do you want to keep the event going? Is it for your own pride?"

Growling, he leaned forward. "I don't bloody care about fame and glory. Everyone's worked so hard on it, and I really believe the collaboration will help foster new relationships. And most importantly, if we cancel because of a threat, then it'll show the hunters how easy it is to get their way in the future."

Finn nodded. "Aye, that last point is exactly my thought as well. But I needed to be sure we were on the same page."

He hated how he was still passing tests with the Lochguard leader, but in some small way, he understood it. Not only was Lachlan human, but he'd also worked for the DDA for roughly a decade. And the DDA hadn't always been that understanding when it came to the dragons until the last few years. He asked, "So what's the other option?"

Finn shrugged. "It's a much harder sell, I'm afraid. You'd have to convince your sister and her family to move here, at least temporarily."

He frowned. "I've never heard of a random human family moving to a dragon clan, at least in the UK."

"Aye, you're right, I don't know if it's been done before, or at least for a long time. But if you mate Cat, it might be a wee bit easier to explain and convince the DDA, especially if they know the hunters are poking their heads up again."

Maybe he should be grateful for the suggestion and keep his questions to himself. But Lachlan liked laying out all the options to craft the best possible outcome. And how he and Finn acted now could negatively affect the future. So he asked, "But if the DDA finds out the hunters are issuing threats, won't they just deny all human-dragon matings in the future?"

Finn shook his head. "There are secrets you don't know about, ones happening both inside the DDA and within the dragon clans, but I can't tell you what they are. Just know that the last thing the DDA wants is to stop matings and isolate the dragon clans again, lest it spoil their plans."

Finn's words were bloody cryptic. And yet, it wasn't entirely bullshit to think there was some sort of covert project going on inside the DDA. He, merely an event planner, wouldn't be privy to that sort of information.

Although given how his child would be half-dragon-shifter, Lachlan wanted to know everything he could to protect him or her.

Finn's voice interrupted his thoughts again. "Do you trust me, MacKintosh?"

He studied the tall, blond dragonman. Gone were the smiles and laughter, replaced with an almost hard, determined look.

The look of a man used to shouldering the burdens of an entire dragon clan and regularly making decisions that played with their fates and futures.

Well, maybe not played. More like sculpted or wrangled.

Finn Stewart cared about his people. And that included Cat and her family.

Soon to be his family, if he went through with the mating ceremony.

He answered slowly, "Aye, I think so."

Finn snorted as his pupils flashed to slits and back. "Not exactly a ringing endorsement, but I'll take it." The dragonman leaned forward. "Mating Cat is something I think you'd intended to do anyway, aye?" He nodded, and Finn continued, "Then what's wrong with doing it a wee bit earlier than planned? I won't force you, but I can't really help your sister and her family without this step."

And still, Lachlan couldn't let the details go. "But let's say I mated Cat. How would you get my sister and her family here without the hunters noticing?"

Finn shrugged one shoulder. "Rafe Hartley from Stonefire could fetch her husband from his job site— he's a human mated to a dragon-shifter, works for the military, and knows a thing or two about staying under the radar. As for your sister and her children, I'd have one of my Protectors sneak down to them and do a combination of driving and flying them back."

He blinked. "Fly them back?"

"We have wee baskets we can clutch to carry humans in our dragon forms. We don't use them very often, but it's possible. It'd have to be done at night so the dragon would be harder to see. The drive would be first, then flying for only the last few miles. The hunters might have weapons to attack us in our dragon forms, but I know for a fact that the twenty-mile radius surrounding Lochguard is safe from them."

He didn't know all of Lochguard's security precautions. And frankly, he didn't care as long as they worked.

He wanted to scream yes and put the plan into motion. However, Lachlan blurted, "As much as I appreciated all of your offers—I truly do—I'm not sure if I can convince my sister to move here." He paused but decided Finn deserved some sort of reason, so he added, "We're not as close as we once were."

Finn's eyes flashed a few times before he replied, "You either convince her today it's the best option, or we have to cancel the event and hope it doesn't set a dangerous precedent with the hunters. It's that simple, MacKintosh."

He could do nothing but sigh. *Fucking fantastic.* His sister and her family's life could hinge on him being able to mend things with Sarah.

Something he hadn't been able to do in a decade.

He'd just have to try a wee bit harder this time. Lachlan replied, "I'll do my best. But I'm still not sure how you can convince the DDA to go along with this so quickly."

Finn waved a hand in dismissal. "Leave the politics to me. But I think before you go convincing your sister, you should probably ask Cat if she wants to mate you. Unless she agrees, I'm not sure I can get your sister's family permission to stay here." Finn searched his gaze. "I already know how you feel. But will asking Cat be a problem?"

He had a feeling Finn knew quite a bit about Lachlan's relationship with Cat already.

And aye, he wanted to mate Cat. But it all seemed so rushed. He didn't want Cat to resent him asking her so he could save his sister and her family.

Although that wasn't the main reason he wanted to claim her as his own. He loved her but had only wanted to give her time to make sure she wanted to spend her life with him, a man who'd always be a bit broken and damaged. Aye, he was doing so well now. But the dragon equivalent of marrying him meant Cat would have to stay with him for the long haul.

And no one knew exactly what the future held.

Finn said softly, "You're a very cautious male, and that's not always a bad thing. But what does your gut feeling say? In situations related to family and love, that's what I tend to go with."

His gut said he loved Cat and wanted to spend his life with her. Aye, he had a lot of shit to work through and would always have to be careful not to regress with his alcoholism.

But everything was simply better with Cat. With her, he could finally imagine a family, a future, and even a happy ending.

All things that had been foreign to him for years.

Finn spoke again. "I think you have your answer. Go talk to the lass and see if she says yes. And if so, then see to your sister. Let me know ASAP about their answers."

He nodded, still not believing Finn would do so much for his family despite the fact he'd been on Lochguard for barely two months. "Aye, I'll go see Cat now. I'll let you know either way."

Finn merely smiled as Lachlan left. For once, he was going to have to be spontaneous and not plan out every last detail of his proposal.

He only hoped she said yes. Not just for his sister's sake either.

Chapter Seventeen

The smell of paint usually comforted Cat. But after a close call in her studio earlier, when she'd tried to mix her paints and had ended up running to the toilet instead, she decided to fill her day with paperwork and prep work for the other artists arriving in about a week.

Which was why she was stacking supplies on a series of shelves inside the big art space, her dragon asleep from boredom, when Lachlan burst into the room.

She turned at the sound, but she paused midair in placing some paper towels on a shelf when she noticed his face.

Something was wrong.

Her dragon stirred. *Then find out what it is.*

Cat tossed the paper towels aside, closed the

distance between them, and placed a hand on his chest. "Talk to me."

Lachlan cupped both sides of her face with his hands before leaning in to kiss her quickly. The action almost felt like an apology, which sent off warning bells inside her brain. Searching his gaze again, she stated, "Lachlan, just tell me what's going on, aye? You're worrying me."

His voice was soft as he answered, "I'm sorry, I just didn't think the moment would go like this." She growled impatiently, and he continued, "My sister came to Lochguard because of a threat to her family, and the only way to save her means I need to ask you to mate me."

Her dragon sighed. *He's right. That's not very romantic.*

Since when do you care about that sort of stuff?

Not giving her dragon a chance to reply, Cat told her human to fill her in on all the details.

When he finished telling her about the note and the hunters, as well as Finn's idea, she finally said, "Of course I'll mate you, Lachlan. You could've asked me weeks ago, and I would've said yes." She paused a beat and added, "I knew you needed time, so I wasn't going to rush you."

He leaned closer. "It wasn't so much me being unsure, as wanting to make sure you could deal with me and all the baggage that comes with it."

She tilted her head. "You're worth a whole lot more than you think, Lachlan MacKintosh. And if you're going to be my mate, you need to realize that."

"I do know that," he said quietly. "But it's not easy to erase a lifetime of history as quickly as I'd like."

She cupped his cheek. "Aye, I know. And I don't expect it. But I love you, Lachlan. So of course I'll mate you."

He blinked. "You love me?"

"Of course I do, you bloody human. And not just because you'll be the father of my child, either. I've told you before—you make everything easier to endure, to enjoy, not to mention how you help me handle my family so that I no longer want to kill them." She smiled wider as she caressed his cheek with her thumb. "You also have a hidden sense of humor that I like knowing you show me and almost no one else. Maybe one day you'll share it with other people, but for now, it's all mine."

Her dragon added, *And the sex. He's good at that too.*

She snorted, and Lachlan raised his brows in question. "My dragon likes your cock and your tongue."

Lachlan's lips curled a fraction upward. "Well, it's good to know the whole package is included."

She laughed and tilted her head upward. "So, do you believe me when I say I want to mate you now?"

He strummed her cheeks with his thumbs, leaned

down to kiss her gently, and whispered, "Aye, I do. And I love you too, Cat. I hope you know that."

She did, but it was still nice to hear it. "I do."

Her dragon spoke up. *He can convince me a wee bit more later.*

She ignored her beast, kissed her human for a few beats, and then pulled away. "So now what? Tell me what you need, and I'll do it."

He frowned and glanced down at her belly. "Are you well enough? I don't want to make you sick again."

"As long as I don't have to cook a three-course meal or fertilize a garden, I think I'll be fine." He looked dubious, so she added, "I vow to tell you if I don't feel well. And you know how seriously dragon-shifters take their vows."

He nodded without hesitation. "Aye, I know." He let go of her face and took one of her hands in his. "Now I just have to convince my sister to move here. I might need your help with that."

She raised her brows. "My help? How? I've never met her before."

He shrugged. "Sarah's more comfortable around women than men, and I think that would be doubly so for dragon-shifters. She'll probably have questions and will protest at our solution, but we need to do everything we can to convince her this is the best choice in the long run. Because if the hunters think they can start threatening family members of anyone tied to the dragons, it could get rather dangerous fairly quickly. Not to mention the DDA could eventually stop any sort of matings between humans and dragons if things get too out of control. We have to nip this in the bud now."

He was right. Only in the last few years had more and more humans started mating dragon-shifters in the UK. If it became known that any human connected to a dragon-shifter could become a target by the hunters via their extended families—especially if people got hurt or even killed in the process—then the DDA would probably halt any more humans from living with the dragon clans, end of story.

She nodded and said, "Then lead the way and I'll do whatever I can. Just maybe don't run, aye? I'm not sure if my stomach would like that."

He raised her hand to his lips and kissed the back of it. "Of course, lass. Now, let's go."

He led her out of the warehouse and to the main Protector building. Whether because of the urgency or simply because he was thinking, Lachlan kept quiet.

But Cat didn't mind. His family could be in danger, so of course he needed to focus on them.

Her dragon said, *We're his family too.*

Aye, but apart from a queasy stomach, we're just fine. If you care about Lachlan as much as I do, then try to be quiet when I'm talking with his sister, aye? I'm not sure what flashing dragon eyes will do to her.

Her beast sighed. *Fine.*

Even though her inner dragon sounded exasperated, Cat knew it was an act. Dragons, for the most part, treasured family. Well, especially so on Lochguard. And her inner beast wouldn't want to hurt Lachlan's sister if she could help it. *Don't worry; I'll make sure you get some extra attention when it's safe. That should make up for staying silent.*

Maybe Sarah's sons will scratch my ears. I could use a few more people doing that.

We'll see, dragon. We'll see.

It wasn't long before they reached the room where Cat assumed Sarah was waiting. Lachlan knocked once, and they both stepped inside.

Even though she'd seen pictures, in person, his sister looked even more like him—same dark hair, cautious blue eyes, and slightly too-long nose. Her skin was a little less pale, but Cat knew from Lachlan that the human female liked to garden and probably spent more time in the sun. She was also quite a bit shorter than her brother.

Once they were inside the room and the door was closed again, Lachlan gestured toward her. "Sarah, this is my fiancée, Cat MacAllister. Cat, this is my sister, Sarah."

Sarah frowned before her eyes darted to the tattoo on Cat's bicep and then back to her brother.

"A dragon-shifter is your fiancée? When did you get engaged?"

Apparently, when Lachlan had called his sister, he hadn't mentioned much of anything. She wondered if Sarah even knew Cat was pregnant or not. She was going to have a chat with Lachlan about that later, for sure.

Lachlan merely said, "Recently."

His sister studied Cat a few beats, and she debated what to do. Staying quiet wasn't her way, and yet she didn't want to scare the human. Or, worse, leave a bad impression. If they were going to convince Sarah to stay on Lochguard, they needed to keep her calm and open to the idea.

Her inner dragon stirred but remained quiet. Usually the pair of them made decisions together, or at least talked them out.

This time, she'd just have to go with her instincts. She decided talking would help. "I love your brother, Sarah."

The human frowned. "Why does that matter right now?"

She decided to keep it light. "Aye, well, just so you know, I didn't kidnap him and keep him captive, forcing him to marry me."

Lachlan met her gaze and shook his head, although she could see the spark of humor in his eyes. He said, "I'd like to see you try to kidnap me one day, love. You're strong, but are you *that* strong?"

She grinned at him, but Sarah's voice garnered her attention. "You really are different, Lachlan."

He met her gaze and nodded. "Because of Cat."

She was about to say it wasn't entirely because of her that Lachlan had finally allowed himself to hope for the future, but Sarah's voice prevented her from saying anything. "And whilst I'm happy for you, truly, I'm not sure how she's going to help me. Unless she works with the clan leader?"

Lachlan replied, "No, she doesn't. But I did talk with Finn, and to make it all work out, I need Cat's help."

Sarah's gaze turned wary, and Cat had a feeling Lachlan might try to retreat a little to protect his sister. As much as she loved him for thinking about his sister's feelings, Sarah seemed made of sterner stuff than Lachlan probably realized. After all, she'd been willing to face her brother at his lowest, wanting to help him even if it meant getting hurt.

So Cat decided to jump in. "I think it might help us all if I'm blunt and lay it all out. Lachlan found a way to protect your family. We move up our mating ceremony—the equivalent of a human wedding—and we bring your family to Lochguard. You'd stay here for a while, allowed because of the family connection to Lachlan, until everything gets sorted. That way, the hunters can't hurt you, and they also learn that intimidating us won't work. At least not always."

Sarah met her brother's gaze. "What is she talking about?"

Her dragon wanted to speak up at the dismissal, but Cat sent soothing thoughts to her beast.

As her dragon calmed down, Lachlan replied, "It's the best way, Sarah. In the long run, if we give in to hunter demands, it means they'll use the tactic over and over again, until anyone associated with a dragon-shifter becomes a target. And if that happens, all the progress made in the last few years will disappear."

Sarah's mostly calm exterior faded a fraction, and she reached out for Lachlan's hand. "Can't you just cancel this once? Rob will never live with dragon-shifters, and…and…"

Lachlan's voice was gentle when he asked, "What? There's something you're not telling me."

Sarah swallowed, and Cat's every instinct was to reach out and hug the female.

And yet, she didn't know if she should.

It was bloody hard for her to imagine how comfort could frighten someone or make them uncomfortable, but she had a feeling it was the case with the MacKintosh siblings. Well, at least with strangers, and Cat was definitely that when it came to Sarah.

She barely resisted putting a hand over her abdomen and murmuring to her bairn that she loved them, even now.

Sarah finally murmured, "Rob owes money, a lot of it, to some dangerous people." Her voice lowered. "He has a gambling problem. He's been trying to be better about it but keeps stumbling. I have a feeling that if he just disappears and moves to a dragon clan, those dodgy people will go after members of his family until he pays up."

Bloody hell. For the first time, Cat realized how easy her life was on Lochguard.

And any problems with her mother seemed extremely trivial by comparison.

Lachlan squeezed Sarah's hand. "Why didn't you tell me this sooner?"

She looked to the side, avoiding his gaze. "I noticed your addiction so easily and fought until you saw reason. I missed it completely with Rob until he was in so much trouble, and even then, I couldn't convince him to get help on a regular basis." Her voice dropped even lower. "I was ashamed, especially because I found out about his problem right after I thought about divorcing him."

LACHLAN HAD BEEN DOING his best to remain calm and collected. But at his sister's revelation and the crack in her voice, he pulled her into a hug and held her a few beats.

With hindsight, he could see how his isolation

and forced distance, and how thinking both would help those he loved, had done the opposite.

To the point, his sister had found herself in trouble and hadn't bothered to ask him for help.

He wasn't sure what the bloody hell he could do now, but he had to do something. But first he needed all the facts.

After a few beats, he finally leaned back until he could see Sarah's face. "Don't be ashamed, Sarah." He released her and continued, "We knew each other our whole lives, aye? I imagine it's easier to notice if something is off the longer you know someone. Even after all this time, you've only known Rob roughly ten years or so. And from the few interactions I've had with the bloke, he's not the most forthright person."

Well, unless he needed to blame his wife or children for something. But Lachlan thought it best not to mention that right now.

"Maybe," Sarah murmured.

He hated how defeated his sister sounded.

He most definitely needed to get her to Lochguard, not only because of the hunters but so he could make sure her bastard husband didn't harm her further.

First, focus on the current set of problems. Squeezing her shoulder gently, he said, "What I need right now are all the facts about Rob and his debts. What you know—names, amounts, places he goes, anything that could help."

She looked up at him again, her eyes looking far more tired than they should be for a woman not even thirty. "Why? What can you do? Unless you suddenly have a fortune I don't know about, only money will solve this problem."

He was about to say he'd think of something when Cat spoke up. "You live in Glasgow, aye?" Sarah nodded, and Cat continued, "Lochguard has contacts in the bigger cities of Scotland. I don't know all the details, but I know they exist. If you talk to some of our clan members, they can probably help." She hesitated, but before Lachlan could ask what she meant, Cat added, "We collect favors. I think most dragon-shifters do, but especially Lochguard in the last few years. If you agree to move here—at least for a while—I'm sure my clan leader will find a way to keep your family members safe from your husband's gambling debts."

He studied Cat a beat. For all Lachlan thought he knew about dragon-shifters, it seemed he learned more every day.

Maybe someone would be angry about the secrets, but he knew better than anyone how trust came in increments. And simply the fact Cat was sharing them now, even if maybe she wasn't supposed to, told him how much she wanted to help.

He focused back on his sister. "You can say no and walk away, but then I can't help you, Sarah. But please consider it, aye? You fought so hard to help me when I needed it. Trust me to do the same now."

His sister searched his gaze, and he willed for her to see this was the only way. Even if he canceled the event, she'd still have the problem of her husband's gambling addiction. At least if her husband was on Lochguard, Lachlan could maybe talk him into recognizing he had a problem and gently persuade him to seek help. Maybe even attend a meeting with him at some point in the future, since not all of them were strictly for alcohol but rather for addiction recovery in general.

Sarah finally replied in a soft voice, "I want to say yes, but there's no way Rob will live here. None." She glanced nervously at Cat and then back at him. "He hates dragon-shifters. Once when he was drunk and falling asleep, he mentioned something about capturing one to wipe away his debts. I-I wouldn't trust him here."

Lachlan resisted curling his fingers into fists. His brother-in-law was more than a mere arsehole. He was a fucking selfish bastard who had harmed his sister in his own way.

And yet again, he cursed himself for ignoring the world for too long.

However, that was the past. All he could do was try to be there for his sister now.

Which really only left one option. Taking a deep breath, he asked softly, "If you hadn't found out about his problem and felt guilty, would you have left him?"

Sarah looked at the ground and plucked at the material of her jeans. "I don't know. Maybe." She looked up again. "But I can't just leave him now. You saw the note—they'll kill him. And no matter what I think, he's still the father of my boys."

An idea hit him. One that maybe was severe, but a hell of a lot better than dying. He turned to Cat. "You have jail cells here, don't you?"

"Aye, but—"

"Then we'll bring Rob here and keep him locked up whilst we sort out the fucking mess he created. He can't kill anyone or run away, and the sod will still be alive." He turned toward his sister. "You'll stay here, Sarah. I'll have Finn send someone to retrieve your boys, and someone else to get Rob. It's only temporary. And before you say the debt collectors will start killing people, we'll figure out what to do before that happens." Silence fell, and he looked between the two women. "Unless you have any other ideas?"

They both shook their heads. He grunted and said, "Aye, then let's get to work. The sooner everyone's safe, the sooner we can think of how to solve everything." He moved to the door. "Cat, stay here with Sarah. I'll be back soon."

Before either woman could protest, Lachlan walked out and headed back to Finn's place. It seemed he was going to have to beg for favors, but there was no other way to help his family.

And for once, Lachlan was going to be the rock his sister needed. It wouldn't make up for all the hell he'd put her through over the years, but it was at least a start.

As Lachlan left the room, Cat frowned. She admired him for wanting to help his sister, but holding his brother-in-law hostage on Lochguard? Really?

Her dragon murmured, *I agree with him. It's the only way.*

Sarah gasped, and Cat mentally kicked herself. Her pupils flashed when her dragon spoke, which scared most humans in the beginning.

She expected to see fear in the human's face, but there was merely surprise.

Wanting to distract Sarah from the upheaval of her life, even if temporarily, Cat asked, "Have you ever met a dragon-shifter before today?"

Sarah hesitated before answering, "Only once, and it was by accident."

Well, at least an accidental meeting was better than never. Still, Cat added, "We're not all bad, despite what certain people say. But if you're going to stay here a wee while, you should probably just ask some of your questions now. About dragons, I mean. We'll have to wait for Lachlan to come back before we can even begin to sort out the bigger picture."

Sarah hesitated again, and Cat resisted the urge to try to comfort the human for the hundredth time. She was definitely going to try and befriend Lachlan's sister as much as possible while she stayed on Lochguard. Maybe the lass merely needed a friend.

Sarah finally asked, "The thing with your eyes— is that normal?"

She smiled. "Aye, it means I'm talking to my inner dragon. I have two personalities inside my head, and we like to talk with each other."

"I can't imagine that, having another voice in your head all the time."

She shrugged. "When you're born a certain way, you get used to it."

For a second, Sarah said nothing but then asked, "Can I see it again?"

Her dragon huffed. *I'm not a trained circus animal.*

Hush. This female's life is coming down around her. Humor her a little, aye? Besides, you talking showed her anyway.

Her dragon grunted and kept silent.

Sarah took a step closer. "I wish we'd met under better circumstances. Granted, I haven't seen my brother in a while, but he seems better. Happier. Less angry. I suspect it has a lot to do with you."

Cat smiled at the human. "Some is probably

because of me since I'm not exactly shy about asking questions. And I think Lachlan needed that—someone more outgoing to help bring him out of his shell. But it's more him being accepted, I think, that's made the difference. My brothers have already initiated him into the family in their own way. And my sister fills him in on clan gossip. Truth be told, we're a bit like a whirlwind, except instead of destruction, we try to make people laugh or roll their eyes in our wake, with perhaps a wee bit of irritation thrown in." She risked taking Sarah's hand and mentally sighed in relief when the female didn't snatch it back. "You'll be welcome too. Whether you like it or not, so I'm just warning you."

The human smiled slightly, and Cat counted that as a win.

And as she went about answering Sarah's questions, the human relaxed bit by bit. Aye, there was always a touch of worry in her gaze, and the human showed her nervousness when she plucked at her clothing, but it was still something.

It would take time to win over Lachlan's sister, but it was a start. She only hoped Sarah would be as pleasant once she was forced to live on Lochguard for a while. Even if it meant her family was protected, Sarah would be a sort of prisoner.

Cat still didn't like the idea of Lachlan locking up this Rob person. But once the human was on Lochguard, Cat would try to find out more about the male. Her dragon would be a better judge of character anyway.

However, she couldn't do any of that until everyone was safe and sound in her clan. So Cat tried to focus on Sarah's questions and keeping her stomach in line, doing what small part she could to help Lachlan with his sister.

Chapter Eighteen

Sylvia MacAllister flipped off the kitchen lights for her restaurant and headed to the main dining area to finish locking up, like she did almost every night. However, as soon as she set foot inside the room, she noticed Cat sitting at a table near the window, looking out at the dark garden beyond.

The sight of her eldest daughter always brought a mixture of joy and guilt. Sylvia knew she'd put a lot of responsibility on Cat's shoulders in the years since her mate's death, and yet she was also extremely proud of her for shouldering so much so well.

Her dragon spoke up. *We did the best we could. In the old days, some dragons would follow their true mates into death. That would've been worse.*

Sylvia's grief had been all-consuming when her mate had been murdered. She'd mated young, had children young, and ever since she'd met him at sixteen, Arthur had been the solid, steady center of her life, the one who could make her laugh when she needed it most.

Losing him had been like losing half her soul.

She finally replied to her beast, *Regardless, if we avoided that old tradition, it was unfair to Cat, forcing her to grow up sooner than she should have.* She paused a beat and added, *I need to step up for our unborn bairn and make sure Cat knows I can handle things.*

It pained Sylvia to even have to think she needed to convince her daughter of such a thing, but it was true. While she'd eventually sprung back from her mate's murder, a mysterious illness and the ensuing decline had sent her spiraling back into depression in recent years.

But the one night she'd spent with a human male all those months ago in Glasgow had changed everything.

And as she placed a hand on her ever-growing belly, she was almost glad of the one-night stand and for more than her child. He'd made her laugh, made her feel beautiful, and had shown her she could be with another male and not feel guilty.

Aye, she didn't know where he lived exactly—the greater San Francisco area was a big place—or how to reach him. But at least she'd had that night, and maybe she could find someone else in the future. Not to replace Arthur, but to make room in her heart for another to share her love, if she were lucky.

She never would've reached this realization if not for the human male showing Sylvia that she had a lot more life left to live.

Her dragon huffed. *Of course we do. You never listened to me.*

I did, dear. But…I know you're always on my side. It took a stranger to make me realize it was more than my dragon being supportive.

Her beast sighed. *No matter how it happened, it's a good thing. Because soon we'll have another child to love.*

Even though she was exhausted at the thought of raising a child all over again—she was in her forties this time, not a teen or early twenties—she couldn't help but rub her belly and feel a surge of love. *And this time, I'll do whatever it takes to be there for him or her.*

Not just because the accidental bairn had most likely saved her life, according to the doctors, either.

Cat finally noticed her presence and smiled up at her. "Are you tired, or can you chat a wee while?"

She slid somewhat clumsily into the chair opposite her daughter, knowing that six months was nothing compared to the size she'd be at eight or nine. She answered, "Of course I can talk, love. I heard about your male's sister and how her family is coming here. Is that what you wanted to chat about?"

Cat blinked. "How did you learn about that so quickly?"

She shrugged. "I'm not as good as Lorna or Meg, but I hear my fair share of gossip from the customers." She reached across the table, took Cat's hand, and squeezed. "You can tell me anything, Catherine. You know that."

Cat bobbed her head. "Aye, I know. But I merely want to sit and chat for a wee while, until my stomach calms down and I can walk without feeling sick. I'm pregnant now, too, so I know how you can be fine one second and then feel either sick or exhausted the next." She studied Sylvia's face. "Tell me if you're tired, Mum. I mean it."

It was still strange to think she and her daughter were pregnant at the same time.

Focusing on Cat's question, she replied, "The bairn is behaving for now, I promise. I have done this before, you may recall, and more than once."

Cat snorted. "To my everlasting frustrations, aye, I know it well."

The love in her daughter's voice told Sylvia that the words were merely for fun. She was lucky that all her children were fairly close with one another.

A beat passed, and Cat asked, "Will you ever tell me about the father?"

An image of a tall human kissing her as he stroked her hip, her thighs, and then between her legs flashed in her mind. It took everything Sylvia had not to blush.

Her dragon murmured, *We should find him.*

Clearing her throat and ignoring her dragon, she shrugged. "I don't know a lot myself. But it doesn't matter. The bairn may have saved my life and chased away my illness, or so the doctors think right now, giving me a second chance at life." She squeezed Cat's hand again. "And this time, I'll be the mother he or she deserves."

Cat frowned. "Don't start saying things like that. You're a brilliant mother who did the best she could under the circumstances, and I love you. I wouldn't want any other."

Her words brought tears to Sylvia's eyes. "You deserved more after your father died, and you know it. But you have your own child to worry about now. That will keep you busy enough so you won't have to keep worrying about me." She smiled. "I'll admit I never thought this would happen, us having children so close in age. I'm going to be a grandmother and new mother at the same time."

Cat grinned. "You're still fairly young and bonny for a grandmother-to-be." She leaned forward a little. "Let's just hope neither one of us has twins, or there will be far too many new MacAllisters at once, and we all know there are plenty of us already."

Sylvia shook her head. "I've already had twins, and as much as I love Ian and Emma, once was enough. Not only for the extra work, but I was the size of a wee barge by the end of it."

Silence fell a beat, and Cat shifted in her seat. Sylvia knew it meant Cat was a little uncomfortable with something internally and was trying to think of how to say it. However, before she could ask, Cat blurted, "I'm sorry for complaining to you during the last couple of months and all the times before that. Lately, I've realized how lovely I've had it compared to others."

She studied her daughter and asked quietly, "You mean like your male and his sister?"

Cat nodded as she traced shapes on the table with her finger. "I know we had a hard time after dad died, but he loved us until the day it happened."

She smiled at the memories. "Aye, your father was special. Loving, charming, and able to stand up to my father, which is saying something."

Cat grinned. "Given how his father's Grandpa Archie, yours would've been a piece of cake."

Sylvia chuckled. "You don't remember my father much since he died when you were quite young, but he was intimidating. A Protector who didn't talk much, but when he did, you listened. He actually threatened to tie a rock to your father's leg and drop him into the North Sea if he did anything to upset me. And you know what your dad said to that?" Cat shook her head, and Sylvia chuckled at the memory. "It'd better be with steel cable because otherwise, he could just slice the rope with a talon and fly right back to me."

Cat snorted. "Leave it to Dad to make suggestions on how better to plot his demise."

A rush of longing filled Sylvia's body. She missed having a male, a best friend, a companion in her life.

Above all, she missed Arthur. But she knew she'd never get him back.

Her dragon spoke up. *I still say we should go looking for that human. He made you forget your sadness for a wee while.*

How, exactly? Beyond his name, the fact he's American and works in some restaurant in San Francisco, I know almost nothing else about him.

I bet Ian and Emma could find out if you asked them.

Aye, and then they'll get caught hacking into who knows what and be carted off to jail. I think not.

"Mum?" Sylvia met her daughter's gaze again. "If there's anything I can do to help you, be it with the bairn or anything, just ask, aye?"

Since Sylvia wasn't going to ask her daughter to find her males to date, she merely nodded. "Aye, I will. I miss us chatting alone like this. We need to do it more often."

Cat squeezed her hand. "I agree. As much as I love my siblings, it's nice not to have to compete with four other strong personalities."

Sylvia laughed. "You have no idea. Trying competing with all five of you in one room."

She was shy and reserved outside of her restaurant, which was out of place among all her late mate's extended family. Not to mention she had almost no family left on her side still alive.

Sylvia was, quite simply, the odd one out. It didn't bother her much, but it could be exhausting at times to explain how she liked—or, rather, needed—spending some time alone.

Her son Ian understood the need for peace and quiet more than the rest, but he was still more charming than Sylvia could ever hope to be.

Her dragon sighed. *Stop looking for faults. I think they're excuses to use so we don't go looking for another male. Or maybe even one particular male.*

The human from San Francisco had been outgoing and charming. And for a day and night, Sylvia had been someone else, almost as if being out among the humans in Glasgow had coaxed out a different side of her. Because they were human or simply because she wasn't surrounded by people who expected her to act one way, she didn't know.

However, it wasn't who she truly was here at home. He'd soon see how she wasn't the bold, spontaneous person she'd been that day. And she didn't need the rejection.

Ignoring both her beast and the memory of the mysterious American, Sylvia chatted about everything and nothing with her oldest daughter. And she couldn't help noticing how happy Cat was. Her daughter's true mate had turned out to be what she needed. Aye, he'd brought a bit of trouble to Lochguard, but it wasn't anything the clan couldn't handle.

But it did make Sylvia realize she wanted a similar sort of happiness again too.

So, aye, it was time to stop making excuses and do a few things for herself. Her children were grown, and after she settled into a routine with her new bairn, she would have the rest of her life to think of.

And as much as she'd always love her late mate, she knew he'd want her to find some happiness outside of their children. And so, for only the second time in a decade—the first being her one-night stand with the human—Sylvia decided to be more than a mother. She was also a lonely female with needs of her own.

It was high time she did something about that, as long as it wasn't with a certain human but rather someone who knew who she was and would accept it.

Chapter Nineteen

Lachlan wasn't sure how the dragon-shifters had managed it, but somehow they'd snatched his brother-in-law and two nephews and brought them to Lochguard without anyone raising alarms or calling the police.

Maybe some would be relieved at that, but it only made Lachlan more aware of how easy it would be for the dragon hunters to do the same.

At least his sister had seemed to warm up to Cat a little. His dragonwoman had helped Sarah and her sons settled into a temporary cottage while Lachlan had tried visiting his brother-in-law.

Which had resulted in nothing but the man cursing at him and disparaging all dragon-shifters.

He'd had to leave before he punched the bastard in the face.

On the walk home, he tried his best to forget the

arsehole and focus on the next item in the never-ending list of things to accomplish—mating Cat.

Lachlan arrived at Finn's cottage, knocked, and Arabella, Finn's mate, opened the door. She raised an eyebrow and said, "You look like crap."

Her words made him smile. He preferred the dragonwoman's bluntness to any sort of small talk. "It's been a long twenty-four hours."

She stepped aside, her pupils flashing as he walked past her. She murmured, "I hope not too tiring. This is supposed to be one of those 'happiest days of your life' sort of events."

Not wanting to go into how kissing Cat the first time had triggered everything else and should be considered the happiest moment, he merely nodded and followed Arabella down the hall to Finn's office.

Inside, the room was filled to capacity with Cat's siblings, her mother, Finn, Faye and Grant, even one small blonde-haired child he knew to be Finn and Arabella's daughter, Freya.

Wee Freya stared at him and smiled.

He must be tired because the child was barely one and looked far too intelligent for her age.

Looking around, he finally spied Cat in the corner next to a small table. She wore a long, flowing dress in dark blue. On the surface, it looked modest, but the silky fabric outlined the shapes of her body, leaving nothing to the imagination.

With a growl, he walked over to her and stood as

if to shield her from the room. He whispered, "Why are you wearing a bloody nightgown in a room full of people?"

The corner of her mouth ticked up. "This is Lochguard's formal dress. You should know that, Mr. DDA Expert."

"I've never attended a formal dragon event before." He moved his mouth to her ear and murmured, "But if I have to in the future, you're adding ruffles. Or maybe extra layers. Lots of them. So other men don't stare."

She laughed, but it was Finn who replied. "If you think her dress is bad, you're aware that dragon-shifters are *naked* when they shift, aye?"

Lachlan swung his gaze toward the clan leader and glared. Hard.

Arabella stood next to Finn, touched his arm, and sighed. "Don't provoke him, Finn. He's human, remember? They're modest and embarrass easily."

Lachlan wasn't in a mood for the usual teasing, but he felt Cat's hand on his cheek, and she gently turned his head back to meet her gaze. She kissed him gently and whispered, "Just focus on me, aye? Mating ceremonies are usually only between two people."

They were having their ceremony in a small, crowded room only because of the rushed situation and urgency to help his sister.

Lachlan's irritation faded, and he nuzzled Cat's cheek. "I'll make it up to you, I promise."

She caressed the side of his neck with a finger. "There's nothing to make up. I love you, remember?"

Not caring who else was in the room, Lachlan took her lips in a desperate kiss, licking, and tasting, needing her calming presence to help control his worst impulses.

When he finally let Cat up for air, they both breathed heavily, and her cheeks were flushed.

Someone cheered, but he ignored them. He murmured, "I love you," kissed her gently, and asked, "What do we do? They don't teach us about the finer details of mating ceremonies in the DDA."

She turned and took an arm cuff out of a box on the table. It was silver and engraved with markings he knew were from the old dragon language, but he couldn't read them.

Noticing his focus on the cuff, Cat explained, "It's my name in the old language. After I say my bit—like marriage vows for humans—I'll put it on your arm. You'll do the same for me, except the cuff has your name instead."

It seemed almost medieval, the literal claiming of Cat with his name. And yet, he rather liked the idea that they'd belong to each other.

While it may not be technically true that a mating ceremony was between two people—the DDA was involved for any human-dragon pairings after all—

the exchange of cuffs was indeed for them and them alone.

Cat smiled at him and waited for everyone to quiet down. Once there was silence, she said, "Lachlan MacKintosh, when we first met, I felt a strange pull toward you. It made no sense since you were so reserved and me the complete opposite. But in those differences, I think we discovered more of ourselves, encouraged more of who we wanted to be. Even though I know our journey has barely begun, I'm better for knowing you, Lachlan. I love you and can't wait to start our family when our bairn gets here. Do you accept my mate claim?"

He nodded, and Cat slid the cool metal around his arm as her pupils flashed. She'd said the ceremony was only between two people, but in reality, it was three with her dragon.

She looked up at him again before darting her eyes toward the other cuff and back, telling him it was his turn.

Clearing his throat, he picked up the silver cuff and said, "I felt the same pull you mentioned, Cat MacAllister. However, more than intriguing me, it quite frankly terrified me. My life consisted of tasks, deadlines, and schedules to keep me in line. I thought it was the only way I could live and avoiding falling back into the darkest depths of myself. However, it took a spirited dragonwoman to show me that the isolation hurt me more than anything. Love, friendship, and even a wee bit of fun helped me more than anything I'd done in nearly ten years to stay sober. I never thought I would ever be a father, but now I can't imagine not having a bairn with you. Aye, I'm still terrified, but for different reasons. I love you, Catherine MacAllister. Do you accept my mate claim?"

"I do."

He slipped the silver cuff around her upper arm, lingering a moment to trace where the metal met her skin, never taking his gaze from hers.

And for a few seconds, he forgot about everyone in the room except for Cat. She had become his guiding star, and he couldn't imagine his life without her any longer.

Needing to feel her in his arms, he tugged her against his body and kissed her again, his lips sliding between her lips as she met his tongue stroke for stroke. She groaned, and he barely resisted lifting her up onto the small table and taking her right then and there.

However, her brothers started catcalling, and he broke the kiss with a sigh. Laying his forehead against hers, he murmured, "I wish we could take a proper honeymoon."

She smiled as she touched his cheek. "Maybe someday. But this is the first time I've ever heard you even think about shirking responsibility for something else, what with the artists arriving soon."

Not to mention dealing with his sister, which, while unsaid, filled the silence for a beat.

Cat stood upright, moved to lean against his side, and faced them toward the crowd. His new bride asked, "Before I take an hour to ravish my mate, where's the paperwork we need to sign, Finn?"

Her sister, Emma, laughed and said, "Now who's being the brash one, Cat?"

Cat replied, "I can embarrass him, but not you. So don't even start."

As he watched the sisters trade barbs, even as Finn laid out the paperwork for Lachlan and Cat to sign, he wondered if he could ever get this close to his own sister again.

All he could do was try. However, as Cat looked up at him with love in her eyes, he decided he could take one hour to celebrate and treasure his new mate, wife, whatever term they wanted to use. She'd already made so many compromises to help him, but he'd give her this at least.

So he carefully guided Cat toward the door and said, "Barring violence or retribution showing up at the clan gates, we don't exist for the next hour."

As Cat giggled, he held his woman close, loving her heat at his side and her scent filling his nose.

Aye, she meant the world to him now. And somehow, Lachlan only hoped he was up to the challenge of protecting and treasuring her as she deserved.

Chapter Twenty

Cat kept staring at the glinting band of silver on Lachlan's arm as he opened the door to their cottage, and both woman and beast were proud to see their name on his arm.

Aye, there'd already been a frenzy and declarations of love. But somehow, the metal bands stoked a more possessive need inside her.

Her dragon said, *Maybe he should tattoo our name on his arm.*

He probably would if we asked, but I don't need that. Lachlan is ours, and that's enough.

Maybe for you.

Lachlan rubbed her back, garnering her attention again. "Are you too tired? If so, just say the word. I can wait."

As much as she loved how he tried to take care of her—something that had been mostly foreign in her adult life—she growled in impatience. Bringing his head down to her mouth, she whispered, "The silky feel of this dress against my nipples the whole way home has made me wet for you, Lachlan. So take me upstairs and claim me for the first time as your mate, or I'll let my dragon out to do it."

She could hear his heart rate kick up before he murmured, "As if that would be a bad thing."

Her beast hummed. *Then let me have him.*

Not yet.

Wanting to drive him a wee bit mad, she moved a hand to the tie on her dress, plucked it, and let her dress fall, right there at the front door.

Nudity didn't bother her, but Lachlan's eyes flared. He yanked her inside and then pressed her up against the door. With his hands on either side of his head, his breath danced across her lips as he said, "What the fuck was that?"

She smiled. "What? I was hot."

"Like hell you were."

"Dragons don't care about nudity, remember?"

"I imagine they fucking do if their mate just told them how drenched their pussy was."

She looped her arms around her neck, hitched a leg around his thighs, and pressed against him. "Well then, you'd better do something about that, aye?"

He crushed his lips against hers, pressing her harder against the door as she rubbed against him. The friction of his trousers against her clit made her moan. In the next second, Lachlan broke the kiss, flipped her around, and placed her hands above her head on the door. He traced down her arm, lingering at the silver cuff around her bicep, and then took hold of her hips. He roughly moved them back before his hand move to her arse. He stroked her cheek a few beats, the warmth of his skin against her shooting even more heat between her thighs, before moving lower. As his fingers stroked through the lips of her pussy, Cat arched back with a cry.

He slowly teased her opening and she tried to wiggle back, wanting more than a finger.

He nipped her earlobe before saying, "Tell me what you want, lass, and I'll give it to you."

She looked over her shoulder, the heat in his gaze sending a rush of wetness to her center. "You. I just want you."

He lightly smacked her bum, the small sting making her pussy throb. "You'll always have me. But just know that right now, I don't have the patience to draw this out like you deserve."

She smiled slowly. "You remember the frenzy. Sometimes rough and quick is just as good."

Raising her arse and standing on her toes, offering herself to him, Lachlan's gaze turned possessive. With a strangled sound, he undid his trousers, freed his cock, and positioned it at her entrance. As he bit the place where her neck met her shoulder, he thrust home, and she moaned at how full she was in this position.

Lachlan threaded his fingers through her hair, tugged slightly to turn her face more toward him, and took her lips in a kiss.

His tongue met hers, stroking, coaxing, and driving her mad.

Fingers tweaked one of her nipples, and she gasped. Lachlan only took the opportunity to delve deeper into her mouth, as if he needed to claim every inch of her or he'd die.

Not one to merely sit by, Cat met his tongue with her own, loving the intimate, possessive dance, one where they were claiming each other yet again.

He broke the kiss long enough to say, "Rub your clit for me, lass. Make yourself nice and wet for me before I do more."

Cat moved one of her hands from the door, down her body, and finally to the sensitive peak between her thighs. Never breaking her gaze, she began to rub and circle the way she liked, each pass making it harder to stand as heat built, and she grew wetter.

The fact she was doing all this with Lachlan inside her, unmoving, was strangely erotic.

As she started to pant, getting close, Lachlan murmured, "Put your hand back on the door."

His command made her shiver, and she did as he said.

He kissed her again as he held her in place at the

waist and moved his hips, thrusting slowly at first but faster with each second, until she couldn't help but make little noises each time his balls slapped against her cunt.

At her little mewls, his thrusts grew frenzied, almost as if he'd die if he didn't claim her harder, faster, needing to brand her pussy with his dick. Only because her hands braced against the door did she stay standing.

Then he broke the kiss to run his hand down her belly, between her thighs and found her clit. She was already sensitive from earlier and groaned at his firm touch. As he rubbed, circled, and lightly flicked her sensitive bundle of nerves, Cat arched her back more, the pleasure building.

He murmured, "You're mine, Cat MacAllister MacKintosh. Come for me, lass. Let me feel your pussy claim my dick in return."

As he pressed against her clit, Cat cried out as pleasure flooded her body, clenching his cock as Lachlan continued to move, each stroke only heightening her pleasure and extending her release.

When he finally stilled and groaned out his orgasm, so deep inside her she could feel his heat, she leaned heavily against the door as she tried to catch her breath.

Lachlan wrapped his arms around her and kissed her shoulder. He slowly pulled her upright until she leaned against his chest.

They stayed like that a moment, their heavy breathing filling their ears and Cat reveling in the feel of his solid form behind her, until Lachlan finally said, "That was better than any frenzy."

Her dragon huffed. *I beg to differ.*

Cat giggled. "Now you've upset my dragon."

He lazily cupped her breast before playing with her nipple. "Well, maybe she should prove me wrong."

Her dragon said, *Gladly.*

Cat let her dragon take control of their mind, turned around, and pushed him to the ground. She extended her talons, sliced off his clothes, and went to work on claiming Lachlan in her own way as well.

And for the rest of the hour, Cat and Lachlan took turns claiming one another in new ways, determined to leave their mark upon one another forever.

Chapter Twenty-One

C at and her new mate made it as far as suppertime on their mating day before Lachlan's brother-in-law needed their attention again.

The human male had tried to attack a Protector, threatening to kill the dragonwoman slowly. He'd failed spectacularly—Iris was female and one of the strongest Protectors on Lochguard—but it only reinforced what Sarah had said about her husband hating dragon-shifters.

And by the next morning, with neither she nor Lachlan getting much sleep because of worry, she started to wonder how this situation could ever be fixed before people started dying.

Her dragon said softly, *Trust Finn. He'll find a way.*

As much as she usually trusted her clan leader, the entire bloody situation seemed impossible.

Still, she'd managed to get up and *not* vomit before heading downstairs to make some toast. Just as Lachlan joined her—he'd finally dozed off, and she hadn't wanted to wake him up—someone knocked at the front door.

Cat moved to get it, but Lachlan kissed her cheek and murmured, "The less you have to move in the morning, the better, lass." He gently touched her lower belly before heading out of the room.

She still felt the lingering heat of his fingers against her abdomen when he came back, Finn and Grant right behind him.

Before she could even offer them some tea or coffee, Finn spoke without prompting. "The dragon hunters are going to remain an issue, but you don't have to worry about your brother-in-law's gambling debt collector and its ramifications."

Lachlan frowned. "I didn't think you knew people in that world."

Finn shook his head. "I don't. I have contacts in Glasgow, true. But not with the debt collectors. Grant can tell you more."

He gestured for Grant to speak, and the quieter dragonman picked up the explanation. "Someone I trust sent a message, which basically said that the group who holds Rob Carter's debts is currently being targeted by some unknown group. If we ruin all the groundwork they've laid for the takedown by trying to talk to them or investigate in any way, they'll punish all of Lochguard."

Cat frowned. "Who the bloody hell would order that?"

Finn and Grant glanced at each other before Grant replied, "I don't know for sure, but I've suspected for a while that some dragon-shifters have been recruited to work as sort of special ops agents by humans. There's a Skyhunter male I knew a long time ago who was declared dead—one with extremely valuable skills he acquired in the army that everyone still talks about—but I swore I saw him in Glasgow not that long ago."

Lachlan grunted. "That's a rather thin amount of evidence to make such a conclusion."

Finn nodded. "Aye, but there's more. The DDA sent a message this morning saying that they're still reviewing your mating application, your request to remain part of the DDA, and that of your sister to stay here temporarily. While not explicit, it implied that if we went after the criminal arseholes, they might deny the lot."

Cat's frown deepened. Just who had Lachlan's brother-in-law got involved with?

Her dragon said, *He might not have known how established or corrupt they are. He doesn't seem bright, though, if he's racking up debts with dangerous people.*

She focused on the others in the room and asked, "What about Rob's family? Regardless of whatever trouble he got himself into, are we really going to let the human criminals kill them because of his unpaid debts?"

Grant shook his head. "No, of course not. The message said they would be protected and to keep the human locked up here until we receive word to let him go."

So in other words, they were going to keep Rob as a prisoner for who knew how long.

Cat looked over at Lachlan, trying to gauge his expression. If they followed the order, then it could deepen the rift between Lachlan and his sister, if for no other reason than his nephews would keep asking where their father was. And that would mean Sarah either had to lie or tell them the truth.

Neither of which Cat wanted for the boys who were only five and seven years old.

Finn spoke softly, "I know it's a lot to ask, aye? But if we go against the request, it would ruin more than one life in the process. Isn't that worse than disappointing your sister a wee bit?"

Cat opened her mouth to say it was more than that, but Lachlan placed a hand on her lower back and beat her to it. "I'm not sure we have a choice." He looked down at Cat and added, "I've done far worse to Sarah in the past. This is barely anything."

She placed a hand on his chest. "Lachlan, you shouldn't be so dismissive. Once things are safe, she could decide to be done with you and flee with her lads. By keeping Rob prisoner, it could be the last straw with Sarah, and you might end up never seeing any of them again."

He pressed gently against her back in reassurance. "I'd rather they be alive and not speaking with me than them thinking tender thoughts right before they died."

Anger boiled inside her at the whole bloody situation. Lachlan had done so much, tried so hard to be a better person toward all, and it could all come to nothing.

Well, not nothing since Cat would stand by his side. But she hated to think he'd lose his sister after all this time.

Needing to feel his skin against hers, Cat took his hand and threaded her fingers through his.

The choice was his, she realized, and she could see the decision made in his eyes. However, Cat would fight to help him any way she could.

Her dragon murmured, *And me.*

She whispered, "No matter what happens, I'll still be here, Lachlan."

Her mate squeezed her fingers and gave her a loving glance before looking back at Finn. "What about the artists arriving in less than a week? Is it safe to allow strangers to stay here?"

In the recent chaos, Cat had forgotten all about the event. Leave it to Lachlan to remember every detail, no matter what else was going on.

Grant was the one who answered. "Every single participant has been vetted by the DDA, as well as by us. If any of them are a threat, they're bloody good at hiding it. The best we can do is to keep them situated in the cottages just outside Lochguard's gates for everyone's safety, as well as watch everything carefully whilst they're inside the warehouse during the day."

Lachlan looked at her again. "Is there anything I can say to convince you not to be near any of these people?"

She raised her brows. "If you're there, I'm there. I wish we could cancel, but with the threat from the hunters…"

He nodded. "Aye, I know."

As she stared up at her mate, Cat just wanted to wrap him in a hug and say everything would be all right.

And yet, she had no bloody idea if it were true.

The whole mess with the art collective and the dragon hunters was a "damned if they did, damned if they didn't" type of situation.

All they could do was make the best guess and be vigilant.

Although Cat hated how she'd have to constantly look over her shoulder. Art was special to her, one of her greatest joys, and it somehow had become tainted because of the damn dragon hunters.

Her beast murmured, *One day, they'll be gone too. Just like with the Dragon Knights.*

I hope so. Sooner rather than later would be fantastic.

Finn's voice interrupted her thoughts. "Stonefire, Skyhunter, and Snowridge are all sending one or two Protectors to help monitor things whilst the artists are here. One of them paints on the side and will be in the warehouse the whole time as nothing more than a participant, to keep an eye on things without being noticed. Chase McFarland is going to install extra security—locks, hidden cameras, and panic buttons —as another precaution. Protectors will be in one of the small offices in the building, ready at a moment's notice." Finn paused, looked between them, and added, "I know it's not foolproof, but it's the best we can do."

As Finn and Grant discussed the final details with Lachlan, Cat had an idea. Once she was alone with her male again, she said, "I should be the one to talk with your sister and explain the situation."

Lachlan frowned. "She just started feeling comfortable around you. So, no, I should be able to do it."

She shook her head. "You said she does better with females, aye? Let me talk with her. Maybe there are some things she doesn't want to tell you, afraid it'll upset you. If she went to such great lengths to get you help when you needed it, I also think she'd avoid causing you distress if she could help it, to keep you from relapsing." She could see the indecision flash in his eyes. Cupping his jaw with her hand, she said, "I'm your mate now, Lachlan. We share everything, including burdens. Let me do this for you because it would break my heart if this was the final straw to push your sister away for good. Let her hate me, not you. I can handle it."

As she waited for his response, her dragon paced inside their mind. Cat knew her beast wanted to do more than talk—she'd rather join in the fighting.

But Cat wasn't a soldier, a Protector, or anything like that. She was good with people—talking with them, bringing out the good in them, and so much more.

And she wanted to use those strengths to help.

Lachlan finally sighed. "I'm still getting used to having someone at my side, having my back. It's going to take some time to not want to do everything by myself."

She raised her brows. "So is that a yes, you'll let me tell Sarah what's going on?"

He cupped her cheek with his free hand. "Aye, I will. But if she makes you cry, I'll be visiting her myself."

Her dragon snorted. *We're stronger than that.*

Ignoring her dragon, Cat replied to Lachlan, "I doubt it'll come to that. Now, tell me anything that can help with your sister."

And as Lachlan did so, Cat started to formulate her approach.

It seemed all the years she'd been handling her siblings—finding ways to soothe them, scold them, or merely be there when they cried—was going to come in handier than she thought.

Chapter Twenty-Two

A short while later, armed with Connor on one side and Jamie on the other, Cat reached the cottage where Sarah and her sons were staying. She looked to either side of her as she said, "Remember, make them feel welcome but don't start wrestling or anything that could be construed as hurting them and making their mum upset."

Connor rolled his eyes. "Jamie and I both have worked with the children at the school before. And whilst I can't exactly teach them to cook in a garden, Jamie brought his football. I'm sure we can play some footie and not break any bones."

Jamie tossed the black and white ball, bounced it on his knee, and caught it. "Even if I just do tricks, that'll keep them entertained, aye? If not, Connor and I will think of something to distract them. Don't worry about them, Cat. You have enough to do as it is. Leave this to us."

For one of the first times she could remember, Cat finally saw Jamie as more of a grown male than a child.

She sometimes forgot he wasn't the wee lad following her around everywhere anymore.

Her dragon sighed. *Aye, aye, he's grown. Now let's hurry. You know Lachlan will be pacing a hole in the carpet if we don't.*

Taking a deep breath, she knocked on the door.

Even though Sarah had been told Cat was coming, the human opened the door a crack, looked at each of Cat's brothers, and then said, "Aye? What do you want?"

She gestured to each brother in turn. "My brothers Connor and Jamie often volunteer with the school here. Since your sons will be attending soon, I thought they could answer your boys' questions out here in the garden whilst we talk alone."

Sarah looked suspiciously at Connor and Jamie. Since the human was a wee thing by comparison and unused to dragon-shifters, she could understand how they were intimidating to her.

So Connor lifted the container he'd brought with him. "I made some biscuits to say welcome. We're family now, after all."

Sarah looked at the container. A small voice behind her asked, "Can we have some, Mum?"

A small dark head popped up at her side, the older of Sarah's sons—Mark. Before Sarah could answer, the wee lad's eyes caught sight of the football and widened. Mark looked up at Jamie. "Are you the coach here? I want to play, but all the boys at schools say I'm rubbish."

Jamie smiled at the boy. "I used to be rubbish too. But with lots of practice, I became one of the best players in the Highlands."

"Of all the dragons?" Mark asked in awe.

Jamie lowered his voice. "Of all the humans as well." He shrugged. "I can't play for any team, though, because I'm a dragon-shifter. So I just teach lads and lasses for fun. If your mum says it's okay, I can teach you a few things out here in the garden."

Mark looked up at his mother. "Can I, Mum? Please?"

Sarah looked undecided, so Cat spoke up. "I promise on my unborn child that I'd trust my brothers with my life, Sarah. They'll watch over the lads like they were their own, I promise."

Sarah searched her gaze a few beats before finally sighing. She swiped the container of biscuits from Connor's hand and said to her son, "Fetch your brother."

"But Mum, he's so slow."

Sarah raised an eyebrow, and Mark wilted a wee bit, the way children tended to do when they knew they couldn't win. "Aye, I'll get him."

He dashed away, and Sarah opened the door. "We'll sit in the kitchen, which overlooks the front garden." Sarah pinned first Connor and then Jamie with a stare. "I'll be watching you both, so remember that."

Well, at least in the case of her children, Sarah was stronger than she looked.

And while not exactly a warm-hearted embrace of Cat's brothers, she knew complete trust would take time. Cat would take it.

The boys both appeared in the doorway. The younger one also had dark hair but was a bit shyer than his older brother and hid behind Mark.

As if sensing he needed to break the tension, Connor ran further back, and after squatting, he flipped in the air before landing back on his feet.

The younger boy—Joey—gasped. "Do it again."

Connor grinned. "Only if you come out into the garden."

Mark went first, following Jamie as if he were some sort of god. It took Joey a few seconds, but once his mother gently pushed him forward, he raced over to where Connor stood.

As each of her brothers began entertaining the lads, Cat smiled at Sarah. "They'll both be ready for naps when my brothers are done with them."

Sarah nodded but didn't say anything. However, she gestured inside, and Cat followed the human into the small kitchen that indeed overlooked the garden.

Once Sarah filled the kettle with water and turned it on, she asked, "Why are you here? No one would tell me the reason for your visit."

Cat leaned against one of the counters. "First, let me say that Lachlan wanted to do this, but I made him let me do it instead."

Sarah shook her head. "No one makes my brother do anything. At least not anymore."

She smiled. "Maybe not before, but he's changed." Sarah opened her mouth, but Cat beat her to it. "But we can talk about your brother later. I'm here because I need to explain what's going to happen to you and your family."

She expected Sarah to demand, or freeze, or show some sort of emotion. But the human merely raised her eyebrows.

Cat had a feeling the female had suffered through heaps of explanations over the years. Ones that had, in reality, merely been excuses for hurting her.

Her dragon sensed her unease but remained quiet for the moment to avoid distracting Sarah. Cat decided to just be blunt. "We've figured out how to protect you, but there are a few conditions. As to what they are—you and your family are to stay on Lochguard until we receive word it's safe."

"I knew that."

"Aye, but unfortunately, it means keeping your husband locked up until that word arrives."

She watched the female closely, but she couldn't read any emotion off her.

Maybe, like Lachlan, she'd learned to conceal her feelings to protect herself at a young age.

Sarah finally said, "I suspected as much. He hates your kind, aye?"

"But you don't, though. I'm curious as to why?"

The kettle clicked off, and Sarah turned to pour the hot water into the cups. "I met a dragon-shifter once, although I didn't know he was one until he told me as he left. His eyes didn't even flash once, at least not until after he told me what he was." She laid out some biscuits on a plate, and Cat held her tongue, waiting for Sarah to continue, hoping she'd share the full story.

After another few beats, the human did. "We took a trip to the Lake District last summer, and Joey disappeared somewhere near Keswick. My husband had gone off somewhere that morning, and I was doing my best to handle the situation. The dragonman was randomly in the same area with his own son, overheard about Joey's disappearance, and helped me find him." She paused to turn back toward Cat. "He was nothing but kind to me and my boys. When he revealed he was from Clan Stonefire, I almost didn't believe him until he let his pupils flash to slits and back again. It was the first time I ever took a second to wonder how dragon-shifters were in reality versus what floated around via the news and rumors."

Cat nodded, wondering if she could find out who the male had been. Maybe he could help Sarah build more trust with the dragons in general.

Sarah stared at her a second before asking, "What I don't understand is why are all of you so willing to help us? Aye, you're Lachlan's bride. But marriage doesn't instantly make a family care for you."

The statement revealed more than Sarah probably realized. Cat suspected Sarah's husband's family were all horrible too.

Her dragon rumbled but remained silent. Cat replied to the human, "Much like how that dragonman helped you find your son without asking for something in return, the dragon-shifters often like to help those they can. Not to mention Lochguard takes care of its family. Even if loosely related to the clan, it's enough." She took a step toward Sarah. "Although I'll admit that I'm surprised you aren't more upset about the fact Rob will have to be locked up the entire time he's here."

"They let me talk to Rob earlier, you know." Sarah's gaze moved to the window, where Connor and Jamie played with her lads. "And because of that, I knew I had to make the decision to stay for my sons' sakes, no matter what." She paused, clenched her fingers into fists, and continued, "He flat out refused to even try to behave. Swore he'd do anything to get free and said he didn't care if the dragon bastards killed us all. It'd be better than being their slaves, or some such shite." Her voice was low but still angry as she murmured, "Not even me pleading for him to think of our sons was enough to change his mind."

Cat yearned to reach out to Sarah but held back. She sensed the female was desperately trying not to cry. And as she'd learned with Lachlan, touch wasn't instinctively confronting for the MacKintosh siblings.

Sarah shook her head. "And if Rob won't even try to be kind to the dragons here to protect his sons —let alone try to make plans to keep us together— then he's lost to me." The human sighed and moved closer to the window until she could grip the small ledge. "Especially now that I see Mark and Joey out there playing in the garden. They're happier than they've been in months, with two complete strangers. More at ease than I've ever seen them with their own bloody father." She turned back toward Cat. "I was trying to make it work, hoping I could fix things. But I'm done. My boys need me, and that's all I care about."

Cat took a step closer. "And they're lucky to have you." Sarah looked dubious, but Cat added, "I know we barely know each other, but I hope we can become friends, Sarah. I want my child to know his or her cousins, not to mention their aunt." She took another step closer. "And I think you could use some friendship and maybe a wee bit of fun."

Sarah laughed bitterly. "Fun? That's something I've long forgotten, if I've ever had it at all."

She tentatively reached a hand to touch Sarah's shoulder, and the human allowed it. Cat squeezed in reassurance. "Aye, well, that is something my family has in abundance. And before long, you'll rue the day you met us."

Sarah gave a hesitant smile. "I doubt that. If you can make my brother happy, as he seems to be, then I will always be grateful."

Despite everything, Sarah still loved her brother.

And that thought warmed Cat's heart a wee bit.

One of the boys squealed in the yard, and they both watched as Connor did a complicated series of flips before landing on his feet, just as Jamie headbutted the football to him.

Both of the boys clapped, and then they all started kicked the ball around.

Cat gestured toward the small table. "Let's have some tea and biscuits before they come in. With four males, the biscuits will be gone in seconds."

Sarah smiled, carried the tea over, and they sat down at the table.

As Cat asked more about Sarah's sons, and Sarah asked her some more about how she and Lachlan had met, the tension in the room slowly faded away.

It was a small step forward, but one Cat would

gladly take. She may have only met Sarah recently and didn't know her well. But she was Lachlan's sister and Cat would do everything she could to help the female and her sons find a wee bit of their own happiness too.

Chapter Twenty-Three

The arrival of the artists and getting them settled into both their housing and art spaces had gone off without a hitch. Nearly a month had passed, and all of their art projects were well underway. Today was actually the beginning of the tours given to approved visitors, showcasing the murals and selected artwork.

And being the first day, some of the more important visitors from the DDA, important business figures, and the British government were due to arrive at any minute.

The fact everything had gone smoothly to date pleased Lachlan, given how much time he'd spent on putting this entire event together.

And yet, as his eyes passed over Cat talking with one of the human artists, all he could think about was his mate and keeping her safe.

Not that Lachlan had extensive self-defense training—although Faye MacKenzie had been giving him lessons twice a week—but he wished Cat would've reconsidered and stayed home.

But of course she wouldn't. This project was hers as well. Not to mention she glowed when talking with the other participants or how she radiated happiness whenever she worked on a piece or helped with painting a mural.

She would go mad being cooped up all the time. And because he loved her, he hadn't met with Finn to press for her to remain safe at home.

Although his gaze lingered on her belly. To most, they could barely tell she was pregnant, thanks to her apron. But Lachlan knew there was a small bump there, the beginnings of their child making itself known to the world.

At one time, he'd been horrified at the idea of being a father. And now? He couldn't wait. Especially after all the extra time he'd spent with his nephews recently. He'd learned how he did okay with children when he wasn't constantly worrying about a strict schedule, checklist, and narrowing down every second of his day.

Although he thought the visits helped his nephews more than him, given how their father had decided to leave rather than stay on Lochguard once the human criminal gang had been taken care of. Finn and the others had tried to convince him to stay, to avoid the dragon hunters, but Rob had declined.

While Sarah wasn't the happiest she'd ever been, she wasn't as sad as Lachlan had imagined she would be at her husband abandoning her.

He wondered if his sister talked to anyone about what she'd suffered during her marriage. Lachlan still didn't forgive himself for being absent when Sarah had dated the bastard when he might've been able to scare him away to protect her.

But as Cat always told him, he needed to focus on the here and now, as well as the future, because they couldn't change the past.

The male voice of Adam Keith, the dragonman from Seahaven who was going to help him with the tours, garnered Lachlan's attention. "Everyone's nearly here, gathered in the Protector building. We should go."

He nodded. "Aye, just a second. I want to speak with my mate first. Go ahead, and I'll follow soon after."

Lachlan strode toward his dragonwoman before Adam could say anything. He reached her side, and she paused in what she was doing to smile up at him. "If you're here to check on my stomach yet again, I'm fine. I told you, the vanilla oils I put above my upper lip helps hide the paint smell."

"I know I'm protective, but I last checked only twenty minutes ago. I'm not that bad."

She raised her eyebrows. "Aye, you are. As bad as any dragon male, for sure."

The words were said with a smile, though, and he couldn't help but chuckle. "I'll take that as a compliment." He nodded to a passing artist and guided Cat to an empty side of the room. He said, "I'm about to meet the first round of guests before bringing them here. Can you let everyone know and get them ready?"

"Aye, of course." She glanced at the wall of completed murals. "I only hope they like what they see; otherwise, they'll send everyone home and cancel any future events like this one."

Even though he tried to limit touching Cat in front of all the other artists, he couldn't help but take her hand in his and squeeze. "They'll love it, lass. Maybe not as much as I love you, but that would be fairly hard to do."

She lightly hit his chest. "There you go flattering me again. You're getting quite good at it."

He itched to kiss her, but he somehow resisted as more eyes watched them. "It's merely the truth, and you know how much I like that."

She laughed, squeezed his hand, and pushed him toward the door. "Go on, or they might start thinking Lachlan MacKintosh is a lazy, tardy, unreliable employee, and we can't have that." She lowered her voice for his ears only. "Impress them, love. So they'll let you keep your job."

He hated how the DDA kept stringing him along as to whether he could still work with them or not. He sighed. "You're right."

She put a hand to her ear. "What was that? Say it again?"

He growled and fought the urge to lightly smack her bum. "You're right. Now, I'm off." He murmured into her ear, "I love you."

She murmured back, "I love you too."

He reluctantly let go of her hand and exited the main art space. As he headed toward the Protector building, he focused on the facts and rehearsed speeches he'd give to the first round of visitors. He needed everything to go perfectly. Not just for him or for the sake of good public relations.

No, the whole event was about showing how dragon-shifters were just like humans in so many ways, emphasizing how they were more alike than different. And he desperately wanted that to become more mainstream so one day his child would face a better future.

Entering the Protector building, he went to greet the guests and geared himself up to be more charming than he'd ever been in his life.

CAT and the other artists somehow managed to breathe and not cause some sort of major paint-spilling catastrophe as the first group of humans and dragon-shifters were shown around the warehouse art space.

Her relief at how well things were going was only amplified as she met Lachlan's gaze across the room as he motioned for the others to exit.

His look told her everyone was pleased so far.

Her dragon yawned. *Of course they were. We're all brilliant.*

I know that, but it's a wee bit different than having friends around, aye? They were scrutinizing everything, even asking to look into drawers and things.

Which seems ridiculous to me. How can paintbrushes or even pencils be interesting?

Just because you don't have any interest doesn't mean others won't. Remember, this is mostly funded via the DDA and some company donations.

More human stuff I don't care about.

She snorted and noticed one of the human artists named Christopher walking toward her. The male had a shaved head, dark skin, and was one of the quieter ones in the group. Still, Cat was determined to win him over before he eventually left with everyone else.

She smiled at him. "Hiya, Christopher. Do you need something?"

He stopped right in front of her, a slight frown between his eyebrows. "It may be nothing, but I noticed one of the tour members hanging back a bit in the hallway when I was returning from the toilet. I was about to ask him if he needed help when he said no and walked away. However, it was in the opposite direction of the tour flow."

Her dragon was fully alert. *We need to tell Faye and Grant.*

She nodded and asked, "Can you come with me, to tell the Protectors everything you can remember about the male?"

He shrugged. "I suppose."

"Brilliant." She motioned toward the exit. "Let's not waste any time."

They made their way toward the wee room being used for security surveillance. After a quick exchange, she left Christopher and headed back toward the main art space.

She didn't want to be paranoid, but she kept her eyes and ears open for the slightest sound. She may not be a Protector or have worked with the army, but every dragon-shifter learned to make the most of the supersensitive hearing and reflexes as a child.

However, she reached the main art space without incident. She made it halfway into the room before she was bombarded with the smell of some kind of pouring medium, overpowering the vanilla oil she used to try and mask other scents.

The smell was worse than any paint, so much stronger, and her stomach churned with the remnants of her breakfast.

She dashed out of the room and ran for the toilet. Cat reached it just in time to lose her stomach into the porcelain bowl.

Once she finished, flushed, and rinsed out her mouth, she went about washing her hands. She'd just about finished when she heard some knocking and swearing coming from the other side of the wall, where there was another isolated toilet room.

Under normal circumstances, she'd go see if they needed help.

But with someone possibly roaming the halls, she wasn't going to be stupid and check it out herself.

No, she'd tell the Protectors and let them handle it.

Cat slowly left the room and managed to walk about ten feet down the hall before something exploded behind her, sending her flying forward until she landed and the world went black.

Chapter Twenty-Four

L achlan had just handed off the tour group to two Protectors who would lead them back to the main entrance when the building shook as a rumbling roar filled the air.

A beat later, he could instantly smell smoke in the air, meaning fire, and his stomach dropped as he thought of one thing—he had to find Cat.

Lachlan ran down the hallway toward the main art space but was caught from behind by someone. He turned to see Grant. Not caring about anything but finding Cat, he growled, "Let me the fuck go, Grant."

"No. It's not safe."

He still struggled. "Cat, is she okay? I need to see her." Pain flashed in Grant's eyes, and his heart stopped beating. "No, no, no. She can't be dead."

The dragonman shook his head. "I don't know. We're still searching."

Meaning she might still be alive.

No, she *had* to be alive.

Lachlan struggled harder against Grant's arms, needing to find the one person who meant everything to him.

He'd nearly broken free of Grant's grip when another set of arms held him back. He barely noted it was Kai Sutherland—the Protector from Stonefire —as the dragonman said, "If you want to help her, stay here so we don't have to bloody waste resources going after you."

Part of his brain knew Kai was right. And yet, the need to see Cat, to hold her, to kiss her, and tell her how he loved her, still fought with his rational side, and he couldn't seem to stop trying to get free.

When yet another dragon-shifter appeared and looked about ready to hold him as well, Lachlan finally stopped struggling; he'd never win against the three of them.

His eyes prickled with tears—and not from the thicker smoke in the air, either—but he fought them off as he cleared his throat and demanded, "What's being done to find her and the others?"

Kai answered, "The trained fire rescue team is evacuating everyone they can and keeping us informed via walkie-talkies. You need to leave. Now. We don't know if the building is going to collapse yet, and I'd rather focus on finding the other survivors instead of standing here, restraining your arse."

Survivors. The word implied some hadn't made it.

With his whole heart, all he wanted to do was run and find Cat. To make sure she was one of the survivors.

And yet, the dragonman was right. Lachlan would only waste time and resources that could better be used to find his mate. His recklessness could end up costing Cat her life.

As much as it pained him to admit it, standing back was the best way to help her.

He nodded reluctantly, cleared the emotion from his throat, and looked Kai dead in the eye. "Tell me the second you find her, aye?"

Kai gripped his shoulder and squeezed. "You have my word."

After one last glance down the hallway, which seemed to fill up with more smoke by the second, Lachlan allowed someone to guide him out of the building and to a safe meeting point on a slight hill.

From a distance, he could see how much worse it was than even he'd thought.

Smoke billowed from the building. Some windows had already shattered, with flames licking the air. And an increasing number of dragons flew nearby, circling and waiting for some order Lachlan didn't know.

And even though the chaos in front of him all but

signaled the end of his career with the DDA, Lachlan didn't fucking care. All that mattered was Cat and his unborn child.

Because if she didn't survive, he didn't think he would either.

He wasn't self-hating enough to believe it was all his fault, but he could've tried harder to convince her to stay home. Or to talk with Finn to ensure she never set foot in the building while a possible enemy waited in the distance.

Despite everything, he still hadn't been able to protect those he cared for.

He had no idea how long he stood there, watching the blaze consume more and more of the building, when an explosion broke any remaining windows and destroyed most of the roof.

Lachlan didn't flinch or cry out.

No. Instead, he dropped to his knees and put his head in his hands, a heaviness he could barely breathe through weighing down on him.

The explosion was so much more than a destroyed project. He'd heard nothing about Cat, and he doubted anyone could've survived the explosion that had collapsed most of the roof.

Had he actually lost her? Would he never see her smile again? Or observe the gleam of mischief in her eyes before she drew out the long, dusted parts of him that liked to have fun?

Never touch her soft skin or take pride in how she flushed when he made her come?

Never watch her hold their bairn in her arms, with love in her eyes for the child they'd made?

Fuck. How could this have happened?

Was she truly gone?

He didn't want to believe it, but he might just have to face the ugly truth: he'd lost his love and best friend, not to mention their unborn child.

He expected sadness, but a sense of emptiness engulfed him. Too numb to do anything but sit on the ground, he nearly jumped when someone shook his shoulder.

Lowering his hands from his face, he found Faye MacKenzie's wild hair and brown eyes, her gaze filled with…irritation?

He finally caught her words. "I've been looking all over for you. Come with me to the surgery."

Lachlan looked back to the building. "Why? The doctor can't bring back the dead."

Faye grunted. "Cat's alive, you bloody bastard."

He instantly stood and took hold of Faye's shoulders. "What?"

"I won't lie—she's hurt badly. But she's alive. So if you want to see her, come with me."

She marched and he followed. A light of hope flickered within his chest. Maybe, just maybe, he'd have another chance to protect his mate from the world. To grow old with her.

To have children with her.

Although the thought made his chest tighten. Faye hadn't mentioned the bairn and might have not done so on purpose.

He wanted to ask but feared learning his child was gone might overwhelm him to the point he couldn't help Cat when she needed it.

Focus on what you have now. Cat was alive. That was all he needed to know for the moment.

Whatever grief followed, they'd deal with it together.

Soon enough, they reached the surgery, and Faye took him past the waiting area and to a small room at the end of the hall.

Dr. Campbell and a male nurse Lachlan didn't know finished doing something, their tall forms blocking the bed and any views of Cat.

Turning, the doctor put up a hand to keep him in place before saying, "She's about to go into surgery. I can give you thirty seconds, but no more. And don't move her."

Lachlan nodded, and Dr. Campbell walked out of the room at the same time Lachlan raced to the bed.

Cat's face was covered in small cuts, a few bruises were starting to show, her skin was extremely pale, and she was entirely too still.

Lachlan barely contained a sob.

Taking a deep breath, he laid his fingers over hers

and kissed her cheek. "I love you, Cat. And you'd bloody well better come out of this. I'm the one with the dark, emotional past, not you. So don't think you're going to outdo me."

She didn't move or respond.

And in that moment, he wanted nothing more than for Cat to roll her eyes at him again.

The male nurse spoke. "I need to wheel her out."

Lachlan kissed her lips gently and somehow forced himself to step back.

As he watched Cat disappear down a hallway, a numbness he'd never known settled over him.

That could be the last time he ever saw her alive again.

The floor began to spin, and strong hands guided him back into the room and forced him into a chair. Only when she spoke did he realize Faye was still with him. "Go on and cry. I've never understood the stupid unsaid rule that males are supposed to remain stoic at all times."

Somehow he croaked, "I can't."

Faye growled. "Don't be daft—"

He cut her off and met her gaze. "If I cry right now, it means I've given up. And I refuse to do that."

She studied him a second before sitting in the chair next to him. "Aye, well, that makes sense." She paused a second before saying softly, "Cat's strong, Lachlan. She won't give up easily."

"Aye, I know."

Silence fell, and neither one of them had the strength to fill it.

Eventually, Faye took his hand and squeezed. They remained like that, one as a husband and one as a friend, waiting to see if Cat made it through.

LACHLAN HAD no idea how long he sat there in the room, waiting for information about Cat.

At one point, Faye had left and been replaced by Cat's mother, Sylvia.

And then the various MacAllister siblings rotated through in the chair by his side, murmuring things he didn't hear, until they all sat together in silence, waiting for any news on either Cat or the bairn.

Eventually, a very pregnant Dr. Layla McFarland appeared in the doorway, which only made him feel worse. She wasn't supposed to be working if she could help it, because of her difficult pregnancy.

However, as she started speaking, Lachlan forgot about everything but the words coming out of her mouth. "Let's start with the good news—Cat is alive and has a good chance of a full recovery."

An undefinable sound escaped his throat, and Sylvia took his hand. She was the one to ask, "What's the bad news?"

He tried to steer himself for the worse but still didn't know how he'd survive the loss of his child.

Dr. McFarland's voice softened. "It's still touch and go as it whether we can save the bairn or not. Cat's lost a lot of blood. And even if Cat were strong enough to brave a C-section, the wee female is far too young to survive outside the womb at this stage."

Female. His daughter.

Something squeezed his heart and he struggled to breathe.

After a beat, Lachlan gripped the arm of his chair with his free hand and croaked, "Can I see Cat?"

The doctor answered, "Soon. Dr. Campbell is still finishing up the post-op checks. I just wanted to give you an update."

Sylvia murmured, "Thanks, Layla."

The doctor left with a sympathetic nod, and Sylvia squeezed his hand again. "Out of all my children, Catherine is the most stubborn and determined. If anyone can pull through this, it's her."

He somehow found the strength to nod.

The silence in the room, with none of the siblings arguing, only reinforced how serious the entire situation was.

He leaned his head back, closed his eyes, and wished for it to all be over, with him and Cat lazing in bed, them both protecting Cat's lower belly with their hands, as if the action could guard their daughter against any danger.

Someone else eventually entered the room, but he

didn't have the strength to open his eyes until he heard Sarah say, "Lachlan?"

His eyelids flew open, and he found his sister's gaze. At the sad, loving look there, he nearly started crying.

Then she walked closer, leaned over, and hugged him close.

Even though their childhood had been him always holding Sarah and soothing her tears, for the first time in their lives, their roles were reversed.

Silent tears streamed down his cheeks as he held his sister close. Not because he'd given up on Cat, but rather his sister's presence was comforting and broke through any walls he'd constructed.

They'd once been a team, and now he needed her again.

She murmured words he didn't hear. After a little while, she released him, and he barely noticed everyone else had left them alone.

Sarah sat down next to him, took his hand, squeezed, and they said no more.

And yet, her silent comfort helped more than anything.

Eventually, a nurse came to fetch him to go to Cat. He numbly made his legs work until he sat next to her bed, held her hand against his cheek, and listened to the steady beeping of the heart monitor.

There was so much he wanted to say to her, yet he couldn't bring himself to treat her as if she were dying. The doctors thought her prognosis was good, but not guaranteed.

So he merely sent his love and wishes at her, reveling in her cool touch, and gently placed a hand over the small swell of her belly.

All Lachlan had to offer was strength for his mate and daughter.

He only hoped it was enough.

Chapter Twenty-Five

L ittle by little, an awareness of pain shot
through Cat as she heard voices coming from
somewhere. Two masculine ones, if she heard right.

But she didn't have the strength to do more than
lay there and try to make out what they were saying.

As she did so, the weak voice of her dragon filled
her mind. *I want to wake up.*

But it will hurt.

Still, we should wake up.

The voices started to become more defined, and
one of them was more familiar to her than the other
—Lachlan.

All she remembered was a loud noise before the
constant pain and male voices.

If she wanted to find out what had happened, she
needed to open her eyes.

Not to mention she desperately wanted to see

JESSIE DONOVAN

Lachlan, have him kiss her, and borrow some of his strength to help fight the aches and pains that became sharper with each passing second.

And she couldn't bloody do any of that if she didn't open her eyes.

Never in her life had her eyelids seemed so heavy, as if they were made of stone rather than small bits of flesh.

Then she made out Lachlan's question, "And the bairn?"

Her wee one. If she was in this much pain, how was her bairn?

Had she lost it?

If so, Lachlan would need her as much as she'd need him.

She pushed aside the rush of sadness and thought only of her mate and bairn, which was enough to give her a wee bit more strength, and her eyelids fluttered open. She didn't hear whatever the reply was to Lachlan's question because instead, he rushed to her and gently touched her cheek. "Cat? Are you awake?"

All she could manage was a groan.

Dr. Campbell appeared on her other side and said, "I'm going to give you a quick examination, Cat. Don't try to talk yet, aye? Blink once if you can do that to answer my questions."

Even though it took concentration, she managed it.

The doctor nodded. "Aye, we'll keep one blink for yes and two for no."

However, as the doctor went through poking and asking questions, Cat couldn't tear her gaze away from Lachlan.

Smudges under his eyes and the bristle on his face told her he hadn't slept or even bothered to shave for a while.

Just how long had she been unconscious?

Dr. Campbell finally finished and stated, "I think Cat's out of the worst of it. As for the bairn, you need to take it easy for at least the next month, maybe two, or risk a miscarriage. The fact you weren't far along is probably what saved her, but we still need to be cautious." He glanced at Lachlan and then back to Cat. "As much as I wish I could give you more definitive answers, there's always a little uncertainty when it comes to medicine. Eat, sleep, and rest is my best recommendation." He moved toward the door. "I'll be back in fifteen minutes with a nurse. If you can't stay awake that long, that's fine, Cat. Rest when you need it."

As soon as they were alone, Lachlan sat in the chair next to her bed, brought her fingers to his lips, kissed them, and murmured, "I love you."

The heartbreak in his words, as if he'd thought she would die, did something to both woman and beast. "I love you too. Now, tell me what happened." He frowned, but she quickly added before he could deny her, "I won't be able to sleep until I hear it."

It was probably one of the only lies she'd ever said to him since she could barely stay awake, but she needed to hear what had put her in hospital and risked their bairn.

He sighed, turned her hand to kiss her palm, and replied, "One of the tour group visitors was bought off by the dragon hunters. And aye, the DDA was supposed to have completed thorough background checks. From what I can tell, heads are rolling as we speak."

A flash of memory floated through her mind. "The person in the toilet."

Lachlan nodded. "The bastard was killed instantly, although experts think he accidentally triggered the bomb early. And given the location in the building, far from the main art space or any of the offices, they think it was meant to scare rather than kill. Although it was close to a supply closet, which only made the fire worse in the end."

Her heart skipped a beat. "Did someone die? Besides the terrorist?"

"No, but one of the rescue team ended up losing a leg. He had to have his rescue partner cut it off, or he'd have been trapped and died."

Sadness at the unnamed person threatened to make her cry. She knew everyone on Lochguard, which meant she knew the male. And even if it were one of the visiting Protectors here to help, some of whom were also fire rescue trained, it wouldn't be any less awful.

She could ask who, but Cat didn't think she couldn't quite handle knowing their identity just yet. When she was stronger, she'd handle the grief.

But for now, she needed to remain calm and strong and manage her stress levels to help keep their bairn safe.

Lachlan spoke again. "Finn and the DDA are handling everything. For now, your duty is to get well." He kissed her wrist. "And protect our daughter."

"Daughter?" she echoed. Dragon-shifters usually didn't learn the gender until birth.

He smiled. "Dr. McFarland let it slip. And I couldn't keep it a secret from you, even though I know dragon-shifters usually wait until the birth to find out."

She glanced down at her abdomen. *A daughter.* She'd always wanted one but had assumed she'd have a male since they were more common among dragon-shifters.

Having a daughter was a precious gift for a dragon, and Cat was determined to do whatever she could. "I guess this means I have to suffer bedrest for a while to make sure she shows up and eventually becomes Daddy's wee girl."

He smiled, chasing away some of the sadness

from his gaze. The sight warmed her heart. He replied, "I'll do whatever it takes to help you, lass. Cravings, entertainment, anything. You'll be so sick of me that you'll sigh in relief when I have to use the loo."

She shook her head, not caring that it sent a twinge down her shoulder. "Never. Well, mostly never. I'm sure my temper will flare at some point, and I might need a few minutes' break to tame it again."

He stood and leaned over her, gently pressing his lips to hers. She wanted more than the chaste touch but knew she couldn't. Not yet.

Her exhaustion alone told her that.

He moved away a few inches and murmured, "I'm rather fond of your temper. The last time it flared, we ended up in bed, and I had marks down my back."

"And as I recall, you didn't mind them."

"Not one bit."

She smiled, but it took more strength than she wished to admit.

She was so bloody tired.

Her dragon's weak voice said, *We should sleep again, to help us and the bairn.*

I thought you wanted to be awake?

We were. We saw our male, helped ease his worry. I want to sleep now.

For all the times her beast said some human

emotions were a waste of time, her dragon had a soft heart when it came to their mate.

She must've not kept that thought to herself because her beast huffed. *He is* ours. *We must take care of him. He's our treasure.*

Despite what stories always said about dragons hoarding jewels and the like, the only kind of treasure dragon-shifters truly guarded was love and family.

Most of her kind did, at least. And she was most definitely one of the majority.

Lachlan stroked her forehead and said, "Sleep, lass. I'll be right here."

She searched his gaze. "Only if you promise to sleep too. You probably look as bad as I do right now."

He placed a hand over his heart. "Such flattery from my mate."

Her lips twitched. "Just promise to take care of yourself too, aye? This child needs both of her parents."

Stroking her cheek, he murmured, "I promise. I'll sit here until you fall asleep, and then I'll take a wee nap myself."

Her eyes drooping, she muttered, "I'll ask later for how long, so you better."

His warm chuckle finally enticed her to sleep, dreaming of the day she could cuddle her mate in bed again without worry.

Chapter Twenty-Six

After six weeks spent mostly sitting in a bloody bed, slowly losing her mind each day, Cat was determined to convince both Lachlan and the doctor that she could leave it, at least for a few hours a day.

The only question was how.

It wasn't as if she wanted to make trouble, especially since Layla had only recently given birth to twins, meaning Dr. Campbell was handling everything on his own until Dr. Innes came up from Stonefire to help.

And she, of course, would do anything to protect her own daughter, even if it meant more boredom.

But surely, if she was in a wheelchair, she could sit outside for a while. Or visit her family. Or even have Lachlan take her to her studio.

She hadn't really had a chance to paint anything since the warehouse bombing. Oh, she could've sketched or painted something even in her bed. But it'd been hard to return to the happy place inside herself where she found her inspiration, especially with so much that could still go wrong in her life.

However, a wee bit of freedom might help her from snapping at Lachlan so often. Her male didn't deserve it.

Her dragon snorted. *He's worse than a hovering male dragon around his mate.*

Be kind, dragon. He thought he'd lost us. Of course he's going to be protective. You're just cranky because you haven't been able to shift either.

Her dragon huffed. *And if the doctor has his way, we won't be able to until after the bairn is here.*

And yet, Cat knew her dragon would refrain from shifting to protect their child.

They were both merely cranky, it seemed.

Cat went back to thinking of how to convince everyone to let her spend some time out of bed for more than the toilet, taking a shower, or her short walks to keep her muscles from atrophying when someone pounded on the front door. A minute later, Lachlan raced into the room. "Your mother's gone into labor, and the doctor thinks the bairn will be here shortly."

She scooted to the edge of the bed. "Then I need to be there when my sibling arrives."

Lachlan hesitated. "Should you be out of bed?"

Reaching for his hand, she waited to see if he'd

help her up. He gave it. She took his hand and squeezed. "You can carry me if need be, but my mum needs all of us there."

Because she still hadn't mentioned the father or reached out to him was left unsaid.

Finally, he pulled gently on her arm and helped her up. "The surgery is close enough. As long as you promise to sit whilst we wait for your brother or sister to arrive, I suppose it should be okay. The distance isn't much more than what you do on your required daily exercise around the house." His gaze turned protective. "But you tell me the second you feel tired, or if anything else seems off. Promise me, Cat."

After nodding, she kissed him. "I really do love you, you know?"

He raised an eyebrow. "Because I'm going to let you walk? The bar has sunken rather low, aye?"

Despite the words, humor danced in his eyes. She stuck out a tongue a moment before replying, "More because you're going to have to deal with my family—including my extended family—once my sibling arrives. And that most definitely earns some love from me."

He sighed. "Just try to keep your granddad away from me, aye? I'm glad the man has people to care for so late in life, but I'd rather not hear about his latest exploits."

She giggled. "What? My grandfather mentioning

how he likes to be tied up doesn't get you all hot and bothered?"

He put an arm around her waist and moved her toward the bathroom. "You're most definitely going to owe me, lass. Now, let's get you ready."

She continued to tease her mate the entire time, never ceasing to be amazed at how far he'd come since that first day he'd set foot on Lochguard.

His sister, too, was becoming less hesitant around most everyone inside the clan. Although Cat thought the human female would be cynical for quite a while yet, which was understandable given her family history and arsehole of a husband that would become an ex soon enough.

As they walked toward the surgery, Cat leaning against him more than she cared to admit, everything almost seemed normal again.

Well, except for how the DDA kept Lachlan in limbo about whether he could work for them again or not.

But she pushed that worry aside. It should be a day to celebrate, and nothing else.

The second they walked into the surgery's waiting room, they were greeted by about twenty people from the MacAllister family. The sight warmed her heart. Even though her mother was only related to them through her former mate, they still considered her one of their own.

Grandpa Archie headed in their direction, but

they were saved by Holly MacKenzie—the human was a part-time nurse—walking out to them with a smile on her face. "Your mum had a wee girl. Both are well, and Sylvia's children can see them both now." Protests erupted, but Holly gave what Cat thought was her stern nurse's look. "Only her children, born or through mating. We can't overwhelm her, aye?"

Mutters died down as Lachlan and Cat joined her four other siblings. Once they were all together, Holly motioned for them to follow.

Connor was the first to speak as they walked. "Cat's having a girl, and now Mum? Isn't that quite the coincidence?"

Holly spoke. "I have a theory about that, actually."

Connor asked, "Which is?"

The human nurse shrugged. "From all the pairings I can think of, it seems when the father is human and the mother is a dragon-shifter, the probability of them having a girl is extremely high."

Emma blurted, "But you had two girls, and it's the other way around."

Holly answered, "Aye, but that happens sometimes, even with two dragon-shifters reproducing. But when you look at the hard data, what I say about human fathers and dragon mothers makes sense. I'm surprised no one noticed it before."

Cat couldn't bear to mention that it was a recent

phenomenon where dragon clan leaders allowed human males to mate with dragon females. For most of their recorded history, the dragon males had refused to share them with humans.

Oh, the males could take humans, but not the other way around.

But regardless, *if* Holly was correct, her mother's lover had a higher chance of being a human than a dragon-shifter. Not a guarantee, but it would make more sense about her not wanting to reach out to him or let him know about the surprise bairn.

After all, dragon-shifters always had to live with a dragon clan, which would include her mother's newest child. And maybe it was impossible for the male to leave where he was to move to Lochguard.

Holly might even know if the father was human but couldn't say outright because of confidentiality agreements.

However, Holly stopped in front of a door and smiled, garnering Cat's full attention. "I know it's a lot to ask anyone on Lochguard, but try to be a wee bit calmer than normal, aye? Since your mum's older this time around, it took a lot out of her. Try to keep it brief."

They all bobbed their heads and entered the room.

Her mum lay in the bed, cuddling a wee bundle in her arms, somehow looking happier than Cat had seen her in a while.

Her mother noticed them and motioned them closer with her head. "Come see your sister." As soon as they all gathered around the bed, she pulled back the blanket to showcase a wee thing with lots of dark red hair. "Say hello to Sophie Rose."

Cat traced her sister's soft cheek. "Hello, Sophie."

As everyone took their turn admiring her, Cat watched her mum closely. She looked tired, aye, and held her newest daughter protectively. And while she *did* seem happy most of the time, Cat caught flashes of sadness—or was it regret?—in her mum's eyes when she thought no one was looking.

Maybe she wished the father was here after all.

Her dragon spoke up. *We should find out more about him. I think she wants to see him again.*

Aye, I think so too. But there's not much I can do. She won't say a word about him. And I don't think even Ian and Emma could find him with so little information.

Her dragon sighed and fell quiet.

As if sensing her sadness, Lachlan wrapped his arms around her from behind and placed his hands over her ever-growing belly. He murmured for her ears only, "We'll all help her, lass. And maybe drop a few hints about how we can help find the father if she wants. Otherwise, love will have to be enough. It helps more than anything else. I should know."

As she leaned against her mate's back and rested her head against his shoulder, she nodded.

Lachlan had tried to hide away from the world

and had become miserable from it. All Cat and her siblings could do was ensure they loved their mum and new sister, and hoped it was enough to keep her from hiding from them or falling into depression again.

Just knowing that Lachlan would always be there, love her, and stand by her side no matter what, suddenly made everything easier.

She never would've guessed that the punctual, overly organized, cool DDA employee would've ever become the warm, loving, supportive male at her back.

Love had truly transformed him. She had to hope love would also help her mother through it all too.

Although as Lachlan held her a wee bit tighter, Cat sighed and took a second to revel in her mate's warmth. Together, they could accomplish anything.

And she couldn't ask for more than that.

Epilogue

Four Months Later

As Lachlan held his wee daughter, Felicity, for the first time, a jumble of emotions all fought for control.

Happiness. Love. Fear. Protectiveness. Uncertainty.

He'd known his daughter for mere minutes, but he knew without a shadow of a doubt that he'd lay down his life for her.

No one would ever hurt her, if he could help it.

And as she squirmed a wee bit before settling down again, he couldn't comprehend how any father would want to hurt their child.

Kissing her forehead, he lingered a second before

murmuring, "I love you, Felicity. Daddy is going to spoil you rotten. Just wait and see."

Cat's tired snort garnered his attention. As he maneuvered Felicity into one arm, he took one of Cat's hands with his other. "What?"

"Everyone thought you'd been the strict one and me the laid-back one, but I told them they were wrong. You're going to give her whatever she wants, and I'll have to step in. I should've bet money with Connor and Ian and made a wee fortune."

Sitting next to her, he gently squeezed Cat's hand. "I'll spoil her, but there will be rules, of course."

She raised her brows. "The way you've been staring at her, as if she were the most precious thing in the world, it makes me doubt you can say no to her."

"You're precious to me, too, but who was the one who had to make sure you rested and took it easy all these months?"

She sighed. "Bedrest is the absolute worst, even with the artbook project to help fill up the time. And as much as I'm happy our daughter is here, I must admit just below that is how happy I am that I can walk without everyone thinking I'd break."

He kissed her forehead. "You're strong, lass. Of course you are. But not everyone survives a bomb blast, aye? It was better to be careful than not."

She leaned against him and traced their daughter's cheek. "I know. I'm sorry for being so cranky. Especially with all the new duties you've been dealing with from the DDA the last couple of months."

Lachlan had eventually received word that he still worked for the DDA. Not in his old job as event coordinator, but a new one—helping human and dragon businesses form partnerships or beneficial working relationships, something he understood being a human living with a dragon clan. The job mainly consisted of him educating both sides, but it was something he could do from Lochguard, as long as he had a phone and a computer.

Between that and helping Cat coordinate her artbook, it'd been a busy few months.

He maneuvered Felicity so that Cat could hold her, and he wrapped his arms around his mate and daughter. "You grew and carried a new person. I think that excuses any mood swings or bursts of temper."

Although her enforced bedrest wasn't the only thing that had stressed Cat in the last month or so of her pregnancy.

The father of her youngest sister had shown up out of the blue at Lochguard's gates one day, which had caused all kinds of trouble and awkwardness.

Although even that seemed to be working itself out. The human had warmed up a bit to Lachlan, and he thought the man was trying his hardest to woo Sylvia. But how that ended would ultimately be up to Cat's mother.

Felicity squirmed again, and they both merely watched her. They stayed that way until the nurse, Holly, entered the room and said, "Let's deal with the afterbirth and then your family. I don't think Layla and Alex can keep them waiting much longer."

Holly offered to take the bairn, but Lachlan shook his head and took her. "I'll watch her." He kissed Cat and went to a chair on the side as Dr. Alex Campbell and Holly dealt with what they needed to do.

By the time Cat was settled and ready for visitors, he didn't like the dark circles under her eyes. He sat next to her again and murmured, "I'll tell them to bloody wait if you need a nap."

She smiled up at him. "As much as I'd like to see you try, you look about ready to fall asleep on your feet too. So let them come in, aye? Then we can all three of us sleep."

Cat held out her arms, and he easily settled Felicity back into them.

And even though he'd been holding their daughter for a wee while, he itched to pick her up again.

His mate was probably right—he was going to be the one to spoil her.

Not that he felt bad about it one bit.

Cat's siblings burst in first, followed by Sylvia with

wee Sophie, and then his sister, Sarah, with her sons. As they all took a turn holding Felicity, cooing over her, and offering their congratulations, Lachlan merely sat next to Cat, his arm around her, gently stroking her arm with his thumb.

The two of them leaned against each other for support in silence, knowing without words how lucky they were to be surrounded by love and family.

And for someone like Lachlan, who hadn't known what it was like, it was almost overwhelming.

But then Cat took his hand, brought it to her cheek, and he kissed the top of her head.

For her ears only, he whispered, "I love you."

She met his gaze and mouthed it back.

And just like that, a sense of peace settled back over him. Cat was his lodestone, his guiding star, and as long as he had her, he'd be the happiest man alive.

Author's Note

Thanks for reading Lachlan and Cat's story! I hoped you liked it. Their tale was a little different than most of my others, and not just because it's less common for me to have a female dragon-shifter and a human male pairing, either. Having a recovering alcoholic male lead is a little risky, especially since it's not the most in-demand or trendy type of guy out there. However, Lachlan was special and he needed his story told. While I have never suffered from addiction, I first really thought about it when one of the guys remodeling my bathrooms told me his story (after months of chatting right before he went home each day). His was a gambling addiction, and it was his fear of losing his then girlfriend (now wife) that he admitted he had a problem and sought help. Ever since then, the idea percolated in my brain until Lachlan came onto the page way back in *The Dragon*

Warrior. I've tried my best to research and make him believable (too many stories or TV shows make light of how serious addiction can be, and I didn't want to do that), and his motivations reasonable. In the end, this is one of my favorite stories to date. It's also tied for the fastest I've ever written a full-length book (Lachlan really, really wanted his story out there, lol).

This book also sets up a lot of future stories. Next will be Sylvia MacAllistair's tale in *The Dragon's Chance* (Lochguard #9) where you'll meet the father of wee Sophie, as hinted in the epilogue of this book. As for Lachlan's sister, Sarah MacKintosh Carter will be the heroine of Stonefire #14, *Trusting the Dragon*, with the dragonman she met in the Lake District a year ago, as of this book (hint: it was Hudson Wells who helped her). And yes, Connor and Aimee will eventually have a story as well, but it's going to take some time to get there, so be patient. Emma MacAllister's story will come before their tale, and her book will be Lochguard #10, with a certain Logan Lamont (and may, just may, have some unrequited love and amnesia-related shenanigans in it). There are a few other whispers of future books in *The Dragon Collective*, but I think that's enough to tease you with for now!

And now, I have some people to thank for getting this out in the world:

- To Becky Johnson and her team at Hot Tree Editing. Without Becky's comments, you wouldn't have had the scene with Lachlan sliding down Cat's dragon's side!
- To all my beta readers—Sabrina D., Donna H., Sandy H., and Iliana G., you do an amazing job at finding those lingering typos and minor inconsistencies.

And as always, a huge thank you to you, the reader, for sticking with me. Writing is the best job in the world and it's your support that makes it so I can keep doing it. If you've read the books and want to support me in another way, almost all of my dragon-shifter audiobooks either are, or will be soon, available in libraries around the globe. Take a listen and enjoy some lovely accents!

Until next time, happy reading!

PS—To keep up-to-date with new releases and other goodies, please join my newsletter on my website at www.JessieDonovan.com

Craved by the Dragon (SD #11)

Persuading the Dragon (SD #12)

Treasured by the Dragon (SD #13)

Trusting the Dragon / Hudson & Sarah (SD #14, Jan 20, 2022)

Stonefire Dragons Shorts

Meeting the Humans (SDS #1)

The Dragon Camp (SDS #2)

The Dragon Play (SDS #3)

Stonefire Dragons Universe

Winning Skyhunter (SDU #1)

Transforming Snowridge (SDU #2)

Tahoe Dragon Mates

The Dragon's Choice (TDM #1)

The Dragon's Need (TDM #2)

The Dragon's Bidder (TDM #3)

The Dragon's Charge (TDM #4)

The Dragon's Weakness (TDM #5 / June 10, 2021)

WRITING AS LIZZIE ENGLAND

Her Fantasy

Holt: The CEO

Callan: The Highlander

Adam: The Duke

Gabe: The Rock Star

About the Author

Jessie Donovan has sold over half a million books, has given away hundreds of thousands more to readers for free, and has even hit the *NY Times* and *USA Today* bestseller lists. She is best known for her dragon-shifter series, but also writes about magic users, aliens, and even has a crazy romantic comedy series set in Scotland. When not reading a book, attempting to tame her yard, or traipsing around some foreign country on a shoestring, she can often be found interacting with her readers on Facebook. She lives near Seattle, where, yes, it rains a lot but it also makes everything green.

Visit her website at: www.JessieDonovan.com

The Dragon Collective
Copyright © 2021 Laura Hoak-Kagey
Mythical Lake Press, LLC
First Print Edition

Cover Art by Laura Hoak-Kagey of Mythical Lake Design
ISBN: 978-1944776275